SHIELDING INSTINCT

CERBERUS TACTICAL K9 TEAM CHARLIE
BOOK 3

FIONA QUINN

THE WORLD OF INIQUUS

Ubicumque, Quoties. Quidquid

Iniquus - /i'ni/kwus/ our strength is unequalled, our tactics unfair – we stretch the law to its breaking point. We do whatever is necessary to bring the enemy down.

THE LYNX SERIES

Weakest Lynx

Missing Lynx

Chain Lynx

Cuff Lynx

Gulf Lynx

Hyper Lynx

Marriage Lynx

Strike Force

In Too DEEP

JACK Be Quick

InstiGATOR

Fear The REAPER

Striker

Uncommon Enemies

Wasp

Relic

Deadlock

Thorn

FBI Joint Task Force

Open Secret

Cold Red

Even Odds

Kate Hamilton Mysteries

Mine

Yours

Ours

Cerberus Tactical K9 Team Alpha

Survival Instinct

Protective Instinct

Defender's Instinct

DELTA FORCE ECHO

Danger Signs

Danger Zone

Danger Close

CERBERUS TACTICAL K9 TEAM BRAVO

Warrior's Instinct

Rescue Instinct

Hero's Instinct

CERBERUS TACTICAL K9 TEAM CHARLIE

Guardian's Instinct

Sheltering Instinct

Shielding Instinct

Trusted Instinct

Acting on Instinct

CERTIFIED CERBERUS TACTICAL K9

Beowolf

Radar

Tank

CIA COLOR CODE

Red Line

This list was created in 2025. For an up-to-date list, please visit www.FionaQuinnBooks.com

If you prefer to read the Iniquus World in chronological order you will find a full list at the end

of this book.

Cerberus Tactical K9

Team Charlie

FIONA QUINN

*This book is dedicated to the wonderful people I met in St. Croix
while researching this book,
especially the real-world Beans and Lucky,
two amazing young men.*

THE PLAYERS

Cerberus Tactical K9 Team Charlie

Hawkeye Kesse and K9 Cooper
Halo and K9 Max
Levi and K9 Mojo
Ash and K9 Hoover
Reaper Hamilton – trainer

FBI

Petra Armstrong
Tamika Bradly
Rowan Kennedy and Avery Goodyear
Frost
Finley
Prescott

1

———

PETRA

From the moment she first blinked awake to answer the phone, Petra Armstrong knew today was destined for the crapper.

This morning started with a five-thirty phone call that Petra snatched up on the second ring. "What?" she'd croaked. "Who?"

"I was at the emergency room last night." It was her friend Tamika, and she sounded rough. "I have a bad case of norovirus, and it is truly an experience to behold."

Petra flung her covers to the side. "Okay, I'm coming. Are you home? What do you need me to pick up?" She pulled her legs from the warm nest of blankets and planted her feet onto wooden floorboards that radiated cold into her bare toes.

"Nothing," Tamika said. "Right now, I'm set. Diamond's daddy came to pick her up last night to get her away from my kooties. He's getting her to school today. And I've got backup to help me if necessary. Though child, I'm just sayin', no one should come near me cuz no one needs to catch this mess."

"I'm so sorry this happened." Petra flopped back onto her pillow and pulled the covers back in place. The sound of ice pinging against her windowpanes made for the kind of morning when it felt good to snuggle under the covers. "Are you home now?"

"Home, and I'm all set up. I'm tucked into a sleeping bag that I laid out on the bathroom floor, and I've got bottles of electrolytes and a box of saltines within reach."

"Gross."

"You don't even know the half of it," Tamika's voice was weak and raspy.

Petra looked at her phone to get the time. "Okay, you just rest and recover. I'll call the airlines and cancel our seats."

"You'll do no such thing. Now listen, I know you hate changing things up. You are, my friend, the antithesis of spontaneity. And if I didn't see first-hand how fast you shift gears to become the go-to gal in any emergency, I'd never believe it. You know it can take a lot of patience and cajoling to get you on board with a new plan. You're like a barge on the ocean."

"Too early. Too preachy," Petra already knew what Tamika would tell her—go without me.

"Now—I'm saying this with love in my heart—you're still going to St. Croix even though I can't be there," Tamika said. "Period. End of sentence."

Yup. There it was. "But—"

"No buts. You just go on and pretend that I'm in the bathroom, which is, in fact, where I'll be. You do what we planned. The only thing that'll be different is that I'm not sitting next to you," Tamika was using her mom voice, the one she used on Diamond when Tamika was laying down the law.

Petra pulled her brows in tight. "But—"

"Uh-uh. Off you go. Have a cocktail on the beach for me. Call me from St. Croix and tell me you love it."

Petra blinked at the patch of light on her wall made from the glow of the streetlamp.

St. Croix by herself; she tried on the idea.

Petra traveled alone all the time for work. She couldn't remember a time when she went on a solo trip for pleasure. That wasn't, in her mind, fun at all. Travel was for creating shared stories.

That wasn't even the issue. Petra just wasn't a St. Croix kind of person. She had only been going down to the island to support Tamika as she went to see where her parents got married, and to scatter their ashes in the ocean.

Petra couldn't bring herself to make the shift from supporting a friend to being down there all alone and without purpose. "Cocktails on the beach feels kind of sacrilegious given our reason for going in the first place," she said softly so as not to sound like she was rebuking her friend.

"I *knew* you'd say that. So how about this? Do a rethink and make this a retreat of sorts—communing with nature, stilling your mind, exercising your body, getting ready for your new job title."

"That feels like it ticks the right boxes. Although, St. Croix isn't a place I would've chosen to do on my own."

"Listen, a body in motion tends to stay in motion. Just keep going with the plans. Take nice hikes, enjoy beautiful sunsets, get good sleep, and maybe find a fine man to tumble around with. Cuz when you get back, you're going to be busy saving the world."

"Yeah, I'll get right on that," Petra laughed, "as soon as I get home." She laid a cool palm on her forehead to focus her thoughts. "I'll admit I was looking forward to eating without needing to cook and clean up after myself." She tried to rally some enthusiasm so Tamika wouldn't feel bad that their plans had gone awry.

"Admit it, you were just thinking about pizza in bed in front of a movie."

"Guilty pleasure," Petra retorted. "Don't judge."

Tamika was panting loudly, then mustered, "I shouldn't have said pizza. Ugh. Got to go—in every sense of the word."

The phone clicked; the call had ended.

Petra wrinkled her nose, feeling a wave of sympathy-nausea sweep over her. Once it passed, she toggled on her bedside light, climbed from her bed, and headed toward her toothbrush.

She made it as far as the bathroom when, at five-forty, a text from the airline struck her with the next blow of bad news.

Winter weather elsewhere rerouted their plane. The airline was consolidating two smaller flights onto a single larger plane. Please check your tickets for your updated seating assignment.

Elsewhere? It wasn't even six in the morning. What plane could have been in the sky when it hit winter weather?

Petra hadn't upgraded and paid for a better seat on this flight because Tamika was pinching pennies as she saved for Diamond's inevitable braces. Before she even tapped the link, Petra knew that choice would come back to bite her.

All through her military and FBI careers, Petra was taught to preserve her reaction space—keeping people or situations outside of arm's length gave her time to observe, decide, and react.

On a plane, that wasn't simple to accomplish.

When traveling for work, Petra did her best by choosing aisle seats on emergency exit rows.

Why yes, she was able and willing to be helpful should the plane go down.

Today, though, she'd be traveling in the backety-back-back. The farthest seat from an emergency door.

While Petra didn't love flying, she also didn't hate it. Flying was a conveyance, a means to get from Point A to Point B. So, the seats in and of themselves weren't upsetting. It was just that the images of the upside-down plane on the Canadian runway with people dangling from their seatbelts and the exit with the jet fuel waterfall were all pretty vivid in her mind's eye.

At the back of the plane, in her new seat, with a plastic indentation for a window and the toilet behind her head, Petra would be the very last passenger off the plane in an emergency.

Normally, Petra's brain wouldn't immediately go to the possibility of escaping a crash, but today kind of had the taste of a soup sandwich.

She rolled her lips in and gave herself a minute to adjust. "This is fine," she cajoled herself. "You had a plan all along. In this seat or that, you can still work your plan."

And she did have a plan. Borne of both nature and career training, she always had a plan. And a contingency plan.

In this case, her plans might be helpful, but they could also be making life so much harder than it needed to be.

Like Tamika, Petra was exhausted.

Unlike Tamika, Petra's exhaustion was by design. She'd purposefully stayed up all night reading a thriller, thinking that once seated and up in the air, she could sleep through the whole event and not fight the fidgets and discomfort of being on a flight for seven hours.

Her plan had been to sleep until she and Tamika reached St. Croix, where the beautiful white sands and clear turquoise waters would surround them—it would have been good.

"It's *going* to be good," Petra rallied herself. She knew that Tamika would, for sure, suffer a guilty conscience if Petra didn't go to St. Croix and come back with some good stories.

Petra did as was required of her—she got ready, got into a taxi, and got to the airport. She deposited her suitcase on the conveyor belt and made her way through security.

Sure, they lost her shoe in the X-ray machine.

Then, with her hands over her head, she got buzzed twice before she got a full pat down by TSA.

And when she filled her water bottle, the gasket was missing, so it leaked on *everything*.

But these were minor annoyances.

She reminded herself that it was a trick of the brain, amplified by fatigue, that made her hyper-aware of the things that went awry.

It was merely the idiom, "I woke up on the wrong side of the bed."

While linguists speculated that the phrase dated back to ancient Rome and that it referred to getting out of bed on the left side (sinister being the Latin word for left), Petra had always believed that it was a reference to waking up with bad thoughts or to a bad turn of events—a direction of the mind and environment more than the person's actual body placement. After all, who would get out of bed on the left if they knew that bad would follow them around all day? "Yeah, that didn't make any sense at all," she murmured under her breath as she hiked her way toward the gate.

There were, in fact, psychological studies that supported the theory that the way you woke up determined the way the day lay ahead. Those first moments imposed a rudimentary lens through which the brain saw things unfold.

It was a survival filter.

On sunny, happy days, the brain relaxed. On high-stress days, the brain agitated the waters to see what hidden awfulness lay beneath.

After all, it was the brain's job to keep its body alive.

And since Petra woke up to a shit show, a shit show today would be.

Tomorrow, she'd wake up to a glorious sunrise, and life would be golden.

Right?

2

————

In her fatigue, Petra swayed back and forth, her backpack hanging heavily from her shoulders. There were zero chairs available in the waiting area, but once seated on the plane, she reminded herself, it would be noise-canceling earmuffs, a blackout eye mask, and some much-anticipated sleep.

She looked around the room at the other passengers, many of whom had decided to wear pajamas for the flight. They must have the same strategy in mind.

With a glance at her phone, Petra realized it was only half an hour until loading. She slid a foil packet from her pocket, tore it open, and extracted the film with the medicated patch that helped with travel sickness. Peeling off the backing, Petra stuck it behind her ear, then squirted hand sanitizer on her hands and wiped them with a tissue.

Petra found the medication to be an overall boon to flying. It relieved any nausea; it took the edge off any unease during turbulence, and it did a great job keeping her just fuzzy enough

—like a couple of cocktails without the inebriation and the day-after effects—to rest if not sleep – the whole way to her destination.

Just a few minutes more, an anxious moment of disorganization as people settled into their places, an announcement from the flight crew, and she'd be asleep.

That sounded so good.

On today's flight, humanity would be packed in tightly. The attendant had already begged the travelers to come forward and let ground crew check in roller bags for free. There wasn't going to be enough room in the cabin. If things weren't sorted voluntarily, they'd just stop folks at the door.

Some people dragged their bags toward the desk.

Petra had learned long ago to keep two days of supplies in her backpack and send a prayer to the gods of flight that her suitcase arrived at the same time she did. But wrangling a roller bag onto a plane jumbled her nerves, and Petra didn't like that sensation.

She hoped that even though she was in a bottom-scraper of a seat, there would be space in the overhead bin. In a window seat, she wouldn't be able to wrangle the depth of her backpack properly under the seat in front of her.

Patting over her heavy winter coat—an absolute necessity for today's Washington D.C. December weather, but something that she wouldn't touch once she was down in St Croix with its steady daily temperatures in the mid-eighties—Petra was considering the deep pockets. Could she move items from the backpack so that she had a better chance of keeping her bag with her? She was loathe to hand it off to anyone since her laptop was stowed inside.

The attendant lifted the microphone to her mouth. It looked like she'd been dealing with peoples' feelings all damned day long.

It was only eight thirty.

Petra braced for news about delays, but instead, she heard, "Hermione Armstrong, please see the desk attendant."

Petra blinked.

It was unexpected that her legal name be called out—and Petra didn't like it. It felt like a violation of privacy. She moved forward quickly lest the woman call her name a second time and maybe throw in her middle name like a child summoned to the principal's office.

Was she getting bumped? Par for the damned course. If she *were* bumped, that would be her sign that she should go home and stay there with her cozy bed and new book.

"Hermione Armstrong?" the woman staffing the desk asked.

"That's me."

"We have an unusual situation. Your name was chosen for an upgrade. Your points allow us to upgrade you to our comfort designation with the added benefit of bulkhead space." A little too cheerful, a little too smiley, this woman was trying to sell something to Petra.

As her mind sprinted around looking for a reason that an upgrade would need a sales pitch, the only thing Petra could land on was an article she read about a couple that had to fly next to a corpse because the man in their aisle seat had suddenly died on their flight.

Petra wasn't down with anything like that. "Oh?"

"The person assigned that seat would like to switch because they don't like dogs."

"Dogs." Petra's gaze followed the attendant's line of sight to a woman in a cat sweater. "Does she know where I was sitting? She'd prefer *my* seat?"

"She was informed that we upgraded by list and that she'd have to accept whatever seat was being vacated. And she said she prefers that."

That seat would have been a claustrophobic squeeze for Petra and this woman…

Who knew? Maybe she liked the feeling of compression.

"This is the situation." The staffer leaned forward, pulling her smile even wider. "We have four working dogs who are traveling to the island. The dogs need the extra room of the bulkhead. On the left-hand side, the dogs will sit in the bulkhead seats at A, B, and C. Their handlers will sit right behind them. On the right-hand side, there will be a handler in bulkhead seat D, a K9 in E, and the seat we are offering you is the window seat, F."

"With the bulkhead space." Images of the K9s at her base in Afghanistan came to mind. They were deadly dangerous. "What kind of working dog?" Petra glanced around, but only the hand-held-sized dogs were in view – the kind their owners could stow in a carrier under the seat, or hug to their chests for emotional support; like that chihuahua over there.

"The one in your row," the staffer looked down at a piece of paper with a scrawl of illegible blue script, "is a German shepherd named Cooper." She threw her shoulders back and nodded with emphasis that Petra read as pride. Or satisfaction? Patriotism? No, Petra couldn't figure out what the woman was trying to convey with her body language.

For her part, the look on Petra's face must not have read as enthusiastic because the staffer added, "You'll receive free drinks and the upgraded meals and services of the comfort seat section."

Before Petra could game out this change of events, she found herself saying, "It's fine with me. I like dogs." If nothing else, maybe she'd walk away with a good bar story, *The time my flight to St. Croix went to the dogs.*

"Thank you." The staffer looked relieved. "You'll board

when we call for those who need assistance so you can get settled. The dogs and their handlers will load last."

As the lady with the cat sweater mouthed "thank you" to her, Petra wasn't sure the woman would feel the same by the time they got all the way down to St. Croix.

Stepping out of the way so more people could bring their rollies to get checked in, Petra found an empty spot to stand in by the window. There she watched the ground crew turn and stop their ant-like activity, focused on something just out of her view. Petra changed her angle until she saw the distraction.

Each of the four men, dressed in the easily recognizable Iniquus camo gray tactical uniform pants, topped with winter bomber jackets and visored caps, stood wide-legged with a K9 sitting at attention between their feet.

Something about the team—the level of calm and orderliness around them—made her yearn to have that, too.

A well-trained dog and an orderly man would be nice additions to her life. Petra felt a bit like a child looking at the glossy tarts in the bakery window, hungry for that kind of connection.

Up until now, Petra's job had been crazy hours and crazier assignments. She wasn't sufficiently reliable to have any kind of relationship that included someone who depended on her— not a pet, not a romance, not even a plant.

People often talked about the boredom of schedules and routines. Petra craved it.

You always want what you don't have. The grass is always greener.

But in her case, Petra believed she'd shoveled enough shit in her day to properly fertilize that greener pasture. And she was looking forward to a slower, more reasonable way of life now that she had her own research lab at the FBI.

Petra had high hopes that things were about to change. She liked the idea of setting her roots in one place, with a routine and the work-life balance that made a more rounded existence possible.

When her phone buzzed, she pulled it from her pocket, Avery Goodyear. Petra might not have a dog or a man in her life, but she did have good friends.

Avery: **Rowan told me about your new position! Congratulations! I'm taking you out to celebrate. When are you free?**

Yup, with her spanking new title and her own research lab, she did feel like a celebration was in order. But right now, Petra was more interested in the Iniquus operators below her, so she tapped to make a phone call just as a jet took off with a woosh of noise.

"Good morning." After a pause, Avery asked, "Are you at the airport? I thought that was over."

"For work, it is. This is personal. I'm flying down to St. Croix."

"Good that you're getting out of this weather mess. I'm surprised the airlines aren't delaying your flight."

"Shhh. We do not speak such things into existence."

While Avery chuckled. Petra added. "I'm looking at a group of men from Iniquus. You and Rowan are friends with a bunch of people from there, aren't you?"

"It's a big place with lots of people," Avery said.

"Yeah. I know. But these guys are wearing operator uniforms. I'm sending you a photo." Petra did her best to get a clear shot, then tapped the send button. "It's a bunch of their dog people who will be on my plane. Do you recognize any of them? Got any scuttlebutt?"

"Okay, let's see." There was a pause as Avery looked at the picture. "I can't make out the guys with their hats pulled down like that, but I know two of the dogs. First, that blue logo on their coat means they're on Iniquus's Cerberus Tactical K9

Team. But I'm sure you already figured that out since dogs … Okay, the Malinois on the right is Max. His handler would be Halo St. John. He's an ex-Australia Commando."

"Australian, huh?"

"Down, girl. He went off on assignment with Panther Force and came back engaged," Avery said. "They were married three weeks later. That happened just recently, too. Like October, maybe? You missed the window of opportunity."

"Wow, whirlwind."

"When you know, you know," Avery countered. "You know?"

"Obviously, I do not. Okay, and the other one that you recognize?"

"Cooper is the German shepherd closest to you."

"Okay, he's the one I wanted to know about," Petra said. "The staffer said Cooper would be sitting next to me on the plane. Who's his handler? Her handler?"

"*His* handler goes by 'Hawkeye.' I don't know him very well. He's new to the area, new to Team Charlie. He did some time in the field with Strike Force and then Panther Force— that's how I first met him at a Panther Force cookout when he got that assignment. Then, I did some brainstorming work with their team. Yeah, nice guy. I've enjoyed talking to him the few times we've ended up in the same room. He seems interested in everything, able to discuss anything. Quick thinking. Kind. And," she put a lilt into this last part. "I know he's single."

"I can almost hear your eyebrows popping. I'm not looking for a date. Especially today."

"Why? What's going on today?" Avery asked.

"Oh, nothing really, just I woke up on the wrong side of the bed."

Avery sighed. "Yeah, I hate days like that. So, you're at the airport. Where are you headed? Did you say St. Croix? When will you be back? Who are you with?"

"Me alone. Tamika was supposed to come, but that's a whole story I'll tell you when I get back. So yeah, St. Croix for a couple of days. I'll be home Monday night."

The staffer brought the mic too close to her mouth, so her words were garbled when she announced, "We are preparing for our direct flight to St. Croix. Families with young children or those needing extra time or assistance may board now."

Petra started walking toward the ramp. "They told me to load with those needing extra assistance, so I was settled when the dogs got on."

"How fun is that?" Avery asked.

"We shall see. Got to go. I'll call you with my report about how it went flying next to Cooper for seven hours."

As she slid her phone into her pocket, Petra felt the eyes of the room following her toward the ticket taker.

It made sense. After all, Petra always looked over to see who needed extra help. Why was this her habit? She had no idea. Cute babies, sure. Maybe to know who might need her if things took a bad turn.

But here she was, walking up the aisle without a babe in arms, looking physically fit and capable. As she moved, she could feel the eyes of the room tracking her with what felt like a smidge of hostility.

With her PhD in brain security that included a hefty look into social media psychology, Petra could admit she was a tiny bit paranoid that someone would video her and slap it up on some site with running commentary, "Look at this chick who wanted special privileges. Does she look like there's a need? #princess #thinksshesspecial #doyouknowher? We heard her name called out; it's Hermione Armstrong. Social media, do your thing!"

And just like that, the Internet could ruin a life.

3

HAWKEYE

When Hawkeye Kesse signed onto Cerberus Tactical K9 Team Charlie, the unspoken rule was that Iniquus Security's reputation would be upheld at all times.

Uniforms were always on point.

The operators' demeanors were always respectful, minds sharp, bodies ready for action.

Their dogs were immaculately groomed, and they presented with impeccable behavior.

Events would unfold in a professional and orderly manner.

What got laid out in *no uncertain terms* was that, to the extent possible, the teams were to keep their images off the Internet.

And in this day and age, that was easier said than done.

With phones clutched in people's fingers and immediate access to social media, when things got out of hand, when emergencies popped up, folks were filming. And posting.

Doing the kinds of jobs Cerberus Tactical did for Iniquus—

jumping into the fray—it was often impossible to maintain their anonymity. Not to say they didn't try.

Luckily, the folks in tech support back at headquarters were wizards at taking down images before they got enough traction to go viral.

And man, oh man, did the tech team have their work cut out for them today.

It had all started out fine.

Team Charlie, the newest K9 team at Iniquus, was heading down to the southern campus on St. Kitts by way of St. Croix. St. Kitts was a convenient jumping-off spot for Iniquus to provide area security and safety support to their clients—the U.S. alphabets, corporate accounts, universities, and other institutions.

In St. Croix, their objectives were to meet the emergency managers, get a lay of the land, and, most importantly, teach their dogs to surf.

Hawkeye couldn't wait. This was going to be a great time.

The first hiccup came when two planes consolidated into a single flight.

Logistics worked what magic they could, and while the team was downgraded from first class, they got the next best thing. They were seated together and grouped at the bulkhead.

With the plane's setup, the business class seats were to the left of the door. All the team needed to do was turn to the right, round the wall to the bulkhead, and sit down.

They'd wait away from the public outside near the support stairs and load last.

It would be seamless.

Easy.

They had a plan.

Out where the workers loaded last-minute carry-on luggage

into place, there was no overhead protection from the ice crystals falling.

Under the operators' umbrellas, the K9s sat between their handlers' legs to keep the dogs as dry as possible.

Even though the K9s all wore "working dog, do not touch" vests, it wasn't enough to keep their fur dry.

Seven hours of wet dog would be tough in such an enclosed space. Multiply that by four K9s, and, understandably, there might be bad feelings and complaints.

So, the handlers did everything in their power to prevent that.

Once the flight attendant signaled to the team that it was their turn to board, Ash and K9 Hoover were the first ones up the metal stairs. Three members of Team Charlie climbed behind him. Arriving on the sky bridge just outside the plane's door, the attendant halted their progress by holding up a hand to signal stop.

"Welcome." She smiled and scanned over the dogs before looking up to catch Ash's gaze. "We're ready for you." She put her hand on her heart as she blushed. "Can I just tell you how excited we are to have you on our flight? It's an honor, sirs."

Lucky for Hawkeye, he was second in line, so it was Ash who had to smile and nod. Hawkeye wasn't one that much liked attention or recognition. It didn't sit right with him. A man took pride in the job he did. That should be enough motivation to do the right thing.

"Your company has an understanding with our airlines," she said. "Y'all have flown with us in the past, I'm sure. We always make an announcement to try to dissuade people from taking videos of the dog teams. That's both for your sake and ours. We don't want people jumping up and getting in the aisle. We're trying to depart on time."

"Yes, ma'am," Ash said.

The woman's blush deepened as she turned away to do her thing.

Today, Hawkeye drew the long straw. He'd be the one who got the extra legroom as he sat in the bulkhead row. He was also the point guy for the four dogs, as his teammates wouldn't have easy access though they were sitting right behind their partner K9s. As tall as the men were, it took a bit of unfolding to get in and out of a regular seat.

This configuration was new to Hawkeye.

In his short time with the company, Iniquus always chose first-class seats for their operators and their K9s.

With the men's large builds, they had the comfort of resting for their upcoming assignment, good food, and the dogs could curl up on the bigger seats or the floor. Disembarking first was helpful, so was being in a curtained space apart from the other passengers who might have allergies or fears associated with bigger dogs or dogs in general.

And just as importantly, they were away from cameras and could let their guard down a bit on long-haul flights.

"Ladies and gentlemen," the attendant spoke into the handheld PA system, "as you settle into your seats, I would like to announce that flying with us today are four K9 heroes. These working dogs are on the Iniquus team that recently made two search and rescue saves in the Washington, D.C. area. Over the summer, K9 Max found a grandmother who had wandered into the mountains during a fierce storm. And here, just recently, K9 Cooper found the four-year-old child who went missing for two days in the cold after the child wandered away from his caregiver. Thanks to this wonderful team, that child has made a complete recovery and is back home in the arms of his family. As the men and their dog partners come onto the plane, we ask that you keep your phones away and that you not take either pictures or videos.

These men and their dogs often protect our nation's lawmakers and diplomats overseas, and it's important they maintain their anonymity for security reasons. We thank you for your cooperation." The attendant paused, then finished with a rousing, "Ladies and gentlemen, please welcome our national heroes."

Ash turned and sent the rest of the team an "oh shit" raise of his eyebrows.

Iniquus culled its tactical teams from the lists of retired special forces operators. True, sometimes their missions did require heroic action, but to all the men in this line, the heroes were the ones who made the ultimate sacrifice.

For this team, work in the field was another day in the office.

Hawkeye didn't like to admit it, but he was a might superstitious on this subject. Someone calling him a hero was a little bit like prophesying the worst.

And by the look on Ash's face, he felt the same.

When the applause broke out, the team adjusted the bills on their caps slightly lower over their eyes.

While the hats gave them a bit more anonymity, Hawkeye also learned in training that obscuring his face came at a price. The forehead was where most people started a scan of a face to identify that person, and it was also the means by which they read the person's emotions. A covered forehead created distrust of the hat wearer.

It was an odd snippet of applied psychology, but once he was aware of it, Hawkeye saw it play out in real-world scenarios.

For that reason, Iniquus operators only wore hats when it made them more effective on the job. Usually, that had to do with glare. Iniquus Logistics must have been concerned about the seat changes when the airline combined the two flights, putting the team on the more public side of the first-class curtain.

Had it not been for their orders, the team wouldn't be wearing the hats.

While it was unusual, Hawkeye was grateful.

As the applause continued, Ash squared his shoulders, gave his K9, Hoover, a hand signal, and moved onto the plane.

Hawkeye followed him on, waiting patiently as Ash signaled Hoover into seat A by the window.

When Hoover jumped onto the seat he turned to put his paws on his headrest, looking out over the plane of clapping passengers, the applause turned to cheers.

Hoover's behavior wasn't atypical. Their dogs were highly intelligent and trained to be observant. When moving into any kind of new environment, the operators let the dogs get a sense of the space, knowing their dogs could hear, smell, and see far better than their handlers could. In a security situation, the team wanted their dogs to have all the information available.

What was not part of the game plan, though, was that the tabby cat at the back of the plane was in its owner's arms instead of in its case. Hawkeye assumed it must be an emotional support animal by the way that the woman clutched the cat to her chest. But even from the back of the plane, the cat must have smelled big, wet dogs.

The cat pressed its front paws against the woman's face, pushing itself into a backbend as it let out an ungodly shriek.

The intake of breath among the passengers seemed choreo-graphed.

They released their seatbelts and whipped themselves around to better understand what was going on and if there was a threat.

Typical human behavior.

Hoover was hard-focused with alert ears, his gaze fixed.

Ash reached forward and wrapped Hoover's lead around his hand in case Hoover's prey drive got the best of him.

Hawkeye swept his gaze down to catch Cooper's eye, then signaled him onto his assigned seat. He sent a glance toward the woman sitting in the window seat to assess her comfort with the enormous German shepherd leaping onto the aisle seat.

In one hand, she had an eye mask, and with the other, she was pressing earbuds into place, seemingly oblivious to the drama in the back.

Apparently, he'd be sitting next to a Zen passenger. At least *that* worked in his favor.

Halo signaled to Max, and they were backing out of the plane to join Levi and Mojo on the platform, giving the flight attendant the space to move toward the disruption.

Hawkeye ducked under the luggage bin, stepping backward into his row, letting the attendant hustle authoritatively by.

By the time she passed, and he was standing in the aisle, the scene had changed.

The woman in the back had lost her grip on the cat.

The cat—a massive orange ball of pissed off—launched itself into the air with a hiss, landing on the seat back and using the available passenger head as a launching pad. That woman startled and screamed as first the front cat legs, then the back pressed into her scalp.

She lifted her purse and whacked at the menace.

"Stop hurting my cat! Don't you dare hurt my cat!" The woman at the very back shoved at the person sitting in the middle seat as she flailed her arm to show she needed to get out.

The whole plane heaved in waves as each person responded —most with laughter, some cheers, dismay, anger, fear—it was chaos.

The cat zigged and zagged, evading the hands that reached out to snag it.

Hawkeye positioned himself in the aisle between the bulkhead walls to try to keep the cat from escaping the plane, which seemed to be the cat's trajectory.

Hands held wide and at the ready, Hawkeye was biding his time.

Three rows down, a man, clutching a chihuahua that wore a tiny "emotional support" vest, batted the cat away.

The chihuahua was *pissed*, snapping his teeth and growling his rage.

The cat stretched its front legs long and smacked the chihuahua across the muzzle.

This momentarily silenced the chihuahua as it sat there with a stunned "oh no, you didn't" look on its face.

While the chihuahua stopped barking, the other lap dogs seemed incensed for their fellow pup and took up the chorus.

The cat leaped to the aisle.

The chihuahua was in hot pursuit.

The other lap dogs cheered him on—as did some of the passengers.

Seeing this, the flight attendant dropped to her hands and knees, making a dam of sorts to trap the chihuahua.

Hawkeye glanced over to give Cooper the signal that whatever was going to happen next, Cooper needed to leave it alone.

But Hawkeye shouldn't have been worried.

The Zen passenger must have raised the arms between the seats because Cooper was stretched out on the first two seats with his head in the woman's lap, getting a gentle rub behind his ears.

It was the same technique that Hawkeye used to help Cooper relax, and she did it absentmindedly as she focused on the journal in her hand, her pink eye mask waiting ready on her forehead, the window shade already down.

Out of the corner of his eye, Hawkeye saw the kneeling attendant reach out to grab the chihuahua.

The chihuahua pivoted in the last second and dashed out of reach.

The woman lost her balance and splatted out flat with a "Haroomph."

The gasps and calls that went out were peppered with laughter as the cat raced across the poor woman's back straight toward Hawkeye.

Reflexively, Hawkeye made the grab, lifting the cat overhead not as a trophy but to keep the claws as far away as possible.

Ash was red-faced, trying not to laugh as he crouched under the baggage bins with a grip on his German shepherd's collar.

As the attendant hefted herself onto all fours, the chihuahua thought he spotted his chance at escape and reappeared, shooting out of a row of children who had their feet on their seats, gripping their arms around their legs to keep them clear.

The chihuahua rounded through the woman's arms and scooted this way and that, trying to find an exit.

Passengers had their hands on the attendant, trying to help her up. The poor woman seemed to have just given up on grabbing the dog because, as she jostled her way to her feet, she didn't even reach for it. Simply turned her head toward Hawkeye with a plea in her eyes.

"I've got him," Hawkeye said, shifting into the aisle to use his booted feet as a barricade.

Once again, Hawkeye grabbed a fur ball up by the scruff of the neck.

Sidling sideways, Hawkeye first deposited the chihuahua into the owner's hands, then handed the cat into the open arms of the woman wearing a sweater with the same kind of cat knit into the design on the chest.

The claps resumed, and Hawkeye tried to wave them off as he returned to his seat.

"Sit down," yelled the attendant, hair in disarray, face red with exertion. "Sit down." She stabbed a stern finger toward the ground to emphasize her directive.

As the passengers complied, Hawkeye arrived at his seat. "Cooper, dude, you only get one seat at a time. Move your butt." Cooper peeked over at him and then walked his hind legs into the middle seat without lifting from the woman, who was now shifting her attention away from what looked like a scientific journal.

The only person on the plane not involved with the shit show was this woman and, by association, Cooper.

Hawkeye swiped his ball cap off as he dropped into his seat to give his teammates room to board.

Halo walked on with Max. Levi loaded with Mojo. Ash released Hoover's collar, and the three dogs, after observing Cooper's relaxed position, lay on the ground up against the wall, curling up as if to sleep.

The noise in the cabin was still electrified by the unexpected chase and recovery.

And the cameras were all out and video rolling.

Ash held his phone up, "I already texted Iniquus to give them a heads up that the mission started off SNAFU. Hopefully, this wasn't a foreshadowing for things to come."

4

———————

The pilot, oblivious to the goings on, came over the loudspeaker to talk about windspeeds and flight times.

Hawkeye kept his attention on the woman cuddling his dog.

Hawkeye normally didn't allow anyone to touch Cooper without his say. But today wasn't normal.

"Thank you, ma'am," Hawkeye caught her gaze. "I hope you weren't inconvenienced."

The woman offered up a Mona Lisa smile.

As she pulled the earplugs from her ears, he was struck by the unusual grey-green of her irises that looked soft and intelligent. His world stilled for a moment as he drank her in, the crinkles near her eyes, the soft scoop of her nose. How silky and touchable her shoulder-length blond hair was with that little wavey flip women get when they've pulled an elastic from their hair. Her skin, void of makeup, looked soft like the flower petals in his grandma's garden that he liked to touch as a small child.

The experience stunned him into silence.

Momentarily disoriented by her—heart hammering against his sternum—he was all sensation without a single coherent thought.

"Sorry?" she asked, holding out the earbud to explain why she hadn't understood the question.

For a moment, Hawkeye forgot that he'd asked her anything. "Oh…I…Thank you for making Cooper comfortable. I hope you weren't inconvenienced."

"Not at all, Cooper and I were becoming friends."

"Are you okay like this with Cooper in your lap?" Hawkeye pulled his seat belt into place. "Or should I get him down?"

"I prefer this if it's okay. He has a calming effect, sort of like the eye of a storm." She sent him a flat-lipped smile. "I'm not a fan of mayhem. Quite the start to this flight. Hopefully, that's all out of the way."

Interesting. So it wasn't that she was impervious to pandemonium like some Zen siren. It was more that she was applying coping strategies. "Glad he could help. I'm Hawkeye, by the way."

She stopped petting Cooper long enough to hold out a hand for an introductory shake. "Yes," she said as if he were repeating something she already knew.

Did they know each other?

Surely, had they met, he'd remember her.

"Petra," she offered. Her hand was small and warm as she shook his hand with confidence.

Hawkeye noticed that there were paint or ink stains on her cuticles and that she kept her nails trimmed short. She wore no rings on either hand.

He probably held her hand a little longer than he should have, but it felt so natural. He liked the sensation. When they released the shake, Hawkeye experienced an odd emptiness, an unsatisfied appetite.

Petra stretched her smile wider and lifted her earbud and journal, signaling she was going back into her cocoon.

"Medical journal?" he asked to keep the bud from going in her ear. He felt a strong need to know something about her other than Cooper treating her like family. "What's the article about?" His attention turned as the attendant stood beside him to start her safety spiel.

The attendant emphasized the rules about animals on the plane.

The Cerberus K9s were curled into tranquil balls, and the attendant carefully differentiated between the animals who belonged in carriers and those who had plane tickets.

By the time the attendant finished speaking, the wheels had lifted from the ground and retracted into the body of the plane.

Now, Hawkeye turned back to Petra with a look of encouragement. "I was curious about the article you were reading."

"Really?" Her brows lifted and pulled together.

"Please."

She slicked her tongue over her lips, and Hawkeye had to work hard at not staring at this stranger's mouth.

"Okay, well, a research team wanted to understand who comprised the unhoused population and why there were so many veterans, especially combat veterans."

"Yeah?" He twisted in his seat and leaned forward. "I'd like to know that myself."

"The researchers found there was a significant number of unhoused people who had experienced traumatic brain injuries before they ended up on the streets." She waggled the journal. "This data helps to account for a large subset of veterans and why they're challenged to find and keep employment."

"That's not how it's portrayed in the news."

"You're thinking of substance abuse?" She waited for his nod before continuing. "There was no data before. A lot of people with brain injuries self-medicate with booze or street drugs when they can't access health care. And we know access to help is a problem for vets."

"TBIs." Hawkeye let that have a minute to settle. As a former Green Beret with time on the battlefield, was there anyone he knew who didn't have a brain injury? Granted, ninety percent of the US military forces served in support roles, but with ten percent seeing combat, the implications were overwhelming.

"Another significant group of people living on the streets are neurodivergent individuals," Petra said. "Testing shows them to typically be highly intelligent, often subject matter experts. But, since they often struggle to fit into traditional workplaces, keeping a job is difficult. And if they can keep their job, they have trouble doing things that require more support like paying their bills on time. Neurodivergent folks, especially undiagnosed neurodivergent folks, also turn to self-medication with alcohol and street drugs."

"I'm thinking of the viral meme that shows a fish in the tree. Of course, a fish couldn't thrive out of their natural environment."

"Or even survive. Exactly." She looked down at the journal. "The article goes on to show how many of the unhoused population tick both categories." She pushed the journal between her thigh and the wall.

"I'd be interested in knowing what changes they're going to suggest to support these groups. Obviously, the idea of someone pulling themselves up by the bootstraps under either of those conditions is impossible."

"Much more difficult, at least." Petra nodded.

"Are you a veteran?" he asked.

She canted her head. "I've never had a man ask me that before. I served in Afghanistan, providing mental health support. While there, I experienced a TBI, among other things. I'm also neurodivergent." She looked down and talked to Cooper. "I wonder if I should be concerned about ending up in the streets."

She didn't look like a woman on the edge. She looked a little fatigued, but that was probably because of that travel sickness patch behind her ear.

"It looks like you might be one of the lucky people who found themselves in an environment where you can swim easily," he offered.

It was interesting that even though she smiled in response, it didn't convey emotion as much as it provided a punctuation mark. Like she was using the smile to buy her some time as the gears whirred. His sister did that, and as his teammate Halo liked to say, Hawkeye's sister was "mad genius."

This conversation jazzed Hawkeye. He liked that Petra dove into a topic and expected him to keep up. He liked the intelligence of the subject.

"I'll add this to the thought pot," Petra said. "There was a study of people living in primitive hunter-gatherer societies. Researchers found that those people with neurodivergent traits such as ADHD are highly esteemed in their cultures. Those who get bored—and are always seeking the stimulation of encountering something new—are much more successful in those societies than neurotypical members are. In our society, however, it's the opposite. Of course, neurodivergence isn't just being on the ADHD or autism spectrums. It's anyone who's wired differently." She held out an open palm as if she were about to categorize him in a pot of neurodivergent folks. "For example, brain scientists have discovered that people who are associated with certain high-risk professions—like free-soloing rock climbing or, say, special operators in the military—often have an *underactive* amygdala. That's the fear-center part of the brain. Those individuals can do things that others can't because they experience less anxiety. They're biologically wired to be less afraid than an average Joe. Like you possibly are, or your pals." She looked back at the row of Hawkeye's teammates.

Hawkeye rubbed a hand over his chin. "Interesting." Walk onto a plane and think you're perfectly normal, sit on that plane, and wonder if you've got a micro-amygdala.

"Isn't it, though?' She asked. "Brains fascinate me."

"And these are studies you're reading for personal interest or work?" He was trying to square the colored stains on her hands with this conversation.

"Both. I chose my profession because of my interests. No, sorry, that isn't exactly right. I chose my profession, and within that, I pursued what was interesting to me. Similar to you, I'd assume. Working with dogs is surely a way of life."

"You're right about that. So, you're a college professor?" he ventured.

She frowned. "Really? Professor? That's my vibe?"

"Wild stab." He found himself grinning at her. He liked that their conversation flowed easily, but she didn't make it too easy. He was up for a challenge.

Might be I'm having fun because of my micro-amygdala.

That thought amused him mostly because it might have some truth behind it. Hawkeye knew some guys who found an intelligent woman intimidating.

"What other careers did you consider for me?" Petra asked.

"A doctor because of the journal. An entrepreneur because of your direct focus and strong handshake game. A creative field of some kind?" He pointed toward her hands which she lifted to examine the stains, turn over, then put back on Cooper. "Psychiatry, maybe? You said brains interested you."

"Better and better." Her focus was on his mouth.

Yeah, he was still grinning. He couldn't seem to help it. "Any of them would be an interesting profession if they fit with your brain wiring."

"Agreed." Her return smile was a bit tentative. Maybe it turned a little shy. Maybe, like his sister, she was starting to get overwhelmed by attention. "So, was I right?"

"I'm with the FBI."

"The FBI?" No, he never would have guessed that.

"Mmmm."

Yup, he needed to wind up this conversation. He could read the signs. She was done.

"I was guessing something less Foggy Bottom. There's not much room for creativity and entrepreneurship in the FBI." Hawkeye turned to the flight attendant who had arrived with her cart.

"What would you like to drink?" the attendant asked as she held out a bag of salty snacks.

"Nothing for me, thank you," Petra said.

"Water, please." After accepting and thanking the server, Hawkeye turned back to find Petra pulling the shade down again.

"Is it okay?" she asked.

"Whatever makes you comfortable. You have your eye mask on your forehead, I bet your patch makes you groggy." He pointed toward his neck to indicate the motion sickness patch.

She blinked at him. And once again, he saw her motors humming.

Finally, she said, "Yes, I need to sleep." There was a

goodbye smile. She pulled her mask into place, inserted her earbuds, and rested her hand protectively on Cooper's head.

Cooper's tail wagged against Hawkeye's leg.

And Hawkeye was left to contemplate her and wonder what the hell had just happened to him.

5

PETRA

Petra roused when Cooper pressed his paw into her thigh in a series of "it's time to get up now" taps.

With her arm trapped between her torso and the wall, she had been leaning on it long enough that she'd lost circulation. Rubbing her fingers over her eyes to rouse herself before dragging her mask to the top of her head, she shoved it in her pocket and out of the way then shifted her shoulder to get her blood flowing. The fingers on her right hand were hesitant to move. But even just lifting herself to a seated position, her arm began to wake up with the buzzing pins and needles pain of a limb that had gone to sleep.

Petra tried to lift her hand to shake her arm and speed things along, but it was heavy and needed more time, so she let it drop back into her lap.

She must have been really out of it.

Reaching across her body, Petra slowly raised the shade just as the flight attendant announced that she would be preparing the cabin for landing.

Her eyes felt dry and scratchy from the stale air.

When had she ever slept seven hours straight? Petra chalked it up to having Cooper in her lap and the Iniquus operator sitting sentinel in the aisle seat.

Petra ran a tongue over her teeth behind closed lips. She wished she had a breath mint in her pocket. Avery had been right with her assessment of Hawkeye on the phone. She had enjoyed their brief chat before exhaustion overwhelmed her.

Changes in plans often drained her, making her zone out and need a nap, no matter how handsome or intriguing she found the person sitting next to her. And today had been a day of switcheroos and mayhem.

But they were landing, and she had no obligations of any kind for the next few days. Petra wondered if, perhaps, Hawkeye might like to join her for dinner during that time.

Deciding that there was no harm in asking, she was stopped when Cooper jumped to the ground and sat facing her with a paw on her knee. He turned his head to find Hawkeye.

Did Cooper need something from her?

She shifted around to see how Hawkeye would respond to this, perhaps giving her an explanation.

Hawkeye's gaze traveled from his dog to her. "You're awake." He stalled as she caught his gaze, and she watched as the man, without actually moving, shifted in front of her.

His demeanor had changed from bored and relaxed to something else.

"Will you do me a favor?" he asked. "Would you smile for me?"

By habit, Petra let her lips slide down her face into a frown, melting her features. She'd practiced this look in the mirror. It wasn't necessarily a frown. It was just letting her facial features go lax. It was her response when men told her to smile. Though clichéd, it happened with alarming regularity. Probably because her resting face was once described to her as "schoolmarm." Not that she knew exactly what was meant by that, but it seemed to make people—men—uncomfortable. Men preferred to be smiled at and fawned over. She couldn't believe an Iniquus guy—on the clock and in uniform—would be so gross.

"Shit." Hawkeye's response was formed on the exhale, but Petra had always had exceptional hearing, too good at times, and she'd heard it clearly.

So good, she thought, Hawkeye got her message; she wasn't the smile-on-demand kind of woman.

He reached up and pressed the attendant's light overhead.

There was a ping, and the flight attendant rounded the corner.

"I believe we have a medical issue," he told her quietly, then turned back to look at Petra.

Petra stilled. *What?*

The attendant leaned in for a moment, then squatted in the bulkhead's extra space.

"Could you smile for me, please?" She, too, changed her tone.

Petra, without any context to rest a thought on, was lost. "What?"

"Are you wearing a medical alert bracelet or necklace?" The attendant asked and, from her crouch, held her hand in the air, making some kind of signal.

Just waking up from a deep, medicated sleep, Petra was confused at that moment. As was sometimes the case under stress, there was a lag as Petra processed the words. She knew each word as an individual word. Her brain was slow in lining them up to form a meaning.

Maybe they thought that her grogginess from the meds was in some way concerning.

Petra scanned down her body. She wasn't leaking anything from anywhere—no drool or snot. No blood. Why would they think she was having a medical emergency?

She looked at Hawkeye blankly as her mind raced, searching for a reason that explained his shift to professional calm. Professional calm was a different beast than regular calm. It had an accent of hyperawareness, a priming of the body that —while held loose and comfortable so as not to expend precious energy until it was needed—was still ready to dive off the X. She'd seen it in theater with the soldiers all the time.

And it usually signaled something very bad on the horizon.

Another attendant arrived with a medical kit, setting it down by Hawkeye's booted feet, then leaned in to see what was going on. "Oh!" She sipped the word into her body with surprise.

Not helpful. Not informative. But obviously, all three of the people crowding around her agreed that something was wrong with her.

Petra felt fine.

Normal.

And also scared.

"Can someone tell me what's going on?" Petra whispered.

Hawkeye pulled his phone from a thigh pocket and opened the camera app. He held it up to her face. "I'm concerned about your pupil," he explained.

Well, lo and behold, what in the *actual hell* was going on with her eye?

"You're a doctor?" the attendant asked.

"I was trained as a medic in the military," Hawkeye replied as he unzipped his thigh pocket and pulled out a first-aid kit.

"Flight attendants, take your seats for approach," the pilot said over the intercom.

Petra kept staring into the camera. One eye looked perfectly normal. In the other eye, her iris was hidden behind her pupil. Her pupil had never been this large before, and the difference from right side to left had to be significant. Frightening.

Hawkeye pulled a penlight from his medical kit and held it up, asking for her permission.

"Sure," she said on an exhale.

Flicking the light across her right eye and then her left, he announced, "Unilateral pupillary responsiveness." He turned to catch the attendant's gaze. "I think we need to treat this as a medical emergency. Could you let the pilot know?"

The standing attendant took off toward the front of the plane.

"Do you have a history of strokes?" Hawkeye asked.

"Strokes?" Was that what this was? Is this how it felt to have a stroke? Because Petra felt fine?

"Could you smile for me?" This time, with context, Petra understood that Hawkeye wasn't a cad but someone moving through stroke protocol FAST – face, arms, speech, time.

This time, she did as was asked.

"Beautiful. Nice and even. Okay, scrunch up your face like the worst sour thing you ever ate. Okay, good. Grab my hands and squeeze. Pull me. Push me. You're very strong."

"Yes," she whispered. Should she tell them that her arm had gone numb? It was mostly back to normal. Still a little tingly, but her fingers were warmer.

"Bilateral strength," he said.

"Yes." She turned her attention to the window. Below them, Petra saw a row of emergency vehicles racing forward. Those would be for her.

This felt ridiculous.

Did she feel like she was having a stroke?

What did it feel like to have a stroke?

Her arm was waking up and was painful with pins and needles. Was that what a stroke felt like?

It was the opposite arm to her weird eyeball. Was that important?

"Ladies and gentlemen, one of our passengers is experiencing a medical emergency. Before taxiing to our gate, we will be landing near emergency services so that the professionals can handle the situation. We ask that everyone remain seated with seat belts in place.

We ask that you respect this situation – a human having a challenging experience – and honor that by affording them privacy. Please refrain from taking pictures or videos. Flight attendants strap in for the landing."

Pictures or videos…

When paramedics show up at the scene of an emergency, one of the first things they did was to cut the patient's clothes off. They did it to check for unnoticed bleeds or injuries, but also to make the patient's body accessible to whatever medical intervention might need to take place once they arrive in the emergency department.

Everyone was going to see her like that, lying on a gurney. Just a moment ago, she was going to ask Hawkeye on a date, and now he was going to see her stretched out like that.

Like an emergency.

Like a problem.

It was crazy. She *felt* fine.

This seemed like a movie scene to Petra, like she could get up, have a lunch break, then head back when the director called out, "Places, everybody!"

As the plane landed with a bump and rolled down to what was obviously the emergency area with rescue vehicles' lights flashing and sirens blaring, Petra could not believe they were there for her.

For *her*.

She knew today was destined for the crapper.

And oddly, since this was about to go viral with people sending out videos despite the plea, Petra found herself wondering, "What the hell underwear did I pull on this morning?"

6

———

HAWKEYE

Hawkeye was glad Cooper had signaled to him that there was a problem before he met Petra's gaze, or his reaction wouldn't have looked the same.

Oddly when he saw that her pupil was blown, his first thought was, "Shit, no, I just met her. We haven't had time." He immediately set that thought aside to examine later. Right now, he had to focus on figuring out what had happened to her from the time they were discussing brain wiring until this moment.

Hawkeye had seen blown pupils before. But they had always been in conjunction with a blast trauma or trauma to the head. And it was always treated as a life-or-death emergency, with evacuations by the PJs if necessary.

She'd mentioned a TBI, but it sounded like it had been back in the past, not something that she was healing from right now.

Since those soldiers had always had bilaterally blown pupils, what he saw in Petra didn't align with his lived experience. But he'd never been around anyone who might be having a stroke. That not one but both attendants came to the same immediate conclusion, told Hawkeye that it wasn't unreasonable to suspect a stroke even when everything else about Petra seemed fine.

"Would you mind if I took your pulse?" he asked as he pulled his arm around to see the face of his watch with its stopwatch capability.

"Thank you." She held her hand out to him, but what he wanted was her in his arms. She looked so scared and confused. He just wanted to hold her to his heart and tell her that everything was going to be fine.

But he couldn't say that truthfully.

Cooper leaned forward and sniffed her hand over before giving Hawkeye the go-ahead. The interesting thing about that exchange was that Reaper, the Cerberus trainer that they were meeting in St. Croix, had been expanding the Cerberus kennels' scent training to include medical issues. Flu, Covid, and pregnancy were the three that they had focused on first. Pregnancy because that would change the way they treated an injured person during a natural disaster; Covid and flu so they could steer their protectees away from a contagion, or if the dog detected the illness—sometimes days before symptoms showed up—the team could get the client to a doctor in time to get prophylactics on board.

With Cooper's all-clear, Hawkeye knew that Petra had none of those conditions. That Cooper checked without Hawkeye's signal meant that Cooper believed this was a medical event.

"I'm drawing a blank," Petra said.

Her voice was calm but from her racing pulse, Hawkeye knew she was feeling anxious. Who wouldn't be?

"I know if you're having a heart attack, you have to inhale as deeply as you can and cough out strongly and keep doing that violent coughing routine as a kind of self-applied CPR until you get to a hospital. But this?" She shook her head. "I'm racking my brain. Beyond checking FAST, What is the newest protocol? I'm thinking baby aspirin. But then I also seem to remember not to do baby aspirin."

"If this is a stroke, all you can really do is get to the hospital as fast as possible. There's a golden hour for getting the medications in. But no to the baby aspirin. You're right, they used to advise that, but not all strokes are caused by blood clots. Ruptured blood vessels can do it, too. Since aspirin thins the blood, it would make any bleeds more severe."

She rolled her lips in, bobbling her head, indicating that she understood.

Hawkeye hated this for her. Hated every second that she was in danger. He wanted the wheels down and Petra in an ambulance. He had no idea how far it would be to get help from here.

As if reading Hawkeye's mind, Halo leaned forward. "Seven miles, brother. Ten minutes if they go lights and sirens once she's loaded up. I can manage Cooper and your baggage if you want to go, mate."

Hawkeye glanced over his shoulder, giving Halo a nod before turning back to Petra to ask what she wanted. "Would you like my support once we're down? I can get to the hospital and make phone calls for you, keep people informed."

For the first time, he saw a reaction from her other than bewilderment. Her eyes got glassy as tears dampened her lashes. "Would you? I was trying to figure out what to do on my own. And since we're family."

"Family..." he left that open-ended because he couldn't guess what she meant.

"Not family. I must have been thinking of home when I said that, wishing my family were here or someone I knew better. But we do have people in common. Rowan Kennedy and his wife, Avery Goodyear, are dear friends of mine. So, I'm grateful for your kindness. I won't feel like a complete stranger in a strange land."

He looked back at Halo. "I'll take you up on that offer. I'll get to the hospital with Petra." Now that they could hear the piercing scream of sirens, her anxiety was rising. He hoped to distract her. "Interesting that you put Rowan, Avery, and me together in your mind."

"Not really. The counter staffer told me I'd be sitting next to the working dogs. And when I looked out the window, I recognized the uniform. I was on the phone with Avery and sent her a picture of you all when you were on the ground by the luggage handlers. You were below my window. She told me who you were. Well, since I was above you, she couldn't see your faces. But she was able to recognize Max and Cooper, and she was able to tell me that their handlers were Halo and Hawkeye."

That explained their first exchange when he'd said his name, and she'd said "yes" like she already knew him. "Friends of Rowan and Avery, yes, that makes us family of sorts. You *aren't* alone. Okay?" It felt good to have the connection and to have a stronger reason to stay with her and offer his support. It also felt good that she was speaking cogently about a timeline.

"Ladies and gentlemen," the pilot announced, "we are coordinating with the paramedics to safely disembark the passenger who is experiencing a medical emergency. The responders are moving stairs into place, and the emergency crews will come on board. Please, keep hands and feet out of the aisles. We have no time frame for this event. Our passenger's health and well-being are paramount. Hopefully, this is your final destination, and this delay will be a minor inconvenience. I'm leaving the seat belt light on. Please remain seated at all times. Imagine if this event took you by surprise, and let's follow the golden rule. Yes?"

Petra's eyes held wide as her lips sank into a frown.

She had to be listening to that, knowing that she was the problem. The surprise was happening to her.

"Hawkeye," she whispered. "I should feel badly, right? Headache? Something? This feels kind of silly."

He got it. From when she kept things contained during the dog and cat scramble earlier in the day, she did not like attention or disruption. Like anyone would, Petra would want to deny that anything serious was wrong with her.

She was a smart woman, capable of dealing with facts. So, he'd just lay it out. "Petra, I'm seeing a blown pupil that's nonreactive. We aren't playing with that. There's a window to get the proper meds in. We need to exercise every caution and get you in front of medical staff so they can determine what's happening." Hawkeye wanted to add that every second she wasn't in the hospital with help focused on her was a second too long for him.

This wasn't about him. Not at all.

This was about Petra's safety.

As the door opened, Halo swung out of his seat to stand in the aisle.

"Cooper," Hawkeye pulled his dog's attention away from Petra. "Go with Halo." Cooper wasn't down with that, and Hawkeye completely understood. If someone were to ask him to step away, there would be pushback. But this was not the time to argue with his dog. "*Cooper*, go sit with Halo." He curled his fingers through Cooper's collar to help guide him over.

Halo moved Cooper into the bulkhead space with the other dogs, then sat in the end seat, scooting down until his knees were against the bulkhead wall, blocking the K9s in and the rescue team out.

Cooper rested his head on Halo's leg, watching intently as the paramedics came on.

"There's a good boy, Coop," Halo crooned. "Your new friend is getting some help. She'll be right, mate."

Hawkeye made to get out of the paramedics' way, but Petra reached out and gripped his arm with both her hands to anchor him in place.

The paramedic watched it happen. "You're fine there. Who are you?"

Hawkeye knew he was asking for a role, not a name. He went to the first thing he could think of to make sure he could stay with Petra. "First responder. I noticed the change in her pupillary response."

"How long ago?"

"Undetermined. She was fine at the beginning of the flight but slept the whole way here." Hawkeye handed out his note-book with respiration and pulse rates that he had taken every five minutes. The numbers had held steady.

"Instead of a gurney, since you're conscious, we can bring up a wheelchair, then carry you down that way. Do you feel like you can't hold yourself upright for that long?"

"I could carry her in my arms," Hawkeye offered. He turned to Petra, "If you'd be comfortable with that. It might be safer than risking an event happening while you're in the chair."

"Event happening…" Petra's voice wobbled. "Like I go unconscious?"

"In the unlikely event that you have trouble staying upright while you're on the stairs." He pronounced his words clearly and spoke just a bit slower to make himself as understood as possible.

"The stairs are steep," the paramedic cautioned Hawkeye.

"We train on them. One of my team could go in front in case of a missed foot." He turned to Petra. "Would that be all right with you? Do you want to make decisions here or would you prefer I make them?" For his sister, Cora, especially under stress, decision-making was mentally and therefore physically exhausting. Cora's brain was constantly going, going, going. Not to say Petra was exactly like Cora—as Cora liked to say, "Once you've met someone who is neurodivergent, you've met one person who is neurodivergent." But Hawkeye did have the advantage of knowing and loving Cora, and maybe his lived experience could be helpful here. "Or we can make the decisions together."

Petra squeezed his arm and said with relief, "You, please. Down the stairs and decision making." She sniffed. "Please."

He hated the fear in her eyes. "All right, you just let me know if you change your mind."

Having listened to them, the paramedic asked Hawkeye, "Do you want to go with her in the ambulance then, in order to provide continuity of care?"

"If I'm able. I can give the emergency department staff the available information."

The paramedic gathered his equipment and made his way to the door, where he called the plan down to his crew.

"Do you have a bag with you?" Hawkeye asked.

"Black backpack." She pointed up.

"Is there anything in there that you need now?" He was careful to ask one direct and simple question at a time.

"No."

"Halo will bring it to you later. Come and slide over into my seat." Before he could stand up, Levi slipped out of his seat and toward the door.

Levi had been on a rescue in Namibia where he had to carry his fiancée down a hillside with a teammate in front ready to break a fall should Levi trip. Levi brought that experience back to the team, where they talked through the different issues, like the areas that had been too tight to get through with someone in his arms; what it felt like to race downward on uneven terrain without being able to see ground hazards.

So, they trained an exfil where the person was carried in the operator's arms when it was counterproductive to do a fireman's carry.

It was one of the ways that Team Charlie knew Petra's friend Avery Goodyear.

Avery, a romance editor, was contracted with Iniquus so when a scenario was presented by an operator, she could think of dozens of ways that the scene could go wrong. "After all," she'd said, "that's what authors do all day long to make a living."

The teams would then test their skill under the circumstances she imagined.

A medical event on a plane was one of those scenarios that Avery had listed.

Hawkeye was grateful that she'd imagined this one.

Hawkeye stood as Petra scooted over to him, then he stooped to scoop her into his arms. The passage being as small as it was, Levi reached under her knees while Hawkeye held her under the arms, her head resting on his shoulder. Levi backed up until they reached the door, where Levi helped shift Petra back into Hawkeye's arms.

It was seamless, and Hawkeye hoped that they had kept Petra comfortable. She didn't need a racing heart right now.

Slow and steady.

Calm and professional.

That's how he'd work to keep her safe.

As she came into his arms, Petra turned to lean her head on his shoulder, clasping her hands behind his neck. And with Levi ahead of them, sliding his hands down the guardrail, ready to grip and block at any moment to prevent a fall, they made their way efficiently down to the ground and the gurney.

"You've got this," Levi said, patting Petra's shoulder, then he climbed the stairs again, getting out of the way.

With flashing lights and blaring sirens, the first responders roared down the street toward the emergency room.

But for Hawkeye, they couldn't get there fast enough.

7

———

Petra felt ridiculous.

But there *had* to be something to this.

The response was the same with every person who looked at her face.

As soon as the paramedics wheeled her into the hospital, the nurse turned toward Petra. Without a single word of information from the ambulance crew, the nurse grabbed the phone to send out the code. "Stroke protocol. *Stroke protocol.*"

Hands helped Petra shift from the gurney to a rolling bed, and that bed speeded down the hall and parked right in the middle of the corridor. "This is where we assess stroke patients. We don't want to waste time angling you out of a room. When we have to go, we have to go. We're clearing the imaging room now."

"What does that mean? Someone was in there, and you're pulling them out?" Petra was horrified that she was displacing another person in need of help.

"Stroke patients take priority," came the response. In her distress, Petra wasn't seeing or remembering faces, just one blue-scrubs-wearing person after another, each efficiently doing the next thing on a list of critical things that needed to be done.

Hawkeye never let go of her hand.

This was real. This was happening. And how strange that she should feel fine, but that her life could change radically. Stroke could lead to all kinds of bad outcomes.

Brain damage. Paralysis. Death.

She could die.

How strange.

It all just felt so normal. And yet, Petra could be dying.

Hawkeye was talking, and Petra forced her attention toward him so she could hear and understand his words. "She was fine when she put on her mask to go to sleep. She slept the whole way here. It could be as much as six hours since a possible event occurred."

"Could you be pregnant?" the doctor asked.

"Not possible," Petra said.

"Any medical conditions I need to know about? Prescription drugs that you use on a regular basis?" The doctor read from her tablet.

"I don't have a chronic condition, no," Petra said.

"She's had a TBI," Hawkeye added.

That's right, she'd told Hawkeye in passing when they were talking about unhoused people. TBI and neurodivergence, a double whammy. "Blast concussion and shrapnel in my abdomen," Petra clarified. "That was in Afghanistan a decade ago. Oh, and I was exposed to burn pits while I was over there. I don't know if that could be at play here. But that's all historic. Presently, I'm healthy."

No, that couldn't be right. Presently, she couldn't be healthy. Presently, she was on a hospital bed in the middle of a corridor so the nurses could race her to lifesaving care, slicing off every extra second so that she *wouldn't die*.

Petra focused on how the doctor received her information. Petra had been a watcher of faces, a studier of nuanced expressions all her life. It was a trait shared by many neurodiverse people as they tried to figure out how to fit in. At this moment, the doctor's face lost its elasticity. It didn't change expressions, but the muscles under her skin became rigid, and Petra knew that the woman's sense of danger had increased. Her body was preparing her for emergency action.

Action to help me, Petra Armstrong.

Wasn't that surreal?

She didn't feel strange. She felt so normal for all this to be happening. Was this the effect of adrenaline? Yeah, that could be what was going on, adrenaline masking.

The attendant had Petra go through the same tests Hawkeye had—face and grip were tested for asymmetry.

Petra asked when that all checked out, "Well, that's a good sign, right?"

The doctor answered with, "This is your husband?"

"Fiancé." Petra reached for his hand again. "He can stay with me if he's my fiancé, right?"

Hawkeye had fixed his gaze on her, staring right into her wonky, crazy eyes, and said, "I'm not leaving you, sweetheart."

The nurse paused while she watched her machine readouts. "It would be good if he stays and holds your hand."

"Yes, please." Petra turned to Hawkeye. "Is that possible?"

The nurse tapped the machine. "Whenever he lets go of you, your heart rate spikes."

Petra looked up to catch Hawkeye's gaze. "Please don't let go," she whispered.

"I won't. I would never. I'll hold on to you as long as you want me to."

Did Petra just make that up? It sounded so sincere, and there was nothing sarcastic about the way he looked at her. Maybe he was play-acting for the medical staff?

In her mind, this seemed like some kind of crazy twist in a rom-com.

No, the hunky hero's hand didn't change her blood pressure, her heart rate—whatever.

This was a dream.

And if it was a dream, it was a stupid dream to have.

After the nurse left, Hawkeye twisted around and planted his thigh on the bed so she didn't have to strain to see him. "Fiancé?" he asked.

"I just met you a couple hours ago. I thought rushing to the altar and calling you my husband was a little too…" She shifted her head back and forth. "Anyway, if you *were* my husband, you'd have my insurance information. You'd also be my next of kin to pull the plugs if this stroke thing gets out of hand."

That unsettled him. Angst clouded his gaze. But he seemed to wrestle it down. "I'd never pull the plug on a woman I just met. Besides, Cooper is too enamored of you, and I'm just not up to that conversation with him. But yes, the husband thing would be hard to pull off without rings. Even as your fiancé, they might think it's odd that I don't know your last name."

"Armstong. No ring. You're not married?"

"I'm not involved with anyone right now. I'm Hawkeye Kesse."

"Kesse. Like kiss."

He raised a brow.

"I'm feeling a bit vulnerable, Hawkeye Kesse, and it's awkward to depend on the kindness of strangers." She gave him a weak smile. "You can go if you want. You've already done so much for me. It was nice of you to do all the things you have.

And, of course, it was also nice that you didn't get scared off by my possibilities."

He lifted a single brow. "Possibilities?"

"I could be an alien." She flicked a finger toward her left eye. "My mask might be slipping."

"Some kind of lizard person with fixed and dilated pupils?"

"Exactly. But you should know, we don't use them for seeing – not like you humans do. I can absorb particles and analyze them in real-time."

He squinted. "Particles of what exactly?"

"Words, emotions, sensations, tastes."

"Tastes?" A reluctant smile slid across his face.

"Yes. You, for example, taste like black coffee and an airplane cookie."

He grinned.

Two nurses hustled around the corner.

Hawkeye jumped to his feet.

One nurse kicked the brakes off her bed while the other swung around behind Petra's head. "We've cleared the imaging room. Sir, if you could wait in the waiting area, no one except for the patient is allowed in that room."

"Okay." Hawkeye kept pace as the women took off at a fast clip, propelling Petra down the corridor. "I'm only going as far as the waiting room. I won't leave you. You've got this." He leaned down, kissed her cheek, squeezed her hand, and was gone.

Petra lay on a bed speeding down the corridor on the way to find out whether she

Might. Just. Die.

8

———

"You look loopy."

She blinked at the man standing there, looming over everything. Broad shoulders, slender hips, and legs that went on and on. Basketball player, probably.

"How are you feeling right now?"

She blinked again, focusing on his face. Nice nose on the smallish side with a little bump in the middle—it might have been broken at some point. Solid jaw. Rugged. Obviously, someone who was outside a lot. He had laugh lines, and she liked that about his face most of all.

All in all, a good-looking man.

"Petra?" He touched his chest. "It's Hawkeye. Do you recognize me?"

Petra stilled. Did she know him? Yes, of course. "Yes. I'm... They gave me..." Petra looked around at the nurse, doing something off to the side.

"We administered a sedative. Miss Armstrong was having difficulty being still in the machine."

"She's neurodivergent. That makes sense," Hawkeye said matter-of-factly. And Petra was grateful. He was right. It did make sense.

The nurse handed him a baggie, sent him a professional smile, and left.

Hawkeye snagged the leg of the visitor's chair and dragged it over, sitting so Petra could see his face without straining.

Petra reflexively reached for his hand. "The sounds from the machine were very electric. While I laid on my back with instructions not to move, it was like nails on a chalkboard and more than my nerves could handle."

He put the baggie beside him and wrapped her hand in both of his. He was an anchor.

"They gave me a helper drug. They told me the name, but I can't remember it." Was that English? Did those words make sense?

"I'm glad you got some relief from the stress. Do you remember talking to the doctor?"

"Me?" Petra didn't feel drunk or high. But she didn't feel normal either. Relaxed.

"You spoke with the doctor. Do you remember the conversation?"

"In the hall when they said you should hold my hand?" The more she moved her mouth, the more limber her thoughts became. She was feeling a bit more in her body, a bit more like herself.

"A minute ago, here in this room." Hawkeye shuffled to the edge of his seat and leaned closer.

"No," Petra said. "I don't remember that."

"Okay. I'll tell you what she said. Ready?" He lifted his brows and waited.

"I don't know." Petra felt very small. Very fragile. Had she had a stroke? She took a moment and wiggled her fingers and toes. She bent and kicked her legs and jiggled her arms.

She wasn't paralyzed.

"I'm not going to tell you anything bad right now." Hawkeye's voice was rumbly and deep. It brought to mind Tibetan singing bowls and how Petra liked the big ones that shook the marrow of her bones like his voice did.

Petra pressed her lips together and nodded, working very hard to stay focused on Hawkeye's words.

"Your brain looks fine. They've ruled out a stroke."

"No stroke." She mouthed the words because her voice couldn't wrap around the syllables to give them volume.

"No stroke." He smiled with his eyes—warm and maybe a little charmed.

Was that possible? Could he be charmed by her confusion?

She wiggled her hand by her eye.

"All the concerns are not off the table," he said. "They don't have an explanation for your pupil, which looks the same as it did on the plane." He held up the plastic bag with what looked like prescription eye drops. "I have this. You're supposed to take it with you tomorrow morning when you have an appointment with the eye doctor to see if he can come up with a diagnosis."

"So, we leave the hospital?" Did they do that? Did they let people with wonky eyes go off to fend for themselves?

"I'm wondering about phone calls." Hawkeye's words were spoken clearly, slowly. Petra had time to put them together in a sentence and find meaning.

"To next of kin?" She tried for sarcasm to lighten the mood. But the look on his face made her immediately regret saying that. "I'm sorry you're being kind, and I'm being—"

"Scared. It's understandable. I was wondering if you had

plans to meet someone on the island and if I should reach out to them on your behalf, so they don't worry. Boyfriend?"

"I'm not in a relationship. I was coming with a friend, but she got too sick to fly. Speaking of friends, we have people in common."

"Yeah?" His thumb painted soothingly over her hand.

"Rowan Kennedy and Avery Goodyear-Kennedy."

"Right," Hawkeye said. "How did you make that connection?"

"I'm good friends with Avery, and I wanted the scuttlebutt on your team since you were going to be on my flight. And she said she knew you."

Hawkeye nodded. "Do you remember when you talked to her?"

"At the airport, I sent her a picture of you guys standing outside with your K9s. And she gave me names and basics."

"Girl talk."

"Yeah, well, we're both women, but I guess. Because of your caps, she couldn't tell who was who. But she did recognize Max and Cooper." She paused. "Have we already had this conversation?"

"We did." A smile wiggled the corners of his mouth. "You're loopy from the meds they gave you. I was asking if you know anyone here. There's an open question about your health status."

"Not stroke, thank goodness."

"And I'm concerned about you sleeping alone."

"Seriously? That's your play? I have an alien baby pupil without a diagnosis, and you want to have a sleepover?"

Confusion crossed his face but ended in a smile. "Petra, you're a friend of a friend. This isn't a play for you in any way, shape, or form."

Well, that was embarrassing.

And disappointing.

Hawkeye was acting in service of a friend of a friend.

A girl can fantasize after the fact. That was an odd thought for her, and Petra wondered where it had come from when she remembered Tamika had suggested that morning—a lifetime ago when Petra knew her day was destined for the crapper—that Petra could turn it around by finding a warm body to make her feel good about life.

This wasn't a rom-com after all.

But at least as the friend of a friend—a degree of distance even farther than being relegated to the friendship corner—Petra could be grateful she wasn't navigating this shit show alone.

"You sound drunk, and Rowan would be pissed if I left you vulnerable so far from home." Hawkeye's tone was light and reasonable.

"You're right. If something bad were to happen—worse — he'd expect you to," she held up her hand and made an expansive gesture, "see it through in some way."

"Do you remember where you're staying?"

"Blue Fin Hotel."

The nurse arrived with a wheelchair.

Petra moved from bed to chair in silence.

They were quiet as the nurse pushed Petra out the main hospital door and then waited while Hawkeye got Petra up into the front seat of what smelled like a rental.

They must have told him to bring the car around, or why would his car be parked here by the door? Had he told her about this?

Okay, still loopy.

He circled the front of the car and climbed in, adjusting the seat back as far as it would go and fixing the mirrors.

After pulling on his belt and checking that hers was

securely clasped, Hawkeye set his phone in the cupholder and focused on the blue directional line.

"SUV, you'd need the headroom," Petra said.

When he turned onto the road, he glanced her way, "I'm going to throw it out there and see what you think." He turned his attention back to the road. "When we get to the hotel, we can ask and see if they have two adjoining rooms available. If they did, we could leave the doors open between the rooms. Cooper would serve as chaperone."

"Cooper." Petra turned and looked over her seat to the back.

"Cooper and your bags are waiting to see how things land, and then Halo will help with logistics. If I stayed in an adjoining room, it means someone could be there and get to you if things take a turn."

Petra swiveled back in her seat to look at him, rerunning those sentences.

He drove silently, not pushing his agenda. He laid the offer down.

An offer. Take it or don't.

As time passed, he didn't up the pressure on her to accept.

He didn't huff and puff that she didn't answer and immediately accept his hero's gesture.

He sat there patiently, hands on the wheel, letting her process as he drove through the twilight sky.

Petra thought about being on the plane with her sleeping mask on and how she had planned to invite Hawkeye for dinner or a drink once they landed.

The clock read eight-thirty. She hadn't had anything to eat since dinner yesterday.

If she mentioned food to him, he'd get her something to eat. But this was a different vibe than what she'd intended. In fact, she'd envisioned seducing him and enjoying some sexy time over the weekend if he could get free from work—a vacation adventure for her, some stress relief for him.

And at that point, all she had was Avery's green flag to tell her Hawkeye was safe. Well, that and Iniquus's reputation for only hiring people with a high thread count on their moral fiber.

Did that make sense? Fiber…thread count…Threads *were* fibers… moral cloth.

Cloth? Fabric.

There, that's what she was aiming for: Iniquus had a reputation for only hiring people with high thread count moral fabric.

But that thought didn't matter. What mattered was that Hawkeye felt like a good guy. Upstanding. Forthright.

If her eyeball had come to his notice, all he had to do to get his good karma points was mention it to the flight attendant and step aside.

But he stepped forward.

"Yes," Petra said. "Thank you. Though I hate to put you out, I think that would be wise. And it's very kind of you to offer. We can see if that can be arranged. And if it's not possible. We could think of something else. Alone, I think I'd feel too vulnerable and isolated."

Hawkeye drummed his thumbs on the top of the steering wheel. "Physically, I know the meds are making you feel off. How about mentally? It's not a small deal that people thought you were having a health crisis that could have profound effects on your future."

"I think I'll have to process all that once I know what the eye doctor says. That's what's happening, right? Tomorrow morning, I go to the eye doctor?"

"You have the first appointment. We need to be there at eight. I'll have time to get you there and back before I head out to train Cooper."

"Thank you." Relieved to take the focus off herself, Petra asked, "What is Cooper learning tomorrow?"

Hawkeye sent her a grin. "Tomorrow, he'll be learning how to surf."

"Surf? But why?" she asked.

"Oh, lots of reasons. We constantly work to build our dogs' confidence. Working dogs need to consistently be challenged mentally and physically. Smart animals get bored when they're not challenged. So, facing a challenge is one reason. Another is, if we're doing rescue work on a coastline, the K9s need to be comfortable in the surf, able to work on the water, and probably most importantly, know how to stabilize themselves on floating objects as a safety measure against floods and currents."

"And when you train them, is that all day?" she wondered.

"We watch the dogs to make sure they're not getting over-hyped. Too much adrenaline leads to poor choices."

"In dogs and in humans," Petra said. "So how do you manage that?"

"If we're introducing a new task? We break it down, building on something they already know how to do. For example, back on the Cerberus campus, we have a wave pool, and they've already been working on getting on a board from the water and balancing. We won't be starting from complete scratch out there on the waves. That's part one of management. We don't let them fail. The next tiny thing will be sitting on the beach and working up to throwing the ball in the water. Give them a break. Then, after they rest in their crates, we'll let them hang out on the surfboards with us if they're up to it. Hoover, that's Ash's K9, big red German shepherd."

Petra gave a nod. "He was the first dog on the plane this morning."

"That's right. Hoover's a big water dog, so he came to provide peer-to-peer mentorship."

"Oh, nice! You said crates. Why not just let them sleep on the sand?"

"Their crate, by themselves, without distractions, is their thinking spot," Hawkeye said. "They go into their private space and rest for twenty minutes, which helps them relive the experience and process it to learn more quickly and with less stress."

"Like they do in Finland with their kids. No homework. Hands-on learning, mixing fun activities with harder ones, then out you go to play in the woods no matter the weather, to process and maybe apply what you just learned to your playtime. It's an extremely effective system." Petra paused and covered her eyes as if to shield herself. "What was that smile?"

"Nothing really, just for someone in the FBI, you have a non-linear way of thinking."

"You're not the first person to say that." Petra rested her head against the side window and felt the coolness of the night air radiate through her hair to her scalp. "Have you worked with Cooper for a long time? Where did you buy him? Here in the States, or did you have to go over to Europe?"

"He's been with me for almost four years now. I didn't buy him, though," Hawkeye said, "I found him in the road."

"What? Found him? An amazing dog like Cooper?" Petra only knew a very little about working dogs. But she did know that when the special operators came through camp with their K9s, the teams treated their K9s like fellow soldiers and held them in high esteem. She also knew that the military bought their dogs from specific breeders, and they could cost more than a car. "How could that happen? Would you tell me?"

"The Hawkeye and Cooper origin story? Sure. I knew Cooper was a special dog from the moment I first saw him. Tiny puppy. I'm guessing about eight weeks old. Scrawny. He ran into the middle of the road, facing down my vehicle and barking his head off. This puppy's whole body posture was so readable. He was determined to stop me, and it was for a damned good reason."

Petra bent her knee and pulled her leg onto the seat to turn sideways, leaning forward to focus.

"So, I'm out in the country, taking a drive to clear my head. And this tiny pup ran out in front of my vehicle, where he squared off and barked at me ferociously. It was comical, really. And I climbed down from my cab to see if he had on a collar so I could get him back to his mama. Cooper was so small; I wasn't even sure he'd weaned yet. I was afraid he was going to run away, so I got into a low squat and was chirping at him, trying to get his curiosity and courage up so he'd come see me. Every time I got close, he'd bound off a bit, then turn to see if I was following. So now he had sparked my curiosity. He stopped at a ditch with tall weeds, and I thought that, since he didn't have a collar on, his litter mates might be in there and be hungry. I was making plans for rounding them up and getting them to a no-kill shelter."

"But it wasn't more puppies," Petra whispered.

"It was a human baby. Seven months old. He must have crawled from his yard toward the street. And was just then coming up the side of the ditch. Determined little bugger."

"Baby! Can you imagine what would have happened without a warning?"

"Especially in the size truck I was driving," Hawkeye said. "I could have easily missed the baby on the road. Lots of bad could have happened. There was cold water in the ditches. If the baby hadn't crawled out, he could have gone hypothermic and died pretty fast if he hadn't drowned first, weighed down by his clothes. He could have crawled into the woods and disappeared, lots of wild animals, coyotes, and the like."

"A random baby in the weeds? Like Moses in the reeds on the Nile?"

"I hadn't thought of that. But, that is about how it looked. When I picked the baby up, he seemed okay, damp and dirty from crawling, mud from head to foot. I could see through a break in the trees that a gravel drive was hidden under the dried leaves. And a few paces in, I could see a house.

"The baby wasn't crying? What was Cooper doing?"

"The baby let me hold him without any fuss. Cooper looked satisfied that he got someone to pick up the baby. I felt there was a lot more to this story. Things seemed too still. If a baby is missing, alarms are clanging."

"Like the cat on the plane. Everyone was in motion. You're right. A still environment was suspect," she said.

"I had no way to stow the baby away safely while I checked things out, so I cautiously approached the house in the shadows. The puppy bounded out toward a patch of sunlight, then he raced back, yipping at me to hurry up."

Petra reached out and gripped his arm.

"I followed, coming up over the mound where I saw a blanket laid out with baby toys. As I walked closer and could see the other side of the elevation, I made out an elderly woman. She was non-responsive. So, I have a puppy nipping at me to get me to fix things. The baby starts screaming bloody murder, and I have an unconscious woman in front of me."

"9-1-1 was far away?" Petra asked.

"I didn't have a cell connection out there. I put the baby in the middle of the blanket and told the puppy to keep that baby on the blanket. The woman didn't have any discernable vital signs, but her skin still had color and was warm to the touch, so she hadn't been down that long. I gave her CPR. Every time I looked over, the puppy was hard at his job. And I was hard listening for a vehicle to come up the road. A few minutes in, I hear one. I lifted a finger to the puppy—and I say here puppy, not Cooper because you know big Cooper, and you shouldn't have that image in your head. This puppy was small enough to curl up in a cereal bowl."

"My goodness." Petra pressed a hand to her chest.

"I held up my finger so the puppy would remember he was to do his job guarding the baby, and I tore off through the woods to intercept the car. It was an off-duty firefighter. He had a radio in his truck and some medical equipment. An oxygen bagger. Soon enough, the paramedics showed up with an ambulance. They loaded Grandma up and took off. The firefighter and I waited for social services to send someone to take custody of the baby."

"How was puppy-Cooper doing through all that hubbub?" Petra asked.

"He never lost focus on his job. He was pushing toys over to the baby with his nose, and he'd bop the baby in the chest when he got close to the edge of the blanket."

What a fascinating story. Petra had so many questions about what was going on in the puppy's brain. But since her own circuitry was buffering, she'd save most of them for a more cogent time. For now, she'd just ask for this much, "From a K9 trainer's point of view, why did that work? How did Cooper know what to do?"

"We became a team. It was a life-or-death situation, and animals of all kinds tend to line up and work toward a common purpose when a life is on the line. Cooper saw me as the leader. I sent him a picture of his duties, and he did them."

"Like a movie in your head? That's what you showed him? Clairvoyance?"

"That's right. Cooper was creative as hell with the problem-solving. Just a miracle puppy on the side of the road."

Petra felt tears sting her eyes. A miracle puppy. The ramifications of his showing up were enormous. "He had to come from somewhere, right? But it sounds like that wasn't his baby or his owner."

"Before the social worker showed up, the baby's mom arrived with the groceries. She said the puppy didn't belong to their family, everyone was terrified of dogs, and she'd never seen the puppy before."

"What did she think of her baby crawling to the road?"

"I never told her about that," Hawkeye said. "I said there was a puppy in the road, and I went to see if it belonged to the house. I mean, it's true enough, and the mom was pretty distraught by all the doings, near hysterical. I drove the woman and the baby to the hospital and got a ride service to take me back to my truck."

"And Cooper, where was he? Waiting on the blanket?"

"In my coat pocket, curled up asleep."

"Tiny then!" Petra wished Cooper were there so she could give him some extra scritches.

"Compared to now, yes. From the get-go, Cooper was an itty-bitty powerhouse of protection, cunning, strength, and fear-lessness."

"Okay, Cooper? Why that name?" Yeah, Petra was pushing herself to have this conversation. She was afraid with the meds in her system that she'd fall asleep, and Hawkeye would feel like he had to scoop her into his arms again. Once a day of the heroine carry was probably a good quota to stick to. While the questions helped her to stay engaged, they were also sapping Petra's resources. And at the same time, she wanted to know everything about this man. The image of bottom watering a drooping houseplant came to mind. She sighed. Maybe she'd come up with some sexier imagery after some sleep.

"Cooper was the name of the baby he saved."

"Ah, now, see? I thought it was because your nickname is

Hawkeye, and you named him after James Fenimore Cooper and the Leatherstocking tales."

"My sister, Cora, was named after that, so you aren't far off the mark."

"Does your given name have a literary bent, too?"

"My given name is Michael George Kesse. Michael for Crichton and George for Orwell. Mom was a high school English teacher." Hawkeye pressed the blinker up and then turned right into a parking lot.

"Would you tell me about that?"

"Curious Petra, we're at the hotel." He pulled into a spot, put the SUV into park, and turned her way. "The drugs must be wearing off because your mind is picking up speed." He sent her a grin. "I'll answer all your questions in a bit. Come on, let's go see what we can figure out about the room situation."

9

The desk staffer stood slack-jawed, staring at Petra. The woman finally coordinated her lips to stammer, "Ma'am, are you all right? Are you aware—" She flipped a hand up by her eye and wiggled her fingers.

Petra cut the woman off by simply raising her arm with the blue plastic hospital band.

"Oh," the woman clutched her chest. "I—" She gripped both hands in front of her. "I've never seen that before." She cleared her voice. "How can I assist you?"

"I'm Hermione Armstrong. I have a reservation for tonight. It might be listed under Tamika Bradly, my travel companion. But I should be on the reservation as well."

The staffer tapped the keyboard.

"I was hoping that perhaps you had two adjoining rooms, and you could move my reservation to one and put the other on my card?" Petra pulled a credit card from the back of her phone.

The staffer rolled her mouse and clicked. Rolled and clicked. Rolled and clicked. And Hawkeye knew the woman was buying herself some time before she gave Petra some bad news. Her frown told Hawkeye the staffer didn't want to add to Petra's already difficult day.

"I'm so sorry." Her voice conveyed her sympathy. "But we let your reservation go."

"Go?" Petra said as if that were a foreign word. She slid her credit card back into its slit.

Hawkeye dragged his phone from his thigh pocket, checked for service, and then texted Reaper.

He was curious as to how Petra would handle the situation. This was a big interpersonal litmus test for him. How people treated others in times of stress – or those with less power every day—was a cheat code that unlocked a view of a person's true character. A person could have a bad day, that gave them no right to spread the pain.

Hawkeye was pretty invested in Petra.

He'd started thinking of them as having an unspoken under-standing. But over time, he'd learned it's better to pull your foot out of a trap before it can snap.

He was old enough now and had been through enough that if he was going to move forward, he needed to be clear-eyed.

Hawkeye wasn't off the mark. The receptionist—braced to take a tongue-lashing—was ready to bear the ire if stress had sanded off Petra's shiny veneer. "We sent you each an email and texted both Miss Bradley and you, asking if you ran into delays in your travel plans. Our hotel is booked solid, and we have a seven o'clock deadline for check-in unless we know you'll be late. No one responded."

Petra fussed with her phone, stared at the black screen, then slid it back into her pocket. "That's my fault. My phone was out of battery. Thank you for trying to reach us. Well," she looked around at Hawkeye, "I knew when I got up this morning that today was for the crapper. If you'll just give me a moment to figure this out." She turned back to the woman at the desk. "Do you know of any other places on the island that might have openings tonight? I'm not choosy—clean and safe is all I need."

The staffer looked relieved by Petra's grace. "I'm so sorry. It's our busy season in St. Croix. I could make some calls for you."

Hawkeye leaned in. "No need. Thank you, ma'am." He touched his hand to Petra's elbow, and she followed him away from the desk. "I have a room for you at our hotel. It's not a quarter mile up the road. The Palm."

"Swanky," she said as she followed him toward the parking lot. "One of the tours Tamika and I were scheduled to take leaves from out front, so we looked into staying at The Palm." She indicated the Blue Fin sign with a twitch of her hand. "This was more in our budget. But I'm not going to worry about that. I'm just— how is it that such a nice hotel as the Palm has an opening when my hotel is giving reservations away?"

They waited as the automatic door slid wide.

"We made a plan while you were having your scans done," Hawkeye said.

She blinked at him and lost her balance, stepping awkwardly out to the side and bending at the waist.

Hawkeye Slid his hand around her waist, and she tucked in under his arm, like she'd always belonged there.

"Not to tell you what to do, but in case our support would be helpful, we wanted to be able to offer you something concrete."

"For a random woman on a plane with an alien pupil? Seems more than would be expected. You've already—"

"I told Reaper that we have Avery and Rowan in common.

In my short time at Iniquus, I've found out that friends and family are high priorities."

"No man left behind?" Petra asked.

"In a broad sense, sure. But in a business sense, we work with Rowan and Avery in two different spheres. Trust is paramount in those kinds of relationships. So, while you were at the hospital, we already had backup plans in place." He didn't add that had that not been the case, he'd still have found a way to keep her safe.

"We?" She stopped to look up at him.

Hawkeye reached out his hand to steady her. "My team and I."

Disappointment tried to tug her lips down, and she forced them into a smile of sorts. And Hawkeye wasn't sure how to read that exchange. But he wanted to kiss her and make whatever he said that troubled her go away.

"That doesn't answer the question of how there is space for me. You're not giving up your room, are you?" Petra asked.

"We'll be in adjoining rooms, the way we discussed at the hospital."

"With Cooper being the chaperone," she said. "Okay, I remember that."

"It's Iniquus policy that when we're staying somewhere as a team, we have an extra room." He fobbed the SUV unlocked and reached for the handle.

"That sounds kind of cloak-and-dagger. What's the extra room for exactly?"

"Nothing that interesting." His hand cupping her elbow for balance, Hawkeye waited while she climbed in. He wasn't sure how unsteady it made her to have her pupils so different. It had to throw off her visual field. "We use it for supplies and staging. Reaper was in the room next to the extra room. The guys shifted things around a bit to leave it open for you. And they took our luggage down with Cooper's crate. When we get to the hotel, Levi will bring Cooper to me."

Hawkeye rounded the car and climbed in.

As he pulled his safety belt into place, he had to watch her lips to understand her whisper, "Normally, I'm very good in a crisis." She cleared her throat and spoke in a natural tone. "I do a good job taking care of myself and everyone around me. I don't feel like myself. I'm grateful for your help."

"Under normal circumstances, you wouldn't have the drugs floating through your system. It was karma that put me next to you on the plane." He pressed the engine button, then flicked on the headlights.

"True about the drugs. Karma, though?"

"What goes around comes around. If you show up for people in a crisis," he threw the vehicle into reverse, "it stands to reason that when you need someone, the universe moves them neatly into place."

"You're saying you're an instrument of the universe?" She screwed her face up to show that she wasn't buying that.

"Seems so." He draped his arm across the seat and looked back over his shoulder as he eased out of the parking spot.

"Not someone named Halo. That seems like it would make more sense."

He pulled his arm around and shifted into drive. "Seems not."

"Those thoughts are whirling around in my head. You're right. Those meds are making me pretty wacka-doodle." As he rolled out of the parking lot onto the road. Petra leaned forward and put her hands on the dash. "How is it that we're in an SUV right now?" She lifted the keys from the cupholder and read the name of the rental company.

"Halo brought it to the hospital and handed over the keys while you were getting your brain scanned."

"When you all made the plan." Her voice trailed off. "I must have been in there quite a while. I hardly remember being there at all. I tell you, from the start, this day was destined for the crapper. I had no idea to what extent or how many people would be swept up in my misadventure. But I can't say that I wasn't forewarned." She folded her hands in her lap. "I'm setting my alarm to wake up with a bright sun shining. The dawn of a new day."

"This means something to you."

"It does, and I might tell you later. My head is so full of noise right now." She reached for his hand and when he clasped her fingers in his, she closed her eyes.

A quarter mile wasn't nearly far enough.

He didn't want to let her go.

The staff was ready with their room cards, so they headed up. Hawkeye followed her into her room to check that she had her luggage. Then he reached out to open the door separating their rooms.

"You're not staying?" Her hand was on the wall for balance as she slid her shoes off. "Oh, you need to get to Cooper."

"I'll stay as long as you like. Levi's out for a jog with Mojo and Cooper. They'll be back soon."

"Great name Mojo. That's a dog, right?"

"The Malinois. Okay, here's the rundown. We have five people down here in St. Croix. Reaper, who arrived before we did, is our trainer. I'm sure you'll meet him along the way. Then Ash with K9 Hoover, Halo with Max, Levi with Mojo, and me with Cooper."

She tapped her fingers and mumbled through each name and looked up to see if she got it right.

"Yup." He leaned his hips back onto the table, reaching for the room service menu. "Speaking of great names, I wonder if there's a story behind yours."

"Petra? It's the female version of Peter, my paternal grandfather. The deal was that Dad got to give me my nickname, and Mom got to choose the name on my birth certificate."

He paused, then said, "You need to eat, and so do I. I'm ordering room service." He handed her the menu folder.

She took it and opened it, looking it over. "The print is small, and the lights are dim." She folded it again and handed it back to him. "I'm not very hungry."

Hawkeye canted his head. "Did you eat breakfast before the flight this morning?"

"No."

He walked toward the landline and lifted the receiver, holding it to his chest. "Are you allergic to anything?"

"No."

"I'm ordering pizzas for us." He tapped number four for room service. "Do you have a preference for toppings?"

"No." She grinned. There was something there, some joke that popped into her mind. He could almost see her tucking it into her pocket to tell someone later.

He placed the order without taking his eyes off her as she curled into the pillows at the top of her bed. "It'll be here in about twenty minutes." He pulled out a chair. "So, your dad gave you Petra, and was it your mom who gave you Hermione Perdita?"

Petra paused and blinked. In her one good eye, he could swear he saw an actual file drawer pull open, get rifled through, a paper tugged out and waved victoriously in the air as she shut the drawer again. "Oh, yeah, I told the intake person at the hospital. My given name is Hermione Perdita Armstrong. You said your mom was a high school English teacher, right? Mine was a classics professor. You got Michael George, and I got Hermione Perdita."

"Hermione Perdita Armstrong."

"A bit of a mouthful."

Hawkeye swung his leg around to sit.

"That chair's too small for someone your height. Come relax on the bed with me."

He didn't need to be asked twice.

"About my name—I was born on the Winter Solstice. Mom thought it would be nice to name me after Shakespeare's Winter's Tale. King Leontes and Queen Hermione had a daughter named Perdita. It's not a very nice story, but it is one of Mom's favorites for whatever reason."

"How does it go?" Hawkeye asked, untying his boots and sliding them off.

"Basically, out of jealousy, Leontes imprisons Hermione and orders the abandonment of their newborn daughter, Perdita. Hermione dies in prison while a shepherd is raising Perdita. At sixteen, Perdita returns home and is recognized as the lost princess. Leontes is remorseful, and his family is reunited." She lifted a hand and let it drop. "A terrible story with a worse outcome. So much better had Perdita stayed in the hills eating bread with butter and cheese."

"I knew you were hungry," Hawkeye said as he pulled out his phone and swiped to bring up a prompt window.

"What are you searching? I'm not on social media."

"Neither am I. You're right. Winter's Tale sounds like a miserable story. There must have been something your mom saw in those characters that she wanted for you." He looked over at Petra. "I don't know your mom, but there has to be an explanation." He focused back on his phone. "I'm looking up, Hermione. I only know it from Harry Potter. In that book, she is—"

"Obviously neurodivergent?" Petra asked. "Most probably high masking, high-functioning autistic like my mom is? There is that. Mom might just have latched on to Hermione because she felt seen."

He flicked a glance her way, then continued scrolling.

"Are you a big reader?" Petra asked as a knock sounded at the door.

"Levi," a voice called.

"Coming." Petra unspooled and headed to the door.

Hawkeye came to his feet. "I like to read before I go to bed and on rainy winter days in front of the fire."

"Dog at your feet. Very romantic." She threw a glance over her shoulder as she pulled the door wide to find a sweat-stained Levi with the two dogs.

Levi stared at Petra's face. "You're still lopsided." He released Cooper as Hawkeye chirruped. "I'm sorry you're going through this, but it was a relief to hear it wasn't worst case."

"You're very kind. Thanks, Levi. Hi Mojo. I like your name."

Levi lifted a hand toward Hawkeye.

"Thanks, brother," Hawkeye said as Levi turned and moved off and Petra shut the door. After scrubbing his hands over Cooper, Hawkeye unclasped his lead and set it on the lowboy.

Petra climbed back into her pillow nest. "Is Cooper allowed up?" She patted the space in the middle.

Hawkeye snapped his fingers and pointed, and Cooper leaped up and went straight over to sniff Petra.

Hawkeye sat back in the place he'd been before and continued his phone search. "Hermione Perdita. Are you an only child?"

"I am, why?" Petra pulled the pillow from behind her head and punched it to make a more comfortable shape.

"If I'm remembering correctly, Shakespeare made up the

name Perdita—I mostly know this because of a 101 Dalmatians."

"That movie made me cry," Petra said, watching as Cooper began circling before he settled, sides still heaving, tongue hanging long from his run.

Hawkeye would fill the plastic ice bucket with water and set it out in a minute.

"As a kid, Cruella terrified me," Hawkeye said. "What level of evil would it take to consider hurting a dog? A puppy, no less? But to get you back to my track, I was thinking that if your mom wanted to use other names that Shakespeare made up for another child, she might have chosen Olivia or Matilda."

"Matilda was a great movie. But it was Agatha Trunchbull who terrified me. Makes sense, you and dogs, me—well, I identified with Matilda, another neurodivergent character, probably autistic, like Hermione."

Hawkeye thought she said that as if she was lifting a flag and waving it at him. *Look over here.* But she'd already said she was wired differently. There was a reason she was repeating the theme and watching his responses.

Over the years, his sister had been frustrated trying to maintain relationships. Cora often talked about how exhausting it was for her to try to function in a world where people couldn't keep up or couldn't understand when she was overwhelmed and bored at the same time. Or when she became anxious for no apparent reason—crowds, uneven surfaces, changes of lights, too much sound.

Cora would put energy and goodwill into relationships only for her friend or romantic partner to bow out. She was too much for them.

But it was also the reason that Cora could make the music that left people holding their breath and why she could paint paintings that made people weep.

That comes at a cost in *this* society. Hawkeye reminded himself of their talk on the plane. Some societies honored people with divergent gifts, and societal acceptance had to make things easier.

Yeah, as Hawkeye ran the various conversations through his mind, he was convinced that if Petra was trying to warn him off, it would be partly to protect him but also in a big way out of self-preservation.

If all that was true, it must mean she was testing the waters for something more. It meant she knew he liked her.

He didn't *like* her. This was something else. It was a crazy sensation that he couldn't identify.

She was *his*.

He stilled with the thought. And rejected it. It was a big leap from morning-stranger to *that* thought. Besides, *his* was possessive, and that's never how he thought of a woman.

She clicked with him.

Yeah, that was a better way to put it. Something slid into place, clicked, and felt like it was going to hold.

He was glad that he'd had his head down during that revelation. Hawkeye didn't need Petra to read any of those thoughts in his eyes.

"You know, Hermione and Matilda both remind me of my sister Cora," he ventured. "When we get back to D.C., I'll introduce you two. I think you'll get along well." He waited, but when Petra didn't say anything, he lifted his gaze from the phone and focused on her. "I think you got off okay with Hermione Perdita. There was always Fallstaff or Florizel."

Petra laughed. "Florizel sounds like a brand of toothpaste. That would be bad."

"Imogen?"

"Sounds like imagine." Her voice drifted off. "I actually rather like that."

He wiggled his phone at her. "Here we go, Hermione traits." He looked down to read. "Virtuous, dignified, and patient."

"I don't really identify with the Hermione character in this story. I'm not an impatient person, but I'm not someone who sits around waiting for things to happen either."

"Are you also saying you're undignified?" he asked.

"On occasion, when called for, yes."

"Virtuous?" His brows went up.

"Sounds like something aspirational rather than something that someone could accomplish, you know, like a phrase in an obituary. And since my experience today—"

"To me, it conjures the idea of being cloistered and reaching for perfection," Hawkeye cut her off. Yeah, her mentioning an obituary was a sharp twist in his gut. "St. Mary, for example. Mother Theresa."

"They're not on my aspirations list. Showing up and doing the right thing seems more doable."

Hawkeye went back to his phone. "I'm looking at the characteristics list for Perdita. They are…intelligent, practical, and noble, with a maturity beyond her years. Loyal and romantic." He looked her way. "Are you romantic?"

"Mmm, You?" Petra asked in response, not answering his question.

"I guess that depends on how you define romantic."

"I define it as someone thinking about the other person, wanting to make them feel special and cared for by preparing something specifically for them. If they like surprises, then a surprise. If they hate surprises, make sure everything is spelled out and predictable. That takes knowing the other person and carving out a gesture precisely for them."

"Do you like surprises?" Hawkeye asked.

"As a general rule, not at all. Everything about this trip from

Tamika's norovirus onward has been a steady stream of surprising events. Do I love it? No. Can I cope? Probably."

"My takeaway from this conversation is that when we're home in D.C. . . ."

She canted her head, a question in her eye.

"You gave the nurse your home address," he reminded her.

"Mystery solved. Yes, that's right, I did."

"When we're home in D.C., and I invite you for a date, you prefer that I walk you through all the things you should expect in advance so you're dressed properly and prepared with whatever you like to have with you," Hawkeye said and he was rewarded with a gentle smile.

"Exactly. Yes, when we're home in D.C., I'd like that very much." Her smile broadened. "And I'll wear matching eyeballs for the occasion."

10

When Cooper nudged Hawkeye with a cold, wet nose, Hawkeye came instantly awake.

Grabbing his phone, he threw his covers aside and swung off the bed.

There, with his bare feet on the short fibers of the hotel carpet, dressed in black boxer briefs, Hawkeye paused to get his bearings.

Zero-three-hundred hours.

Standing in the doorway between their room and Petra's, Cooper held steady, his muscles tight with focus.

Hawkeye moved silently forward. Standing beside Cooper, he could make out Petra in her bathroom with only the night-light shining.

Dressed for bed, wearing a pair of pink panties and a white T-shirt, Petra leaned over the sink, spitting into the water flowing from the faucet. One hand held her hair back, and the other clasped her toothbrush. She seemed steady on her feet, even pitched forward that way.

Yesterday's meds must have given her cotton mouth.

A woman he dated a while back once told Hawkeye that the human wakes at three because of changes in the body's temperature regulation. She said it was only in modern times that it was thought to be a problem. Farther back in history, folks called it 'The Golden Hour' and considered that the time for sex and contemplation.

Hawkeye could well imagine why that particular factoid dropped into his awareness at just that moment.

With his cock standing at attention, Hawkeye backed out of Petra's view, climbed back in bed, and signaled for Cooper to lay down.

While a three a.m. temperature change might be the reason Petra was up and aware that she wanted to brush her teeth, Hawkeye was up because he'd spent the night with his search engine open, trying to figure out what Petra's pupils might mean to her health picture.

Without landing on an answer, finally, Hawkeye had turned his computer off and laid down to catch some shut-eye. He needed to get at least a couple of hours sleep so he was ready for the training mission later that morning.

Even though Cooper woke him each day with pinpoint accuracy, that day, Hawkeye set his alarm a few minutes earlier than usual to give himself time to check on Petra before he started his morning routine.

Cooper always began his days with a quick jog to burn off some energy. It helped him to stay focused and on task all day.

If Petra needed him, though, Hawkeye could send Cooper out with Mojo since they ran at a similar pace.

Hawkeye must have fallen deeply asleep because he had

that thought, and the next thing he knew, his phone alarm was vibrating under his pillow.

After pulling on his running clothes and lacing his sneakers, Hawkeye stole into Petra's room.

He didn't want to wake her, but he needed to know if she was lucid enough that she was safe to be left alone. When she spoke, her voice was husky with sleep but seemed back to normal. She responded to his questions without any red flags, so Hawkeye and Cooper hit the road in the quiet of pre-dawn.

Hawkeye loved this time of the day. He liked knowing that inside the houses he passed, families were snug in bed. He liked being alone with his thoughts as he lined up the day's priorities and let the vibrations of his foot strikes loosen any stress or negativity. It was like a shower for his soul.

Today, all Hawkeye could think about was the miracle and the angst of meeting Petra.

On the plane, he thought he had one shot at getting to know her before their brief intersection was in his rearview. Hawkeye had planned to invite her to dinner to continue their conversation.

He couldn't imagine what it was like to go to sleep just fine and wake up in a medical crisis like that. Life could, sure as hell, knock you off your feet with no warning at all.

His feelings for Petra absolutely knocked him sideways.

And the jog hadn't eased his level of concern. Everything Hawkeye had read boded poorly for Petra getting a good outcome.

Today, though, there might be more answers at the eye doctor.

Cooper and Hawkeye slowed their pace for the last two blocks, catching their breath before they strode through the automatic doors at the front of the hotel. They were back just as the kitchen staff was setting up breakfast. Since he had Cooper with him, Hawkeye made two plates—one for him and one with his best guesses as to what Petra might eat—and balanced them in one hand as he went up to the seventh floor.

Cooper's nose was on the ground as he tracked back to their door.

They slid into the room and set the breakfast plates on the table before moving closer to wake Petra.

Cooper went in first with his nose chuffing and doing his checks. Then, he jumped over the top of her and moved to his spot from last night, where he circled and plopped, giving Hawkeye the all-clear. Cooper thought Petra was safe.

"How are you feeling?" Hawkeye crouched by her bedside.

"Good." She stretched her arms over her head, straining her muscles as she inhaled deeply, then released. "More like myself. Less medicated."

Cooper lifted his foot to scratch behind his ear, shaking the whole bed.

"Hey buddy," she reached out to pat his butt. "Did you have a good run?"

Cooper looped his tongue up to lick her hand before moving to the end of the bed to lie down where it was cooler.

As she turned back to him, Hawkeye reached out and caught Petra's chin between his thumb and forefinger. "Smile for me?" And this time, she gave him a sweet smile that came naturally to her lips. "Beautiful."

"I got up earlier to check my eye. There's a little more iris and a bit of reactivity."

He lifted his thumb and painted it over her lower lip to feel the petal softness. "Both good things."

Petra leaned forward, pressing a soft kiss onto his lips. She tasted like honey and mint.

Lowering his knees to the carpeted floor, Hawkeye slid his fingers around the back of her head into her silken hair. He tipped her so his mouth could find hers, and he could kiss her long and slow.

He kissed her breathless.

And when they stopped, panting, they rested foreheads together.

His heart pounding in his chest, it occurred to Hawkeye that this might well be the *last* first kiss of his lifetime. It might be a kiss that launched an odyssey rather than a weekend adventure.

Petra tipped back again, her lips on his, opening her mouth to his tongue. She wrapped her hand around his bicep and tugged as she turned to lay flat on the bed.

His blood racing as he knelt in front of Petra, it took ultimate control for him to slow his movements, his breath, and the forward trajectory of the now.

He had sensations running through him that he'd never experienced before, and Hawkeye had to make *absolutely damned sure* he did nothing that could negatively affect Petra.

She looked confused that he had stopped, had not accepted her invitation to come onto the bed with her and lie between her thighs.

Heaven on Earth.

But in pulling back, Hawkeye could remember the truth of their situation.

"Beautiful, I'm worried about your safety." Strands of her blond hair had caught in her eyelashes, and he brushed them aside, tucking them back behind her ear. "We don't know what's going on with you yet. You have to see the eye doctor this morning to see if he can figure it out. Changes in blood pressure...I think it's a bad idea until you've gotten an all-clear."

She offered up the sweetest pout.

"Yeah," he sighed. A cold shower was in order. "Me too." That pout might just be his kryptonite. "We have a few minutes.

How would it be if I held you for a bit? I could honestly use some support right about now."

"Why, what's going on?" The pout fell away, and she lifted onto her elbow with concern.

That tickled a smile across his lips. "I got a crush on the lady sitting next to me on the plane, and then I think she's stroking out." He rested a hand on his chest. "It's been a hell of a strain on my heart."

"Crush?" She mouthed the word like it was a new word for her, and she was trying to give it meaning.

"Not crush, that's too childish," Hawkeye corrected. "I'm not sure I have the right word. The one I'm considering is that you've endeared yourself to me. 'Endeared,' is that too old-fashioned a word? I'm thinking about the moments that have gathered since I met you."

"Like Grandma's china cabinet with curios on the shelves. Fragile but interesting to consider?"

"Flowers in a bouquet might be closer to how I meant it." Petra seemed to be okay with this conversation, with him declaring his feelings. At least she wasn't giving him any back-off vibes.

She lifted a single brow. "I was asleep the whole time. What could have endeared me to you? At least I wasn't drooling."

He ducked his head to the side. "Not unduly, anyway."

"What?" It was a shocked inhale.

"You and Cooper were both snoring and drooling. It seemed you were both at ease and getting what you needed, deeply asleep like that." He reached out and rested his hand on her hip, sliding it down to her thigh. "I was completely charmed."

Her eyes sprang wide. "I was snoring?" she whispered in horror.

"Afraid so."

"And you didn't wake me?" She lifted her pillow and

wiggled up the bed until she was sitting against the headboard, pulling her knees up until her feet were flat on the sheet and crossing her arms over her chest.

Miffed, but more play-acting. This was Petra teasing him back.

"Like I said, you looked like you needed the sleep. You were out like a light. And I figured your reputation was safe enough. You were on a plane full of strangers, and you were snoring along with the dogs. I think—" Hawkeye pressed into the bed to move from the floor to the mattress, wrapping his hands around the back of Petra's calves. "I think your falling asleep with Cooper in your lap was like a pack signal. All four Cerberus K9s curled into comfortable fur balls and snoozed the whole way."

"But your team knows I was snoring."

"They were charmed, too, just not in the way I was."

"*Endearingly.*"

"If you broke that word down, it would mean you became dear to me. Which seems like a lot to say to someone at this point in our knowing each other."

"It's been a busy twenty-four hours. Though I've been asleep or drugged for most of it." She leaned forward and kissed him. "I accept your word, 'endearing.' I like it. I'd like it more if you said it while we were snuggling."

"That we can do." As Hawkeye swung over the top of her to the other side of the bed, his gaze scanned for the clock to ensure they had enough time to get ready and head for the doctor's.

Lying on top of the alarm clock, partially obscuring the digital read, was the pink eye mask that Petra had worn on the plane and a flash of beige.

Hawkeye reached over to snag it up.

Sure enough, caught on the edge between the elastic band and the satin cloth was a motion-sickness patch.

Hawkeye flipped around to show her what he'd discovered. "You were wearing that patch yesterday."

"Yes, on the plane." She canted her head, and Hawkeye could see she was putting this through her processors, trying to understand what he was driving at.

"When did you take the patch off your neck?"

She looked to the far-right-hand corner of the room and held her breath. When she turned back, it was with a shake of her head. "At some point?"

"But you didn't wash your hands after you touched it."

Petra turned her head toward the corner again, her gaze searching along the blank cream-colored wall. Finally, she pulled her focus back to him. "I put it on in the airport half an hour before the flight left, for efficacy. I used my hand sanitizer and a tissue to clean my hands. I didn't wash my hands until I used the bathroom in the hospital. Although, I don't specifically remember that. The nurse said seconds were precious and wouldn't let me use the bathroom until after the machine. Since I wasn't uncomfortable in the car on the way to the first hotel, and I didn't pee on myself." Her eyes flashed wide. "Did I pee on myself?"

"Negative."

"Okay, good," Petra scratched her fingers over her scalp. "Well, I must have used the restroom after the machines, and surely, from my years of muscle memory, I would have automatically washed my hands."

"But the patch came off on the plane." Hawkeye lifted the mask.

"It would have had to come off on the plane in order for the patch to be stuck to my eye mask. Yes."

"And somewhere along the way, you rubbed your eye?"

"Probably." She shook her head, not following his line of questioning.

"Assuredly." Hawkeye corrected, feeling the thrill of the hunt, he thought he had found the rabbit and had it in his sights. "When Cooper woke you up, you rubbed your fingers under your mask, pulled it off, and stuck it in your pocket."

"Why are you hammering this?"

"Because I was up last night searching all the reasons that someone could have blown out a *single* pupil that was non-responsive. And all the reasons are significant and dangerous. All require immediate medical attention. You told the doctor you don't take any medications regularly." He lifted the mask. "The travel patch, you didn't mention that at the hospital."

"It's not an everyday med, and I guess I forgot I did that. Besides, if it had been in my system and that had been the reason for my alien pupil, it would have blown out both my eyes. Are you angry with me right now?"

"Not even a little." He leaned forward and kissed her forehead, then sat up again. "With a motion sickness patch, the pupil wouldn't have blown out because of a systemic reaction. The pupil reacts with direct contact with the medication. That's why a travel patch can blow one eyeball and not both. Until I saw the patch, I had forgotten that I saw it yesterday. I remember thinking it was probably making you groggy."

Petra reached for her eye mask. "The patch caused all this crazy?"

"I'm trained as a medic, not a medical doctor. But, it's a new theory we can bring with us to the ophthalmologist today."

"But in your research, it goes away eventually, right?" Petra asked, handing the mask back to Hawkeye. "Or will people be like that staffer at the Blue Fin and look at me for the rest of my life like I might spontaneously combust?"

11

PETRA

Petra stood outside the eye hospital waiting for Hawkeye, who had left to use the restroom and collect the SUV. He said he'd meet her out front.

And since she had nothing else to do but wait, she was ruminating.

Of course, she was.

She could take any little thing and chew on it all day long.

Right now, she was reliving the scene when she'd been half awake in the pre-dawn gloom, nervous about how today would unfold. She stayed still as Cooper stuck his nose onto her mattress and chuffed.

"Cooper, I know," Hawkeye's voice was so soft that she strained to hear even with her sensitive ears. "She's beautiful, isn't she? I hate to do this." He put his hand on her back and squatted by her side. "Petra? Petra, hey, can you wake up just a little bit?"

"Mmm." She opened her lashes only enough to take in the shadowy shapes of the room.

"I'm taking Cooper out for about twenty minutes. Do you feel okay being alone for that long? Do you need me to get Levi to take Cooper instead?"

"Uhm. No. I'm good. Thank you."

Cooper, I know. She's beautiful, isn't she?

"Me and my wonky eyeball, beautiful," Petra said to the seagull who was stalking the crust of bread near Petra's foot. "Can you imagine?"

The guy standing next to Petra turned her way. "What did you say?"

She pointed at the SUV that was rounding toward the front doors. "Just wondering where my ride is," she said, stepping closer to the curb.

This morning, once she heard the door shut behind Cooper and Hawkeye, Petra rolled out of bed and made it to the bathroom to see how she woke up looking beautiful, radiantly rested.

And no.

Nope.

Nopity-nope-nope-nope. She was not, in fact, a radiant beauty. Her hair looked like she'd fought through a windstorm. Her skin was dry and dull from the seven hours of flight time. And she had a wonky eye.

"As wonky as yesterday?" she had wondered, leaning toward the mirror and assessing her pupil size. It wasn't even, but it was ever so slightly better. There was a tiny blue ring.

Petra had slogged her way back to bed in the hopes that there was still time for a beauty sleep miracle and crashed right back out until Hawkeye brought breakfast.

And after all that, after everything that had happened in the last few hours, the conclusion of the *Misadventure of the Alien Eyeball* turned out to be so anti-climactic.

At precisely eight o'clock, Petra arrived at the reception desk and was shown immediately back to the doctor.

In her hand, she held the motion sickness patch in a bag, and Hawkeye's theory on her lips, along with the taste of his kisses.

"There's a circle of iris," the doctor said, accepting the vial of drops the nurse gave her at the hospital. "What color are your eyes normally?"

"It depends on my clothes. On my passport, it says gray. My eyes can also look greenish some days or pale blue. It depends on the color reflection."

"Okay, you're within the normal spectrum of your iris color. There's some reactivity, as you noted. This was discovered yesterday afternoon, not yet twenty-four hours?"

"That's right."

"I'm going with your theory. I see nothing here that fits neatly with any other diagnosis. However, if it's not completely cleared up by the forty-eight-hour mark, I'd like to see you back."

"I'll be home Monday. Can I wait until then to see my ophthalmologist?" Petra asked, sliding damp palms down her lap. This had been scary; she could admit that to herself.

The doctor leaned his shoulder against the wall, considering her, then said, "If you're not back to normal, I'd like to run more tests before you get on a plane with the pressure changes. I say that as a precaution. I think it was the patch. We need a backup plan if it doesn't pan out the way we think it will."

Think it will. Hawkeye hadn't made love to her this morning for fear of changing pressures.

Would she keep that last bit to herself?

Just how horny was she for Hawkeye? She wondered as he pulled up beside her.

Pretty damned horny, she thought, as she tugged the door open and climbed in.

Yeah, she'd be willing to take the risk of eyeball pressure changes for him to give her an orgasm.

Or two.

Petra reached for the seatbelt and then leaned over to kiss Hawkeye before snapping it in place. "Thank you for bringing me."

They started their thirty-minute trek back to the hotel, where Reaper told her to stay for her time on the island. Petra turned to Hawkeye. "Okay – that was an unexpected adventure."

"I can imagine you felt like you got rolled by a wave. Everyone telling you that you were in danger."

"Believe it or not, I'm happy about it all around. Mostly, I'm glad that you figured out my medical mystery, otherwise it would have hung over my head in perpetuity."

"I get that." He glanced at the phone navigation display and took a left out of the parking area. "If no one figured it out, you'd always be looking at that eye wondering if it would happen again and if it was a missed sign of something dangerous."

Petra pulled her lips flat as she nodded. He was right. "I have professional-grade ruminating skills. I'm grateful for all the people who helped me in ways big and small—from Levi helping me on the airplane stairs to Halo managing Cooper. Reaper giving up this room. The people on the plane who didn't complain, not out loud anyway. Kind, competent people all around, not the least of them you." She knitted her fingers together as she watched the scenery fly by from behind the polarized lenses the doctor wanted her to wear. "And I'm glad I had a hand in all of this, too."

"If you're up to sharing, I'd like to hear."

She glanced his way for a moment, then turned back to the passing houses. "I was thinking about how civilians would come in as volunteers at Quantico. We'd have some scenarios— terror events, mass shooters. The organizers would hand out signs that they would hang around their necks with the basics of their fictional medical situation."

"At Quantico, it was the FBI doing this? Why?"

"FBI, yes. In the civilian world, law enforcement has to clear the scene before the medical first responders can go in. This isn't army medics trying to stay under the strafe of bullets while they patch people up. At the FBI, we don't give first aid of any kind until we secure the area. At that point, we could offer assistance with medical aid. The scenarios were set up to teach us to run by screaming, begging people."

"Rough."

"Incredibly. The adrenaline was insane. The volunteers were dedicated to their roles. They didn't just have the sign hanging around their necks. They had moulage, a makeup technique used to apply mock injuries to a person making things more realistic for responders in training. They look like they've been shot or stabbed. They even have these latex limb stumps. The volunteers can bend their legs and pull them on. Put a jacket or bag over the bent real-world limb, pour out a puddle of theater blood, dim the lights, and the brain can believe the scene. And we'd have to run by, knowing they'd bleed out while we secured the building."

"In battle, if you stop and help a fallen soldier, everyone falls. The faster you gain control, the faster help is available. But yeah, I get it. Theory and reality are different beasts. It's hard as hell to do with a stranger. Nigh on impossible when it's a brother. But you stick to your training."

They came to a stop at the red light, and Petra could feel

Hawkeye looking at her, so she turned his way. "When I went through training, we had these dummies that were very lifelike," he said. "They'd be gurgling and spurting blood." He screwed up like he was smelling spoiled meat. "It was a bit of a mindfuck to be trying to do a field trach on this dummy when it looked so real. And sometimes, it would just spontaneously start screaming or sit up. I'm telling you, whoever developed this animatronic thing wanted to plant the seeds of nightmares."

"I happily didn't have that as part of my military training," Petra said, pulling out her seatbelt and adjusting it to fit better between her boobs. "I went through basic. I was hired to provide counseling support."

"Before we stray too far down a new topic trail, let me bring you back to the thought you started with. You said you were happy with this situation. And then you lit into Quantico and volunteers in theatrical blood. Could you take me through that leap?"

"I think my situation was the best of all worlds."

"Starting with the idea that you are probably okay," Hawkeye said. "Yes."

"If that's the outcome, then it was an optimal exercise for everyone involved, right? Everyone—me, you, your team—everyone who came into contact with me believed that what was happening was an emergency."

Hawkeye slowed as he edged past some kids playing kickball in the street. "Not just moulage and plastic leg stumps," he said.

"Exactly, which does impact a human's reactions. In this instance, the two systems—the airline and the emergency crew—got to practice with the belief that this was the real deal, but I wasn't, in fact, at risk. You mentioned karma and helper people yesterday. Well, I might well have been an instrument of the universe. I'll never know."

"Another leap that needs more context, please," Hawkeye said with a grin.

"Maybe the people involved in my rescue needed some practice in advance of a real emergency. Because of this seemingly false alarm, they'll be ready to act and can perhaps save a future life."

Hawkeye nodded.

"And you will surely tell your team about the motion sickness patch, and now they'll know to ask."

"Sort of in that same vein, last night when I was on the search engine looking for answers, I remembered this woman I used to date was fastidious about washing her hands anytime she touched her motions sickness patch," Hawkeye said. "After reading that the medication could dilate the pupils, I wondered if that was why she did it."

Petra held up a finger. "See, in my theory, she was fastidious in front of you to teach you what you needed to know in a future moment, this one. And I think you might even have locked onto that possibility and solved the mystery because her behavior made the patch stand out to you."

"An interesting way to look at things. I'll have to think about that."

"It makes life easier if only in this way—when things go awry, I can see some way to make it useful." She raised her brows for emphasis. "It's not Pollyanna-like."

"Pragmatic," Hawkeye agreed. "Instead of sweeping the bad things or maybe bad feelings under the carpet, you're adding the information to your life's encyclopedia. You now have a motion sickness patch chapter."

"And so do you." Petra smiled. "So, what are your plans today? You're surfing, right?"

"Dropping you off and getting out to the site. They already

have the K9s down on the beach, playing ball and getting them used to the environmental sensory input. You?"

Petra looked at her watch. "I still have time. Tamika and I had planned to go on an off-road vehicle safari to the tidal pools."

"I could drop you off somewhere on my way out to the beach," Hawkeye offered.

"Thanks, but The Palm was my pickup point. One of the reasons I knew it was swanky. Tamika and I ended up making those Blue Fin reservations within walking distance."

Hawkeye reached for her hand. "Do you have plans for dinner? I saw a place online that serves local specialties. Laid back. Outdoor eating on picnic tables. I'd like to hear about your adventures today."

"Yes, thank you. But, to be honest, I'm hoping the adventure part of this trip is over."

As she said that out loud, a shiver raced down Petra's spine.

12

———

PETRA

Did Petra really want to go to bed, stare at the ceiling, and vegetate?

Yes!

Would she allow herself to?

Not today. Not with two people—Tamika and Hawkeye—waiting to hear about her grand adventures. Incentives, she'd take them where she found them.

As Tamika always said, a body in motion tends to stay in motion, so as long as her shoes stayed on and her body had a destination, Petra could keep going and doing.

Burnout was part and parcel of what Petra had to navigate on the daily.

Surprisingly, she didn't feel like she needed to shut down despite all the crazy that had happened since yesterday—not the least of which was meeting one Michael George Kesse and having her world—and her libido – flipped upside down by the touch of his fingertips, his kiss.

That man could *kiss*.

What would it be like to have his hands slide over her naked skin? What would he murmur to her as they made love?

She was determined to find out. That very night.

Dinner and sex.

Maybe reverse the order if she couldn't stand the ache any longer.

And over dinner that night, Petra wanted a story to tell. Something funny. Something light. Something very different from the death's doorstep shit that had gone down.

Sliding her sunglasses in place, Petra went outside to wait for the tidepool tour guide to show up.

There was one guy out there who looked like he was rounding folks up, but his T-shirt was about the Caribbean Swim Club. Just in case, she asked. "Breezy Tours?"

"You're going to the tidal pool?" The guy might be seventeen at most.

"I am."

"They usually run a little late. I'm Mitch. I take folks horseback riding on a trail, then out to the shore." He pointed at his T-shirt. "We usually get people out in the water, swimming with the horses. It's a great time."

"Usually, but not today?" The wind whipped the skirt of Petra's sundress.

"Can't swim them this time of year on account of the Christmas Winds."

Petra looked at the tree canopies shaking like a cancan dancer's skirt.

"The winds, especially out on the open water, can make for some difficult currents. I don't personally like snorkeling in this. The waves can go over the snorkel, and it's not a great experience. You never know if you'll be sucking in air or water."

"I can imagine."

"We're not going to risk swimming the horses through the surf until the winds die down in early January or so."

"Of course not." Petra caught at the strands of hair that brushed across her face—tickling her skin—lighting her nerves on fire. She pushed them back behind her ears for a moment's respite. "But you can still ride the horses on the sand part of the beach? I would enjoy trying that. Do you have a card or something?" She stepped closer to him.

"Brochure?" He reached into his back pocket and pulled one out.

"That will do. Thank you." She looked it over before shoving it in the side pocket of her day pack. "I'll reach out and see if you have spaces open tomorrow. I was going snorkeling off Buck's Island. I wanted to see the underwater park, but I don't want to get waterboarded."

"Yeah, for sure," Mitch glanced over his shoulder as a topless vehicle pulled in. "That's you," he said with a hitch of his thumb. "About Buck's Island snorkeling, not to bite into anyone's business, but the last few days, the people who went out couldn't follow the underwater park trail. They had to hold onto life rings and hang out by the boat because Captain Bill wasn't sure they were strong enough swimmers not to get pulled out to sea. And Captain Bill and his crew couldn't keep their eye on all of them at once.

"These Christmas Winds—" Petra watched a family move through the automatic doors—father, mother, three towheaded children dressed in outfits that screamed, "Mom's getting ready for a social media photo shoot." She forced herself to look at Mitch. "These Christmas Winds, will they have any impact on the tidal pool?"

"Johnson family of five!"

Petra pulled her gaze around to find a man equally as young

as Mitch, maybe still in high school. He stood in his open vehicle with a welcoming grin. "We have to divide up the Johnson family. I'm Jumping Beans. You can call me Beans. I can take three children in the back and one adult in the passenger seat. My man, Lucky—" Beans looked over his shoulder, then lifted an arm to wave at his friend who was pulling up behind. Beans pointed to the second vehicle. "Lucky will take the other Johnson parent and Miss Armstrong." He shot a look at Petra. "You Miss Armstrong?"

Petra stepped forward. "That's me." She finger-waved to Mitch. "Hope things work out for tomorrow." And she stepped up.

It seemed that the Johnson family didn't need to discuss who would be the supervising parent and who would enjoy some alone time. The mother was loading their bags into the back of the open vehicle with all three kids at her side.

Watching her put bag after bag in the cargo area, Petra wondered if there was something she should have packed but didn't. She'd applied sunscreen and wore a bathing suit under her sundress and sunglasses. A towel and water bottle were in the backpack she had slung over her shoulders. That should be enough to keep her comfortable. It was only a three-hour tour. Forty-five minutes out, a short but slow section moving along the cliff to the pools, an hour to explore, and then reverse back here to the hotel.

Yeah, she was fine. Kids needed more stuff.

"Yes?" Lucky's grin was bright and comfortable. He seemed like a young man who didn't have a care in this world. "We go? Climb in, and Lucky will take you through the St. Croix jungles. You've been here before?" As she and Daddy Johnson shook their heads, Lucky said, "Then you are in for a treat!"

"Petra," she said in case anybody cared.

"Herb." Before she could ask his preference for where he sat, he stepped in front of Petra and climbed into the front.

Okay then.

They started off.

"Petra, are you here on the island for work or fun?" Herb asked.

It seemed from his tone that he wasn't really interested in her but anxious to open the conversation so he could start telling her about himself.

"Work," she said. Petra was loathe to tell strangers what she did for a living; it made for all kinds of complicated conversations, so she had a travel persona she'd worked on with her friend Avery, the romance editor. In this role, Petra was an author who traveled the world coming up with ideas for her novels. She wrote under a pseudonym that she didn't tell because yes, she was quite famous. And what with this day and age, social media and all, she wanted to maintain her privacy.

"Yeah?" Herb said. "What business are you in?"

"Author."

"You wrote a book? What's your genre?"

"Books. Women's adventure fiction."

Okay, the look he sent her was uncalled for. What in the world?

"And what qualifies you to write about adventure?" he asked.

"Well, Herb, I'm here on a jungle safari, aren't I? I can certainly use this experience for fodder in a future plot."

"I wish to be in your book, Miss Armstrong," Lucky said. "If you write about me, would you sign it and send me a copy?"

"I can do that." Petra wished she were going to write a story so she could send it to Lucky. That would have been fun.

"While you write made-up stories," Herb said. "I've lived through some harrowing experiences that are movie-worthy."

Here we go.

Herb had turned almost all the way around in his seat and was playing with the pendant of his necklace. It was colorful enough that she had spotted the same necklace on each of the family members and wondered if they had had some kind of special event where they wore them to be unified, maybe an adoption or a renewal of vows that would include the kids.

But if they were sentimental, why wear them to the tidepool?

Herb lifted the pendant and rubbed it over his lip like a fidget toy.

Petra wished he'd let it hang so she could get a good look at it. There was something niggling in the back of her mind that really wanted to see the design. Something that made her think of that shiver through her system when Petra told Hawkeye she hoped the adventure part of this trip was over.

Put it down, Petra thought as hard as she could. *Let me see it.*

"One time, I was in Malai, and there was a coup attempt. A moped was winding through the crowd slow enough that I was able to grab the guy's shoulder and jump on behind him. Scrawny man. No match for me if he wanted to fight. He was terrified."

"Imagine that," she said dryly. Malai, wasn't that Hindi for clotted cream?

"I grabbed his shoulders and hung on tight so he knew he couldn't throw me. He took off, weaving his way through the crowd, and didn't stop until he ran out of gas. There I was on the side of a dirt road, unable to speak the language, with what money I had in my pocket and the city ablaze."

"Wow. That does sound harrowing."

"My wife, Jenny, too. She's had *real* adventures she could write about. She's an adventure racer. They go out and run a hundred miles over all terrains and in all climates all over the world. These are races that are by invitation only. She's not fat. That's all muscle on a short frame."

"I'm sure." Despite being prone to motion sickness (hence that darned medicated patch), Petra was glad she got the seat in the rear. She'd rather keep her eye on this Herb guy rather than have him staring at her head. Something about him was … He seemed like an educated, well-mannered, dadbod, middle-aged man from the suburbs. What was it about him? "I know a romance author who's an adventure racer. I think that's right. Long distances on a team where they have to do all kinds of skilled things to get through the different terrain sections of the race, and they have doctors look you over at each check-in to say whether or not you're allowed to continue?"

"That's it. That's what she does. Jenny likes to read romance. She likes it spicy, too. Maybe she's read your friend's books."

"I'll ask Jenny when we get there. If she has, and even if she hasn't, I can put them in touch. I mean, how many women in the world are at that level in the sport?"

"Here!" Lucky was pointing at a shack on the side of the road as they drove past. "This is St. Croix's social club, home of the famous beer-drinking jig. Would you like to hear the story?"

Before she could answer, Lucky swung the steering wheel, and the vehicle crashed off the side of the road onto a hidden path the width of the wheelbase.

"Hands and feet stay inside," Lucky instructed. "Watch for branches that might hit you in the face and hurt your eyes. We are now in wild St. Croix, and things can get dangerous."

13

Hawkeye stood on a rough boulder, his gaze tracking down the footpath to the sea.

Men and dogs lay in the sand, relaxing under the bright Caribbean sun.

It was a gorgeous scene right out of a travel brochure, with bright crystalline waters touching a line of turquoise to the sweep of cloudless azure at the horizon.

A white pleasure cruiser bobbed in the distance. A streamer of red flags, standing out in bright contrast to the blues, flapped sharply in the wind.

Hawkeye was walking on air. He felt amazing.

He wanted to remember every moment of this, he thought as he reveled in the warmth of the sun, smelling the salty air.

Today was an excellent day.

He was in the good company of his new band of brothers here in St. Croix, doing his job of teaching Cooper to surf.

It was fascinating to him that this was the way he earned his paycheck.

And most of all, this morning, Petra's medical mystery seemed to have an explanation. She was seemingly okay and had been okay the whole time.

Petra was better than okay; she was astonishing.

How did he get so lucky as to be sitting next to her on the plane?

Hawkeye wasn't the only one who thought that. Cooper—who was aloof with strangers—had all but crawled onto her lap.

With Petra, there was none of the warm-up time Cooper needed with all the women Hawkeye had dated in the past. No, "He'll come around after he gets used to you," explanation when Cooper would show indifference to their high-pitched baby talk.

Yeah, Cooper's reaction to Petra from the get-go was telling, wasn't it? An entire plane filled with the passenger's explosive reactions and tumult. Cooper wasn't focused on any of it. His muscles were loose, his attention sleepy. In dog behavior, that meant Cooper felt like things were under control. And the only reason he would think that was Petra.

That Cooper treated her with such relaxed acceptance was unprecedented—that was how Cooper reacted among people he considered part of his pack.

Hawkeye tipped his chin back and filled his lungs with fresh sea air, thinking, "This is amazing. It's a miracle of a day."

With a whoop of joy, Hawkeye bolted down the hill over the sandy berm and surface dove into the sea.

The water was luxuriantly warm and shockingly clear.

He took a few strokes out until he could stand chest-deep in the waves, feeling the buoyancy of the salinity as he bobbed with the tide flow.

The strength of the current brushed sand over his feet and dragged his board shorts against his thighs as the water sloshed past him.

Squinting against the sting of sea salt. Hawkeye shook his black hair like a dog to shed the excess water before scanning the beach.

To the side was a cart that held five neatly stacked surfboards, painted in the vibrant colors of island flowers. Sitting against the side in the shade of the equipment was an islander who looked perfectly at ease watching the waves roll in.

Hawkeye found Reaper sitting on the rock outcropping near where the waves broke in a plume of frothy white. Cooper lay on the sand at his feet.

Big old bear that he was, Cooper's coat was caramel with black tips. It was ideal for camouflage. On the dark rocks, he was all but invisible.

Cooper found Hawkeye first; the sudden pink of a tongue helped Hawkeye home in.

Standing and stretching, Cooper meandered to the water's edge in front of Hawkeye, his tail wagging with slow contentment.

It seemed to be a good day all around.

"Glad you're here," Reaper said as Hawkeye waded onto the shoreline. "Everything go okay this morning for Petra?"

"The doctor said go on about life with sunglasses on. Go back if she wasn't a hundred percent before she gets back on a plane."

"I guess that's the best one could hope for. Glad to hear it." Reaper turned to the team. "Rest time's over. I want to get the dogs on the boards and be out of here before low tide makes things tricky." He lifted the plastic phone holder to read the time.

Every Iniquus operator was contractually obligated to keep their phone within arm's reach at all times.

If they were in a body of water—from pool to lake, from ocean to sea—the phone went with them.

Even in the absence of connectivity, they still had the use of apps and, to a limited extent, satellite. They still had beacons to help Iniquus find them and bring them home.

Reaper lifted a hand to the guy at the surf cart. "T.J., we're ready for you now."

"This is fantastic," TJ called out. 'I've never seen a dog use one of our surfboards before." The guy couldn't have been more than a teenager. His long limbs were smooth and thin.

As TJ approached with a board, Hawkeye said, "This tide is a lot stronger than I thought it would be."

"Christmas Winds. They ease up around mid-January." T.J. held the boards upright and stared past it. "This is stronger today than normal, I think." He grinned as he handed the board over to Hawkeye. "But it makes for good waves."

Hawkeye turned his attention to Halo, reaching a fist out for a return bump. "How'd Cooper do this morning?"

"Ash ran right into the waves like you did just now, whooping it up. Hoover raced in after him like it was nothing at all. The dogs watched for a half-second to make sure all was good, then they got up to some good shenanigans for about an hour. They all had some fresh water, a bit of a laydown, and here you are. Perfect timing. Petra's good?"

"Running theory that she touched her motion sickness patch, then rubbed her eye."

"Wait." Ash came over. "Say what now?"

"Petra was wearing a motion sickness patch on the plane yesterday. We think she touched it in her sleep, then rubbed her eye. On contact, the medication can blow out a pupil like that.

No way to prove that right or wrong. But nothing else is making any sense to the people who should know."

"Where is she now?" Levi asked.

"She was signed up for a tour that took her to the tidepool. She said she felt fine. Last night, the doctor didn't put any restrictions or offer any cautions. This morning, the ophthalmologist asked her to keep sunglasses on today. Other than that, everyone's kind of thrown up their hands."

"How's she taking all this in? I mean—thinking back on the scene—the consensus was, 'child, you're about to die.'" Reaper said.

"She's FBI. I think she's already put it in her rearview." Hawkeye smoothed a hand over the citrus orange and lemon surfboard TJ had brought him. It had been a long time since he'd been surfing. It was hard to find a good wave on the East Coast.

"All right, listen up," Reaper said, and the men formed a semi-circle around him. "From training in the Cerberus pool, the dogs already know how to get on and off the boards in deep water. They've practiced holding steady on the board's surface on waving water. This experience in the sea is still going to be new for them. Tiny advances. We're building confidence through success. If you push your dog, you're going to develop anxiety, and we cannot have a Cerberus K9 who is anxious around water. It comes into play too often on our missions. You know your dog. If things feel tight. Stop. Go grab a ball and do some fetch in the water to get them happy again."

Hawkeye cast his gaze around until he found a towel with a neat pile of hot pink tennis balls and the atlatls they used to toss the ball further.

Reaper flicked a finger toward the water. "Ash how about you go ahead out with Hoover and the board and do a little surfing. Lots of high-pitched praise for Hoover. Though he doesn't need it, we want the other dogs to see what Hoover is doing and that it comes with a prize."

Ash tucked his board under his arm and ran down to the surf with a whistle for Hoover.

"Ash is going to put Hoover on in knee-deep water. I don't want the water coming over your dog's chest. See how Ash presses the back of the board down in the water? That keeps it from nosing out in a wave."

"Hey!" Ash called. "Currents picking up."

"We still good?" Reaper called back.

Ash glanced toward the horizon, then slid his gaze from left to right. "Yeah. The waves might get a little higher than they've been today. But right now, it's manageable."

Hoover scrambled onto the board and Ash started pushing out past the break.

"Hoover got on himself," Reaper said. "I want you to lift your dog on. They need the experience of being hoisted out of the surf so they don't scramble and can relax their bodies. Lift them onto the back in that sweet spot we practiced back at Headquarters."

Cooper was a natural.

He lounged on the back of the board as Hawkeye pushed him out.

It was surprisingly easy.

Ash wrangled himself up on the board with Hoover and was looking around. He cupped his hands around his mouth so the wind wouldn't snatch his words. "We're not supposed to have low tide for another couple of hours. This is wrong. Something's wrong." He scooped his hand over his head in a motion that would send the team back. "Get back to the shore. Go back!"

And with his last word, screams rode the wind, coming from around the other side of the craggy ridge of stones.

The men stilled, assessing if those were shrieks of glee or danger.

The next scream was unmistakable terror.

Then shouts, very distinct yelling, "Help! Oh my God, Help!"

Reaper stood on the shoreline. His fingers at the corners of his lips, Reaper sent up the shrill whistle that superseded any other command. It told the dogs, "To me!"

The K9s were instantly off their boards and in the water, paddling for shore. The men watched until the dogs made it past the break, and Reaper grabbed their collars and hauled them in. "Go! Go! I've got them. Go!"

With Cooper safe, Hawkeye flattened on his board, spinning himself around to point toward the open sea. With his brothers moving up fast to join him, Hawkeye cupped his hands and dug into the water, pulling hard to propel himself forward.

Another scream went up. And Hawkeye could hear his heartbeat pounding over the roar of waves.

With adrenaline-fueled power, Hawkeye was driving hard to get around the rocky stack.

He had no idea what would meet him on the other side.

14

———————

Petra

Petra wasn't wearing the right shoes for this trek.

The website said there would be an adventurous trip through jungle-like St. Croix to the tidepool. Once there, it was a short walk to the pools.

Short *walk,* not a mountain climbing adventure.

There was another way out, which the website described as a short hike.

But Tamika was gung-ho on the adventure part. And she preferred her adventures while sitting down. She couldn't see a reason to hike all that way for a tidepool. "Ride through jungle-like St. Croix. Now *that's* going to be a memorable experience."

And she was right. It was an experience. And Petra would remember it.

Her driver, Lucky, was a hoot and a half. Just a naturally easy-going, wry-kind-of-funny guy.

He was also an ace mechanic who got that engine humming

again when everything cut off, which it did every time his tire slid into a rut. And his tire went into a rut every few minutes.

But he was having a good time of it.

And his happy-go-luckiness (the reason for his name?) was contagious.

Petra needed to cut off any Herb conversation and pretend he wasn't even in the vehicle with her.

Something about Herb made Petra think of a man with a crowbar, who was looking for a crack to wedge into to pry a bigger opening.

Petra didn't want to give him a sliver of space.

She regretted every word she said to the man.

Happily, though, as soon as Lucky parked their vehicle, Herb was darting toward the trail to get ahead of his family as they arrived and parked behind Lucky's piece of shit vehicle.

With a bag slung over her shoulder and the kids in a hand-holding row, Petra followed the Johnson family, and the group moved out of the trees.

The trail was non-existent.

The way to get from dirt road to tidepool was to mountain goat it over the side of a cliff wall.

Normally, this would be easy enough. The wall was craggy, with plenty of handholds and footrests. But Petra was wearing flip-flops with her sundress.

She still had that wonky eye going on, making the light do funny things to her vision. And she, per doctor's orders, couldn't take off her extra-dark sunglasses. They were so dark that Petra couldn't make out anything along the side of the cliff.

Lucky was patience personified as he talked her along. "Your foot needs to go a few inches more. Okay, now let go with your right hand, and I'll put it in a new place for you."

Seventeen? Eighteen? How had this kid learned to be so generous?

As they got to the ridge of the tidepool. Petra stopped and looked out. "Well, that isn't good."

"What is wrong, Miss Armstrong?" Lucky asked, and Beans swung his head around, then came to stand near her to listen.

"See that?" She pointed. "I thought this was high tide?"

"Yes." Beans looked at Lucky. "High tide is now. Low tide will come this afternoon around two."

"But you see what I'm seeing? There's that channel of water over there. See how choppy it is? See the different colors like a streak of one kind of blue flowing through a different color blue? There. And there. And there. Look at that foam and the seaweed. See how it's getting pulled out? Those are—"

"Rip currents. And very bad ones. They shouldn't be here like that this time of day," Lucky said, holding the flats of his hands over his eyes like a visor.

"It's the wind," Beans told Lucky.

"The Christmas Winds?" Petra asked. "They make rip currents?"

"They can," Beans said. "But this time of day?"

"I haven't seen this before," Lucky said as he turned to the people at the tidepool. "Hello!" he called, raising a hand in the air. "My friend Beans and I are looking at the sea. It is very rough and dangerous. We can see what looks like rip currents. If you are not from a place with seawater, you should know that these currents can pull even a very good swimmer like Beans here out to sea. You become so exhausted from the struggle that, unless there is a boat right there to help, it is possible to drown. This is your vacation, and you will do as you wish. We want everyone to have a wonderful time. But you should know that Beans and I cannot swim after you to save you. Please stay here, safe in the tidepool, and choose a different day to go into the sea."

"You did a good job with that, Lucky." Petra's gaze was on Herb. He had to have heard, but he didn't cast his gaze around to check on his children or wander over to have a little talk to make sure they didn't climb over the rocks to the shore.

Jenny seemed to have taken up the task as the kids circled around her, and she was pointing and talking, then collecting shirts and shorts as the kids peeled down to their swimsuits, then walked away with a rolled beach blanket.

They left their necklaces on. And that bothered Petra in ways that she couldn't identify.

So, yeah, she was going to be nosey.

Petra decided to let Jenny settle, then she'd lead with the conversation she and Herb had started, the one where she was an author and, "Your husband says you like to read. He also told me you do international adventure races…"

Petra did write. She just wasn't an author.

It wasn't everyone's definition, but to Petra's mind, an author was paid for their work.

She was a writer, someone who put words on paper in the form of stories. By design, nothing she wrote was for public consumption, and she had no desire to expose herself to public scrutiny.

She wrote because, at night, her mind liked to ruminate, to go over every conversation to pick it apart, to second guess, to dig up some memory from her past. Memories from when she was two years old and that thing that happened.

That thing that someone said.

Ruminating. Ruminating.

Too often, the topic set on replay was from her time in Afghanistan, listening to the soldiers vent to her in their counseling sessions about the horrors that they lived through—about their friends who didn't live through them. About holding their buddy's arm and then realizing it wasn't attached to their friend's body anymore.

She didn't have PTSD.

She had neurodivergence, and the processing and reprocessing and the reprocessing of the repossessing was all part of that packaging—not to say that one diagnosis precluded the other. Just to say that Petra personally didn't fit the criteria for PTSD.

What Petra had was an overly rambunctious mind.

Petra started writing following Rowan's good counsel from back in their days at university, when he told her he handled the memories of his time in the military by writing about it.

When Petra could motivate her butt into a chair and her fingers around a pen, it had proved a successful strategy.

Instead of gnawing at the bone of some emotion, witnessing injustice, or re-evaluating some conversation, Petra could give that experience to her characters, and her characters could work it out.

Petra could chase down all the different ways things could have turned out and follow them to their likely conclusion.

A cognitive trial-and-error written out in long hand.

Petra knew she'd picked that bone clean when she was bored and wanted a new experience.

And so, with the Kennedys as friends—Rowan, the private writer, and Avery, the public editor—it made sense for Petra to make her public cover story that she was an author when she wanted the anonymity of an unexposed life.

Petra had both the lived experience of struggling to get words on a page, and all of the background words and industry updates in her back pocket to sound convincing as she told people things like what she was now saying to Jenny as they sat side by side with their feet in the tidepool, "I was talking a bit with Herb on the way here and he says you like military romance novels."

"That's true and rather an unusual subject of conversation." Jenny scanned the area until she found Herb on a stone, slathering sunscreen on his beer belly. He positioned his things in a place where he couldn't possibly see the children. And he looked like that was where he planned to stay. That left the kids to Jenny alone.

"He asked me what I did for a living," Petra explained. "I told him I was an author."

Jenny suddenly looked interested. "Have I read something you've written?"

"I write in a different genre. But I have a friend who's fairly successful, Holly Smokes."

"Reverse harems with SEALs and Delta Force operators. She's talented."

"Amazing at what she does." Petra had never actually read Holly's work, so she needed to move the conversation in a different direction. "I brought Holly up because your husband says you do adventure racing. I was wondering if you knew her from that?"

"I didn't know Holly was an adventure racer. And there aren't a lot of women who compete at my level." Jenny turned in Herb's direction.

He was sliding a ball cap protectively over his receding hairline.

Then Jenny scanned for her children. The water wasn't deep. There was no current here. There were plenty of family-looking adults. She seemed satisfied that all was safe.

Jenny slid her sunglasses on. She looked like she wanted to lie back and end the conversation.

Since Petra was only talking to learn the story of the matching necklaces, before the "go away, please" vibe got too strong, Petra ventured, "On the way here, I noticed Herb was wearing a necklace with such an interesting design. And now I see that you and the children are wearing the same. They must be meaningful." Petra had no reason to be nervous, but she found herself stimming to self-soothe, rubbing the ends of her hair between her fingertips.

Jenny's gaze swept over her children, then up to Herb, who was staring out at the adjacent cove, paying zero attention to his family. Her gaze moved back to her middle child, the daughter—Petra didn't know if any of these relationships she had mapped were correct. They seemed right, though.

And that middle daughter scowled back at her mother with ferocity.

Their eyes held for a long time.

The child wasn't giving in, and Jenny looked away indifferently.

"Yes, well. Our family had a ceremony, a renewal of vows kind of thing, and we wanted the children to be included and have a remembrance that they kept with them, telling them they were loved and part of a bigger happy family."

The oldest child, a boy—probably eight, maybe seven—turned his head to his mom with his brows knit and a tilt of his head that Petra read as a sincere question about why his mom would say something that wasn't true.

Jenny purposefully didn't look his way.

And Petra found that odd.

But before Petra could ask more questions, Jenny pulled a paperback from her bag and leaned back to read. She was done conversing.

For the rest of their hour in the tidepool, Petra ruminated. And watched.

When Beans finally called out that they would start back across the cliff's edge in ten minutes, Jenny finally roused from the plotline. After pulling the children's clothes from the bag and folding her towel, Jenny stood and caught her daughter's eye, then signaled her in.

The daughter scowled at Beans and glared at her mother. Then suddenly, she flicked a glance towards her dad and ran behind a large rock. Leaning back, Petra could see that the girl reached up, grabbed her necklace, and yanked it violently time and again until it finally broke, leaving a red welt along her neck.

Gripping the chain in her fist, the girl lifted her arm over her head and, with a mighty heave, flung the necklace toward the sea. She seemed satisfied with herself as she scrambled toward her mother.

Was it her mother? That was a leap that Petra had made. It could be anyone.

The whole thing was odd.

Something was *off*.

Petra had watched the necklace land. She made her way carefully down toward the water's edge, where she gathered the chain until the pendant lay on her palm. Taking her first clear look at the design, Petra felt something unsettling mix into her bloodstream.

But in her brain, Petra could sometimes know she knew a thing—a name, a definition, a fact, or a statistic—but that *thing* would hide from her.

If Petra chased after it, working hard to remember, it was like a child on the playground calling, "Come catch me!" and then racing away. A better strategy was to leave the thought alone and move on to something else. Eventually, the information would pop out enough that she could snatch it up.

Why did her brain do that?

Petra had no clue, but it came with her diagnosis. She knew it didn't just happen to her.

For now, she'd just slide the necklace into her pocket.

"Miss Armstrong?" Lucky was calling her. "Where are you?"

"Here, taking a photo." Petra pulled her phone from her pocket and pretended to snap an image. "I'm coming!"

But as Petra picked her way back to the group, her head spun toward the sea, where shrieks of horror rode the wind.

15

———

HAWKEYE

Hawkeye had memories of vacations near the Pacific Ocean when he went west as a child to visit his grandparents.

As an adult, he'd come up through the Army, to the Rangers, and then the Green Berets.

During his time in the military, they drummed into him the rudiments of staying alive in river water.

But he wasn't a SEAL like Reaper and some of the other Iniquus operators.

He hadn't trained for saltwater survival or rescue.

That was the reason Team Charlie was down here in the islands to get the land operators up to the proper skill levels.

Which meant that as Hawkeye leaned over the nose of the borrowed surfboard, plunging his hands into the water and dragging his arm back to his side, he was plowing ever forward toward some kind of crisis that he'd meet with the only thing he had—seat-of-his-pants strategy and enormous will.

As the team rounded the finger of land and could see into

the next cove, each man popped up on his board, coming up on their knees to give themselves a moment to make sense of the chaos and to catch their breath before their next burst of effort.

Nobody liked that. It felt all kinds of wrong to stop the forward momentum.

But, like in any emergency, the first rule of rescue was not to become part of the problem.

Even before Ash pointed and called out his findings, Hawkeye had spotted the problem. By the look of the water with two deep blue lanes and foam cutting through the pale turquoise, those had to be two sections of rip currents that had caught people up.

At least those on the shore knew better than to dive in without a floatation device and try to swim out and help.

That could just double a family's grief.

As those on the shore spotted the team, their screams turned from terror and anguish to hope, from gripping their heads as they knelt along the surf to leaping in the air with pointed fingers.

One woman came to her senses.

Thank goodness for that woman.

She rallied those around her, and as a group, the chant went up, "Six. Six. Six."

"Six in the water, boys. Call them out when you see them," Ash yelled to the team.

Here, where the sea was comparatively smooth, the men balanced with arms wide as they stood on their boards, working to gain perspective.

With hands shielding their eyes from the glitter of sunlight reflecting off the water's surface, they scanned with eyes well-practiced in searches.

None of the teammates called out a find.

Had the victims already gone under?

Hawkeye cupped his hand around his mouth and shouted toward the woman. "Find them! Show us!" He repeated this three times so that if the wind was snatching his words, someone could piece the message together.

The woman rallied the people around her again.

A moment later, groups ran to different positions on the beach. There were two, sometimes three people at each station, and every arm pointed at the swimmer they were marking.

It was brilliant.

"I have number six. The one on the far side," Hawkeye called. "Once I have them, I'll paddle south until I reach that boulder. It looks like it's past the rip current. That's where I plan to turn to shore."

"Go, Hawkeye. Go! Go!" Ash called.

As Hawkeye threw himself down on his board, he heard Ash issuing orders behind him, "Levi takes five. Halo takes four, then three. I have the shortest paddle. I'll go for one, then two, and see if Halo needs an assist with three. Get to shore and reassess."

Hawkeye's breathless "Wilco!" joined his teammates as he drove his board forward.

The lip of land had brought them out just far enough that they were past the current. There was a clear demarcation that Hawkeye tested before he pressed on.

He couldn't risk being caught in the current, too.

First man out, his brothers would be watching his progress to see if that line of travel was safe.

So far, he wasn't battling a cross pull out to sea, so he powered on.

It was tough as hell to pass the people in the water. He thought about the scenes at Quantico that Petra had described. In theory, it made rational sense.

In practice, it hurt like hell.

Hawkeye had to fight his instincts, trusting that his brothers were roaring onto the scene behind him.

That last guy, number six—*his* guy—he had the least expectations of being saved.

As Hawkeye drew parallel to him in the calmer waters just ahead of the man, his face was etched with surprise, exhaustion, hope, and pain.

From here, all Hawkeye could do was cheerlead. He couldn't paddle his board toward the man in the rip current any more than that man could swim for shore. "Sir, let the current bring you to me." Hawkeye rolled off his board. "Try to relax into it. Float. It's pulling you right to me."

The pain on the older gentleman's face worried Hawkeye. He couldn't account for it.

A cramp?

There would be time to assess once they reached the shore.

"You're going to be okay," Hawkeye encouraged. "I've got you. What's your name?"

There was no answer. The man made guppy lips as if trying to sip in some air.

Hawkeye felt his assessment turn from awareness to a clenched gut. This wasn't anything he'd seen before. "I'm Hawkeye. Sir, your name?"

"Roy," he croaked out.

From the sound, Hawkeye began to suspect Roy had swallowed too much salt water.

But if yesterday with Petra taught him anything, it was never to assume. "You've got this, Roy. You're not fighting the current. You're using the current to bring you to me."

The guy attempted a lazy side stroke in Hawkeye's direction with just enough effort to keep his head above water.

His pallor was gray.

Really gray.

Seconds felt like minutes. But, from the expression on the guy's face, Hawkeye knew the exact moment when Roy reached the edge of the rip current, and there was some relief from the power of the sea's energy.

Hawkeye pushed his board toward Roy so the guy could grab hold while maintaining a safe distance between himself and this guy until he was sure Roy wasn't panicking.

If Roy grabbed Hawkeye, they could both drown.

As Roy reached out one hand to clasp the edge of the board, he clutched at his chest with the other.

His mouth agape, Roy's breath was shallow, and had the cadence of a freight train.

"I've got you, sir. I have you." If Hawkeye was guessing, this grandfatherly, overweight man was having a heart attack from fear and exertion.

Hawkeye needed to get him to shore stat.

While culling through videos from the Iniquus library in preparation for this training evolution, Hawkeye had seen a couple of surfboard rescue techniques demonstrated.

There was a way to get an unconscious person onto a board, but to get them back to the shore, the rescuer basically had to lie on top of the victim to paddle.

Hawkeye didn't think Roy could survive the pressure.

On the plane, when Hawkeye and Levi carried Petra to the ambulance, they hadn't trusted she could stay conscious on the stairs. Better to get her configured safely in advance while they had her cooperation.

And now, Hawkeye didn't think Roy was going to make it far without passing out.

Better to get him configured for that potential rather than trying to get him moved in an unconscious state.

Running through memory files, Hawkeye recalled viewing another technique—a much more complicated technique—that kept the victim facing upward and the rescuer facing down. If Hawkeye could figure out how to get himself into the right setup, that might be the best option here.

But truth be told, Hawkeye was winging it.

Rounding the board until he was within arm's reach, Hawkeye kept his voice loud but calm. "Sir, I'm a retired Green Beret. I'm here to help you. If you follow my instructions, I'll get you back to the shore and get you the medical help you need."

The man bobbled his head.

Hawkeye turned onto his stomach, spread his legs, and backed toward the man until his knees were on either side of Roy.

"I'm almost in place, Roy. Do me a favor. Just keep your hand on the board. You're doing great. Now, I need you to turn and face out to sea. I'm going to keep talking you through this. You'll know every step. Okay, Roy?"

Roy didn't answer, and if he made a gesture, from Hawkeye's position facing the shore, Hawkeye missed it.

"You'll feel my legs positioning on either side of you." Hawkeye used the board to slide his thighs along the outside of Roy's ribs. "You should feel my legs around you now. You've seen the rescue harness that the Coast Guard uses? That's what I'm going to do with my body. I'm making a harness for you with my legs. We're going to work together, Roy. And together, we're going to get you to shore. I'm in place now. I'm bending my legs at the knee to bring my feet toward the sky to make that safety harness. Your head leans back and uses my ass as a pillow. Put one arm over my thigh. Good. I've got you. You won't go under. I need you to let go of the surfboard now."

Roy didn't comply.

"Roy. I've got you. You're safe. The sooner we get you in position, the sooner I can get us to shore. Let go of the board."

After a moment when Hawkeye could feel the man's inner fight to obey Hawkeye's command, Roy let go.

"See? Like I said, it's like a Coast Guard safety harness. You just hold onto my shins. You're doing great, sir. I'm going to cross my ankles over the top of you. That's right, hold onto my calf. Don't reach for the board. I've got you."

Hawkeye pulled the board along until he had it heading parallel to the shore.

"This next part, Roy, I need you to be really still so I can focus on keeping us out of that current."

Hawkeye reached to either side of the board and gripped tightly as he pushed the back down into the water and heaved himself up and over the end. Reaching forward and pulling hard, Hawkeye edged his torso on, then his hips, and with this last effort, he was able to get a bit of his thighs on board.

With his head resting back on Hawkeye's butt, Roy's body stretched out in the water.

Getting a man this size far enough south that they could safely tack back to shore was going to be a trick.

The sound of a jet ski gunning its engine pulled Hawkeye's attention seaward.

Someone with a motor would sure make this event easier and safer.

Were they close enough that he could signal for help?

Sweeping his gaze along the horizon, Hawkeye spotted the white pleasure boat he'd seen earlier, the one with the joyful red flags.

Not too far away, considering how sound travels over water. Laughter brewed amongst the group on the deck, but they were all facing away from him.

A guy on a jet ski circled the yacht, popping out of the water and doing a few quick tricks.

The jet skier had his eye on the audience, watching as they cheered him on.

What he didn't see was a monstrous wave rolling over the sea's surface.

With his weight on his elbows, Hawkeye cupped his mouth and yelled, "Wave!" to give his teammates a heads-up.

That swell was so big that Hawkeye changed his plans and decided to ride the crest to shore. It had to be stronger than the rip current. And Roy was struggling to breathe.

"Jeezus! Wave!" Levi called.

"Wave!" Hawkeye could hear the message passing from one brother to another.

The person who didn't hear the warning was the guy on the jet ski wrapped in the cloud of his revving engine noises. The rider pulled up on the handles as he stood and arched backward to make the jet ski flip through the air.

It was a spectacular sight.

The roar of approval from the boaters rode the wind to shore.

Hawkeye tried again, aiming his call directly toward the boat that was about to get broadsided and rolled. "Wave!" he hollered.

Roy started wheezing in a way that reminded Hawkeye of the death rattle he'd heard on the battlefield.

Hawkeye needed this wave to get to them fast and transport them quickly back to the shore, where he could find a hard surface if Roy needed CPR.

The guy on the jet ski did another fancy flip, but this time, as he lifted from the water, the wave pushed him impossibly high, adding enormous energy to the trick. The guy had to be at least two stories up when he lost his grip and fell toward the boat.

The boat rolled onto its side, flinging the passengers into the water.

Hawkeye was scrambling to turn his board facing shore in time. No small feat with Roy serving as an anchor in the water.

Looking over his shoulder to ensure he was in line with the wave, Hawkeye watched as the boat righted itself, just as the jet ski came down and hit.

There was an explosion. Flames shot out of the wheelhouse.

Shrieks of horror sounded from shore to sea.

Hawkeye held onto the surfboard with an iron grip.

And as the wave lifted and thrust them toward the sky, Roy blacked the hell out.

16

To Petra, it was like she was sitting in a movie theater as she watched the wave rolling in from the horizon.

She expected someone to cue the music, and at any moment, the symphony would play the ominous chords designed to get the audience's blood thrumming, wondering how the hero could survive.

For sure, that was exactly what she was wondering.

And in this scene, she was the unfortunate hero.

On this terrain, running anywhere was impossible.

Petra's brain flashed to the rip currents and wondered if that had fed into the enormity of this wave.

Right now, everything played in slow motion except for her thoughts.

Petra's brain flailed for her best next action—a means of survival.

She had *nothing* until she had something.

Suddenly, Petra was moving, leaping, grabbing—not back toward the cliff but southward toward a massive boulder.

As she found a wedge for her foot, Petra cleared her hands by shoving her phone down the neckline of her dress and under her breast into her bikini top.

She grabbed at the jagged protrusions, hugging her body to the surface as the wave crashed, sending a spray of water showering down on her.

The pull of the receding water dragged at Petra's legs.

She strained against it, tensing her muscles and white-knuckle gripping the stone.

With a heart filled with gratitude that she was high enough in the rocks that the water only came to her thighs.

Suddenly, she was suffused by terror.

The children!

Petra turned toward where the group that had been on the cliff wall, edging back toward their vehicles to return to the hotel.

Blinking past the burn of salt water, Petra thought it looked like the turn of events stunned the others from the tidepool, but they were untouched.

Lucky hollered, "Miss Armstrong, another wave! It's coming!"

Petra turned her face to the rock, put her head down, and gripped the surface in preparation.

Again, the wave reached over and around the boulder, tugging hungrily at her legs, trying to loosen her from her perch and steal her away like a pirate with his treasure box of gold.

Panting, Petra turned her head toward the cliff, searching for her best route for escape.

Beans and Lucky were helping the last of the tidal pool revelers onto the path. Both stayed on the cliff as Beans pointed and called out. "Miss Armstrong! Wave!"

How many?

How long would this go on?

Already, she was exhausted from the fight.

This third wave was the highest yet, the water coming to her chest. Her eye—stinging from yesterday's wonkiness—was on fire from the salinity of the spray.

Her grip slipped, and the sheer power of the tidal force shoved Petra to the side, onto her knees amongst the foam.

Scrambling to find something new to hold, or at least get her feet out in front of her so she wasn't tumbling headfirst into the line of boulders, Petra was suddenly jerked backward, held on the land by her hair.

A hand landed on her arm, then released to grab her wrist, and she was hauled back onto her feet.

Lucky.

Lucky had leaped forward and grabbed the only part of her available, protecting her from a treacherous outcome.

His eyes held wide and unblinking with fear and disbelief.

Beans called from the cliff. "That was all. No more waves. No more *big* waves. I'll watch. But hurry."

No one needed to tell Petra twice. Her sunglasses and flip flops out to sea, Petra's dress wrapped her thighs as she reached for the hand Lucky extended to her.

"My lucky day to have such a brave guy watching out for me." Petra tried for light as she tapped her boob to make sure her phone in its waterproof case was still in place.

Lucky looked traumatized as he pointed toward Beans and the cliff wall and started back.

Poor kid needed a stiff drink.

On bare feet, picking her way painfully over the sharp rocks, Petra froze when she heard a second scream.

This one was a different beast.

The first scream was fear and shock. It was the warning that Petra needed to stay safe from the initial rogue wave.

This scream was the anguished cry that goes up when a loved one is pronounced dead. A call to the Heavens.

It sent a wave of horror through Petra's system, making her gag as she tried to vomit the sensation out of her gut.

But body and mind were at cross purposes.

Petra turned and flew over the rocks toward the screams, Lucky following behind.

Hunching over to place their hands for balance, they were crabs skittering along the edge of a wave.

Around an outcropping, they found a young woman standing in hiking clothes, soaked head to foot.

With hands clutching chunks of hair, she looked out to sea.

Her chest heaved as she forced air into her lungs like a bellow, oxygenating a fire.

Then she tipped her head back, and her scream ripped the air, vibrating Petra's skeleton until she could feel the tug on her tendons.

"Hey!" Petra shouted as she approached. "Hey!" Her voice was loud and commanding, but the woman didn't notice.

Here were the bellows heating.

There was the scream.

Petra and Lucky turned toward the sea, scanning to see if they could decipher what was happening.

Petra stilled.

What was that?

Cocking her ear, focusing hard, she listened.

Could that be an echo?

No, the pitch wasn't a lament but pain and terror.

And it was male.

Petra gripped Lucky's arm and tapped her ear. They had to

wait for a wave to come in—the normal kind of wave that she'd seen from the time they'd arrived.

It receded.

And nothing.

The woman was huffing again, and Petra folded a hand to her chest and swung it wide, backhanding the woman's arm in a sting that brought her to her senses, pulling her out of whatever survival reaction her limbic had conjured.

"Be quiet," Petra hissed. "I'm trying to hear."

Another wave came and went.

There it was again. This time, instead of a scream, Petra heard, "Help! Help!"

She squeezed Lucky's arm harder.

He was still wide-eyed, in shock from making his earlier save.

Understandably so.

Petra couldn't imagine the bravery it took for this kid to leap from the safety of the cliff into the swell of the angry waters to grab a stranger by the hair and drag her back from the clasp of a hungry sea.

But Petra needed someone to snap out of it and help her figure out where that man could possibly be.

Petra saw nothing and no one who could be in danger.

The woman turned to them. "My fiancé. He was here. The wave." She flung her arms. "He pushed me." She pointed at the boulder, much like the one Petra had used to save herself.

This next wave was receding, and Petra held a finger to her lips and pointed another into the sky.

"Help! Help!" This time, it was weaker.

"We were holding hands," the woman whispered. "Then we weren't. I saw him pulled out, and then he went under." She pointed toward the horizon where no heads bobbled in the surf.

Petra turned to Lucky. "You heard that?"

Lucky shook his head. "I hear nothing but surf and wind."

Beans scrambled down beside them.

"It sounds like the call for help is bouncing off the rock. Is there someplace like a cave? Someplace where if the first wave dragged a guy out, that the second, or maybe the third wave, could have pushed him in?" When she said that, fear iced her system.

All four turned, with stiff fingers shielding their eyes to scan the horizon.

"Carlos is watching," Beans said. "He'll give us a warning if more waves come." He punched Lucky's shoulder. "The blowhole?"

Lucky was looking at Petra when he said, "It's very dangerous. We warn everyone away from swimming near it."

"Here somewhere?" Petra asked as the next wave receded. And she jabbed a finger into the air and again cocking her head to the side to focus on sounds.

"Agh!"

Petra pointed at Lucky, asking with her gesture if he heard the cry.

Lucky shook his head.

But Beans was moving north along the rocks. "The blowhole is over here. Here and up. And then you can look down."

Petra raced after Beans as she heard a strangulated cry for "Help!"

17

———

Realizing there was an emergency, others who had been at the tidal pool were finding their way to the scene.

Carlos maintained a wave lookout.

Beans threw himself down on a boulder and looked into a round hole that looked like an old-fashioned well. A bit wider. Certainly, large enough for even as big a man as Hawkeye to go in.

Looking over the lip, watching the water rush in, Petra formed a picture of what had happened.

The man wasn't in the chimney. He sounded like he was further under the rock. If he were trying to get out, the waves would keep pushing him in.

These waves weren't as big as the three rogue waves. But the horse guy that morning at the hotel, while she was waiting for her tidal pool adventure ride to show up, had talked about how difficult the current was and that he had suggested not risking the disappointment of a failed attempt at snorkeling.

Petra imagined that the man had been pushed into a small cave.

At least there would be oxygen between waves.

Possibly.

Probably.

But she remembered being a child on the beach body surfing and what happened when a wave hit, and she was rolled without any power against it. She imagined the guy getting battered against the rocks, then using what time he had to suck in air and cry for help.

He needed to stop using his energy to signal.

"We're here," Petra called into the opening. "We're affecting a rescue. You're not alone." Petra got all that out before the next wave hit.

The tourists huddled in one group. The locals stood closer, looking prepared to leap into action.

"Who drove down here?" Petra asked. "Not people in the car, but the person who had their hands on the steering wheel. Can you step forward?"

The men gathered.

Men—these were probably teens still in high school trying to earn a few bucks on the weekend, making the tourists scream and laugh with an adventure that was just an everyday drive for them.

"Okay, guys, in a minute, I need you to go through your vehicles for anything helpful you might have—ropes, blankets, first aid kits, carabiners, climbing gear, tow webbing. I need you to think outside of the box. Something to use as a splint for broken bones. Be imaginative. Just make sure you can bring it back without injuring yourself. One crisis is enough for today. I need those things here so we can figure out what resources we have to try to help this guy." Petra turned to the woman. "What's his name?"

"Terry," she whispered, clasping her hands together and holding them to her chest.

"And you are?"

"M-m-m-melissa."

The wave was going out. "Terry," Petra hollered into the hole, "Melissa is safe. We're working on getting you out. Try to reserve your energy. Your goal is to keep breathing deeply."

There were no cries for help since she'd told Terry they were on the scene.

That might be a good thing.

Or it could bode very badly.

Petra pulled her phone from her bikini top.

No bars.

"Anyone have connectivity?" she asked, holding her phone aloft.

"No one does," Beans said. "We don't get cell reception until we're up on the road."

Petra scowled. "How far up?"

Beans cast his gaze back toward the vehicles. "At The Social Club with the drinking jig."

"Far then. I need someone who has a vehicle that hasn't been breaking down every five minutes like ours was. You all know each other. I need the person with the most reliable vehicle to get to a place where they can make emergency calls." She was using the voice her instructors taught her at Quantico, speaking from the chest. It was an authoritative sound that convinced people to comply. The one that made everyone aware that *she* was in charge.

Did she want to be an authority and in charge?

Honestly, no.

This wasn't a television show. There were no guarantees. There was a man who could very well die in the next few minutes, and it could well be that there was nothing anyone could do.

But if that did happen, everyone would have a better psychological outcome if they knew they had participated in a rescue attempt.

One of the young men half-raised his hand as if he were in class. "My car is solid. I can drive out and get help."

"Okay, good. What's your name?"

"Bobby."

Petra reached out her hand. "Can you give me your phone, Bobby?"

Petra tried to come up with the right message to send to 9-1-1 when it occurred to her that if those crazy waves hit the entire coast, Terry wouldn't be the only person in dire straits today.

Desperate calls could well be overwhelming emergency services.

Petra was going to reach out to Cerberus. If they didn't have the right equipment, at least they'd have the expertise and the brawn needed to attempt the rescue.

Closing her eyes momentarily, she recalled the number Hawkeye had put into her contacts that morning before heading out to surf with Cooper.

What a grand time *they* must be having.

But she was sure that if she sent Hawkeye an SOS, he and his merry band of brothers would drop their surfboards and head her way.

Still, it was a long shot.

Could Terry hold on that long?

As Petra typed out her message, she said. "Bobby, first call 9-1-1." She continued to tap. "This is a message to a rescuer friend of mine." She handed him the phone. "I've pressed send, but it won't go out until it's in range of a cell tower. You have to get it in range, and then you need to wait there. I've put in a code to pull up your GPS location. My friends will follow the signal to you. And you need to bring them here. They can't find me if they don't find you."

"Got it."

"Can you do that?" Petra looked up, locking her gaze on this young man's.

His body swelled with purpose. "Get into cell range, wait for the rescuers. I bring them here."

"Don't forget to call 9-1-1," she reminded him. "Go!"

Bobby raced away on long, thin legs, bounding up the side of a cliff, an athletic blur of motion.

"Okay, those with cars, go gather supplies and come right back here." She reached out. "Beans."

He turned back to her.

"I'm taking the cord from your hoodie. Does anyone else have a cord? Shoelaces? Anything I can use to make a line?"

Very quickly, the group was in motion. Those who weren't given a task moved out of the way, poised and ready to act.

What Petra needed now were facts. Data.

The way to get that? Eyes-on. Well, camera-on.

With the video recording, Petra tied together a make-do line of anything that could be grafted into a length that might reach Terry.

Slowly, she lowered her phone.

Even though she had a watertight case, she didn't want the waves to batter her phone against the rocks, rendering it useless, so she waited for a wave to come in as she started lowering to give herself as long as possible in the hole when the wave receded.

Holding the string steady so it wasn't spinning and collecting a dizzying whir of images was paramount.

Petra moved—slow and steady—to get as much information as she could.

Even so, what she got was mostly an image of a rock wall.

Over and over, Petra lowered the camera down the blow hole.

Every time she did, Melissa became more agitated. "What are you doing? How is this helping? Terry could be drowning."

Before Petra said something sharp to the distraught woman, the drivers were back with an array of gear.

She spread the items out and came up with a plan.

The phone was probably a good idea. But it hadn't panned out.

She needed to go down herself to understand the situation. And with the climbing gear that the guys had produced, she felt like it was doable, if not safe.

Petra held up the bike helmets. "Whoever brought these, you are a genius. Kudos." She strapped one on.

She arranged the people to hold the rope, then tied herself into a hasty—the kind of quick and dirty way someone can get a rope on for a climb.

Was it weird in her sundress?

Only in that the rope between her legs was against her flesh, and she was going to come out of this with some severe abrasions.

Did she care?

Hell to the no.

She strapped the helmet in place, taking the time to adjust it properly—Petra wasn't interested in having her brains bashed against the rocks.

"Listen up," she bellowed over the wind and surf. "When I have information, I'll communicate it to you. You are not to call down there asking for updates. You'll break my concentration. I don't want to hear anything from you unless you're warning me about another giant wave or that there's a rescue crew on site. Not within sight. *On* site, ready to act. Okay?" She looked around the circle. "Is everyone in agreement? Are we all on the same page?"

The body stances of the people around her were an interesting mixture. They all seemed to have some combination of anxiety and relief that someone was doing something.

She could see the adrenaline at work in their systems, telling them to act, but not having a ready way to use it up made them fidgety.

Mostly, they were shocked that this was how their day had turned out.

Rightly so.

Usually, people don't run into circumstances where they are suddenly part of a lifeline.

Petra's focus followed the hot pink climbing rope to the four men, who were gripping a section. Sitting on their butts, legs bent, feet wedged into the rocks the way Petra had instructed, they could use their leg strength, too.

"If things work out the way I want them to, you guys won't be exerting for a while. I'll mostly have my own weight. I just need you to get me over the lip. This is a good opportunity to test how this feels and check your grip. Make sure it's something you can sustain because once I'm down there, my life will literally be in your hands."

She shouldn't have said that.

It didn't rally them the way it did at boot camp or Quantico.

One of the guys released the rope to swipe his hands over his shorts. She could see the rings of sweat at his pits.

"There are lots of people around who can grab onto the back of the rope. Make sure you let them know you need help *before* you actually need the help, okay?" She tried to reassure them.

She got bobbled head nods and wide fixed eyelids instead.

Adrenaline was definitely kicking around their systems.

Good. That would give them extra strength.

Petra sat down, dangled her legs into the hole, and waited for the wave to recede. She bent her head and yelled. "Terry, I'm coming down to you! Coming down now!" She wanted the guy to have a moment to get that thought into his brain.

He had to be in shock.

He had to be thinking that this was a hell of a way to go.

People worried about heart attacks and car crashes, house fires and bad guys. She bet no one ever thought, I desperately hope I don't die by being bashed to death in a blow hole in Paradise.

Petra rolled over until her hips balanced on the edge of the hole and her stomach was toward the ground. She gripped the rope and called out, "Lower away."

The men pulled their elbows into their ribs and braced to take her weight.

With her free hand, Petra pressed away from the rocks, looking up to see Beans doing his job as her spotter and conveyer of her directives.

Glancing over, she made sure that Carlos was still acting as a rogue wave looker-outer—was there a word for that? Wave guard?

Doesn't matter. Here I go.

Below her, seawater swept into the blowhole.

The men lowered her.

On the second wave, Petra was ankle-deep in water. She visually marked that space by focusing on a rock that jutted out. "Hold!" Petra waited for the wave to recede. "Lower!"

Down, down she went.

One of Petra's superpowers was that she genuinely believed she could do anything she wanted to. It might mean a little learning or training, but yeah, in body and brain, anything she *wanted* to do was within her reach or had been so far.

Of course, her list of wants hadn't included such things as professional opera singer, MMA fighter, or Olympian, so there hadn't been anything to dissuade her magical thinking.

Petra's other superpower was a wide range of interests, which led to a wide range of skills that might be part of the illusion that she could conquer anything.

Did she really think that with a length of hot pink rope from a cargo hold and a bunch of good citizens, she could do *this*?

Maybe she was just acting on her military training, which taught her to run toward the enemy.

And then, FBI training.

Okay, she reasoned as the next wave came to her hips. She did have some training.

But this, under any circumstances, was beyond her capacity.

And with a lack of proper equipment, it was foolhardy.

And yet here she was in a blow hole, for crap's sake.

Petra tipped her head up so her voice would carry to the rope crew. "Hold!"

The rope was rough against her skin, abrading the top layer, and exposing her nerves to the salt water.

The pain was a good sign that she was in her body—thinking, rational, following what training she had that she could apply here.

When adrenaline stopped the pain, she'd need to reassess. Adrenaline could tell her body it was fine when, in fact, it hid a life-threatening injury.

Petra did *not* plan to die today.

If she died, it was likely Terry would die as well.

If she died, it served no good. Petra set those parameters, "no pain means I need to come back up and form a new, more plausible plan."

Another wave roared into the hole, and Petra shoved hard

into her borrowed tennis shoe-clad feet to brace as the wave whooshed in.

It was surprising how loud it was as the small space captured the roar and sent it ricocheting up the sides to release toward the sky.

She was surprised at how much space her heart took up in her chest and how the sound of her blood processing through the four chambers joined the roar of the wave.

Sucking in a lung full of air and pinching her nose, Petra squeezed her eyelids tightly together. The wave only came to her chin, but the spray sprinkled salt onto her lashes.

When the wave receded, Petra looked down to see how far it was to the opening. Leaning down, she could almost get her fingers around the lip.

"Terry, are you in good enough shape to follow instructions?"

"Help." Terry croaked.

"All right, Terry, listen up. I need you to count backward from a hundred by twos." It seemed a cruel thing to do, but Petra's brain was conjuring all kinds of scenarios where drowning people pulled their rescuers to their deaths.

If Terry panicked and dragged her down, Petra too could get trapped by the waves and possibly not escape this blow hole alive.

Before Petra went any further, this man had to prove he could—at least at this moment—process rationally.

"Ninety-eight. Ninety-six. Ninety-four."

"Terry," Petra called, "a wave is coming. Brace."

"Please, please, *please* help me."

18

____

HAWKEYE

Hawkeye had never felt so powerless in his life.

Panic was a gladiator in the Colosseum fighting for dominance.

There was no air, no up or down—nothing for his brain to grab onto to make sense of reality.

The single thought that had substance was that he would not, could not under any circumstances, allow his ankle to come unlocked. If he did, he'd lose Roy to the wave.

His surfboard had ripped from Hawkeye's hands.

But from the drag trying to pry his ankles apart, Hawkeye knew that the tether held the board to him. They plunged together.

On this last tumble, Hawkeye scraped his knuckles through the abrasion of a sandy bottom.

They'd reached shallower waters.

As he spread his fingers to anchor himself in that position, Hawkeye reasoned that he must be face down.

And that meant maybe, possibly, Roy was getting some air.

Hawkeye dug into the sand and pulled himself along. Then he felt a hand under his armpits.

"We've got you, brother."

Hawkeye relaxed into the grip, making it easier on his teammates as they dragged him from the surf.

"Release your ankles, Hawkeye. We have the guy."

Easier said than done. Hawkeye had put so much effort into ensuring he didn't release Roy that neither his brain nor his cramped and stiffened muscles complied.

Halo must have understood because he reached out and forced Hawkeye's legs apart.

"In coming! Go! Go! Go!" Ash yelled.

As Hawkeye blinked, he saw feet and legs swarming him. His team grabbed Hawkeye's arms, hauling him, gasping and sputtering, up the beach to the rocks. Halo and Ash threw their bodies over Hawkeye's as a wave slapped over them, then retreated with enormous drag.

They had to be a good twenty yards from the shoreline.

His teammates clapped him on the shoulder and were once again up and running.

Hawkeye swung his head. Roy was nearby on a flat rock where two people were performing CPR.

Farther down toward the shoreline, people were grabbing humans and racing with them back to the rocks.

Hawkeye was in motion, running to help even before he could process why people were flopping on the shoreline like a school of fish beached by a sudden low tide.

Heaving a man's arm over his shoulder, Hawkeye half-dragged the guy as they jogged toward safety, while a third wave drew ever closer.

"Cerberus, move it! Faster! Get off the sand!" That was Reaper's booming voice.

As he laid the guy on the rocks, Hawkeye spotted Reaper on the road with the four K9s sitting in a row. He was flagging down a pickup truck and scoop-gesturing to move them into position.

"My guy Roy is receiving CPR." Hawkeye hollered as he deposited this man beside a boulder, ensuring Reaper was aware.

"He's first to go," Reaper yelled back. "In coming!"

Hawkeye squatted over the man he'd helped to the rocks and used his body to take the pounding of the wave, like his brothers had a moment ago.

The guy underneath him smelled like diesel.

Then Hawkeye remembered the boat accident.

"Listen up," Reaper called through cupped hands. "I'll keep wave watch. That looks like the last rogue wave, at least for now. Cerberus, all six of the rip current victims are accounted for. There were thirteen people on the beach during your rescue effort. That's nineteen. We need to find a good headcount for the number of people on the boat to figure out how many got swept in by the waves and how many are unaccounted for. Boat people, raise your hand if you know your headcount."

Three men raised their hands.

"Sixteen, including crew," one man called.

"Was the crew in uniform?" Reaper asked, pointing at the man so the guy knew the question was directed at him.

The man nodded, then shook his hand along his torso. "White shorts, navy blue shirts."

"Life vests?" Reaper asked.

There was a general shaking of heads.

Hawkeye cast his gaze along the huddled group. No one matched the description for the crew.

"No," a guy yelled, then stopped for a hacking jag. "No, there were twelve of us. We're in for a sales meeting. There were the four crew members, and there was the guy with the jet ski who met us out there. He was doing the flippy doojiggers when the boat rolled. Bright board shorts. I haven't seen him since he was in the air." Then the man turned, looking out to sea.

They all did.

The boat was a torch on the water. It reminded Hawkeye of the 19th-century Bierstadt painting, *The Burning Ship*, he'd seen in a Vermont museum on some family holiday. Hawkeye remembered the horror of it. The idea that there was no way to survive. And that memory was why Hawkeye had gone the Army Ranger route rather than becoming a Navy SEAL.

In general, he wasn't a fan of giving up survival options.

"Nineteen from the beach. Seventeen from the boat event. Five Iniquus. Four K9s, that gives us forty-five. Levi!"

"On it." Levi leaped onto the highest boulder.

"Everyone, stay very still while we get a head count," Reaper commanded. "It's imperative that we get this right. No one moves." Reaper turned his head and spoke with someone, then turned back. "Cerberus, we have a pickup for the CPR victim. You've been accounted for. You—and only you—can move. Put Roy on a surfboard, and let's get him loaded up." Reaper held a stopping sign gesture in the air. "No one else moves."

Levi called out, "We're missing seven."

"Seven," each of the Iniquus men called out.

Cooper gave a sharp bark, "I'm here. I'm ready. Put me to work."

Hawkeye gave him the hand signal that told Cooper to hold, then he ran for his surfboard, lying behind a boulder, and headed for Roy.

"People not on my team, before you leave the area," Reaper called out, "we need to write down your name, so everyone is accounted for. If you have transportation, please offer a ride to those from the boat. Again, I'm asking you to stay still while we continue our rescue efforts of the rip current victim."

Hawkeye snagged up a sopping wet beach towel as he ran toward Roy.

"In the meantime," Reaper called. "I need two groups of four volunteers who are physically capable of searching along the shoreline. One group will head north and the other south to see if anyone washed into a different cove. Each group should include someone with first aid training. Come forward if you're ready, able, and willing."

When Hawkeye reached the flat rock, the bystanders who had performed CPR crawled out of the way, winded from their sustained effort.

"His name is Roy," Hawkeye told his teammates as they moved up.

Reaper's voice boomed out, "People who are, at this point in time, ready and able to render CPR, raise your hands."

Halo was already arranging Roy into position, bending Roy's leg, pulling his arm long, and with Hawkeye pushing the shoulders and Halo pulling his hips, they rolled Roy onto his side.

"You four." Reaper's finger traced around, tagging the people he'd chosen. "Come forward."

Hawkeye laid the towel under Roy, then he and Halo rolled him onto his back.

With a Cerberus brother at each corner—and a "One. Two. Three. Lift."— they transferred Roy onto the surfboard.

It was a struggle to stay focused on this moment, knowing that there may well be seven people fighting for their lives in the water.

Together, the team shifted the surfboard onto a shoulder.

Without handles and for fear that someone's grip would slip on the slick surface, this was the safest configuration, though it reminded Hawkeye of the dancing pallbearers he'd seen in Ghana.

As soon as that thought crossed his mind, Hawkeye thrust it away.

The Cerberus men passed behind Reaper, who was addressing the volunteers. "The CPR team is exhausted. If you're willing, we need to supply CPR on the way to the hospital. The driver will be going slow and steady to get you there, but you will be in an open, moving vehicle. Only agree if you are comfortable with that situation."

Every second counted.

All four fell in behind Roy and followed the team to the pickup, where the men used the towel to transfer Roy into the bed.

With surfboard in hand, Cerberus jumped out of the way.

The CPR team climbed in and got right back to work.

Cerberus was in motion, hustling back to the beach.

During that brief time away, two missing boat crew were located and helped back to the staging site.

"Five unaccounted for," Reaper said.

"Five," the men repeated.

"Take your boards. The waves and rip currents have clouded the waters. That's going to make rescue and recovery more difficult. If you're confident that your dog can function here like they did on the Potomac—since we were just training this—take your K9 with you. If you're not a hundred percent sure, leave your dog in my care."

What Reaper left unsaid was that "rescue" was the term used for the living, and "recovery" was the term used for a body.

The training they'd been doing for weeks on the river was

the dogs' ability to perform water searches, finding a human scent under the water. Of course, the dogs had been working by leaning over the edge of a boat, not balanced on a surfboard.

The team needed to move fast to have any hope of finding the missing five.

Alive would be amazing.

But even if dead, retrieving the bodies would bring closure for the families and loved ones.

The sea was vast, and the conditions treacherous, but Hawkeye and Cooper raced into the waves, determined.

19

———————

HAWKEYE

With Cooper running at his heels, Hawkeye dashed toward the waterline, the surfboard under his arm.

Hawkeye knew his dog.

When they were in mission mode, Cooper was the tip of the spear. He intuited the need and acted.

As Hawkeye sprinted into the frothing water, lifting his knees high to maintain his momentum, he pulled the board around, diving onto the surface. He looked over his shoulder to see Cooper extending his forelegs and leaping after him, landing between Hawkeye's legs.

Cooper moved up until his front paws extended over Hawkeye's shoulder.

Hawkeye didn't realize how much that would help him balance the board and plow through the water until Cooper did that. "Good job, buddy. We're going on a search. Cooper, search."

Hawkeye was digging deep.

Halo, raised on Australian beaches where surfing was a way of life, slid up beside him. "Bloody hell, mate," he called. "It's a bleeding inferno out there. No one's survived on that boat. I'm going west to the boat, then peeling north if you want to head south from here."

"Wilco. Hey!" Hawkeye lifted his voice in warning.

Halo tipped his chin to see Hawkeye.

"The guy I had on the beach smelled of diesel. Keep an eye on the water. If the fuel gets on you or the board—"

"Poof," Halo said. "Stay out of the fuel ring."

Hawkeye should have said that before he hit the water. There were a lot of moving parts. A lot of details.

Details were survival.

"Diesel in the water!" Hawkeye called out.

"Diesel in the water," Levi and Ash called from behind him.

With that out of the way, it would take some time for Hawkeye to paddle out. He'd use the time to his advantage. He went back in his memory and tried to recall the details of the first wave.

There was the man who fell from the jet ski onto the boat. Without a helmet, it was unlikely that he'd stayed conscious after hitting.

Next, the boat rolled, tossing the passengers into the swell.

Hawkeye didn't see the impact of waves two and three. But, in one way or another, most of the people landed on the shore.

From the age of the two crew members who made it to the shore in the next cove, they were servers and probably out on the deck. Two crew members were still missing. Hawkeye thought one was probably a cook and was trapped in the galley.

Could be the fire started there? Hot grease, propane, and the severity of the tilt.

Could be the fire started with the impact of the jet ski?

Knowing the origin of the fire was useless to him. The whole damned boat was aflame.

Hawkeye figured the other crew member might be trapped in the wheelhouse. Not having seen the configuration of the boat, it was speculation at best.

That would account for three of the five missing. Then there were the two other passengers. With a high percentage making it to the shore, what could have happened to the others?

Could be in the latrine. "If anyone had been hitting the head, they were shit out of luck." Hawkeye looked over his shoulder and said, "Gallows humor."

Cooper didn't care; he was hard-focused on the water.

There should have been at least two more people in the water.

Why?

Three possibilities—killed or injured, someone with a disability, someone who didn't know how to swim, or didn't trust their swimming skills to make it to shore.

If alive, Hawkeye thought he might find them clinging to the side of the boat below the fire line or maybe they found something buoyant.

Yes, that was his best guess.

He had used the first wave to make it to shore, and the others probably made that distance because they used the waves to their advantage.

But why were the crew at the second cove?

If it were Hawkeye, he'd have a sense of responsibility. He would have tried to make sure everyone was safe, tried to get to his coworkers.

Hawkeye bet that by the time the third wave hit, they decided they'd done what they could. And he bet they'd somehow angled differently.

If he was right, and the current pulled them farther south—

not much farther south, but enough—then his search should be south, not seaward for this point.

When Hawkeye looked over his shoulder, Halo and Max were in view. "I'm turning here."

Max was up on Halo's shoulders. And, like Cooper, had his nose down, chuffing air, searching for the scent of a human under the water.

It was so strange to be in the pristine clarity of the water this morning and to have visibility change so drastically in such a short time.

As he turned back to the boat, Hawkeye saw that the anchor line was down.

"Halo!" Hawkeye called with a hand cupped around his mouth. The winds were high and strong, and he was covered in goose flesh. "Anchors down! Check to see if anyone is clinging to it. Bobbing into the water so they aren't in the fire. Someone who can't swim."

"Wilco. Heading there now."

Hawkeye could feel a shift in the water and wondered if they were now moving into low tide. And while that might help him get out to the boat, it would make getting back in that much harder.

Stilling for a moment to consider the position of the boat and the direction of the ripples, Hawkeye saw something in the distance farther out to sea.

He squinted at it using a technique from his days as a Green Beret when he willed his brain to make sense of a shape. It often brought something into relief. Hawkeye would swear there was a bobbing white cube—cooler?—with something dark draped over the top—person? It seemed to be floating away from them out to sea.

He spun his surfboard around. Halo was closest, but not in a direct line of sight. If he was checking the anchor, he might miss this. And the person might float past the horizon line.

"Halo!" Hawkeye bellowed, letting the water carry the sound of his voice. "Around the back of the boat, your eleven o'clock."

"My eleven. Wilco!" Halo tucked his head, his hands stabbed into the water as he propelled himself toward the mark.

Cooper scrambled to Hawkeye's other shoulder, whining and crouching as if to dive into the water. Hawkeye wondered if the smell of the fire and the burning chemicals was frightening him. Their surfboard might be as close to the inferno as Cooper could stand it.

Pressing his clawed paws into Hawkeye's back, Cooper released a series of barks that set Hawkeye's limbic on fire.

His body was moving with purpose and power that came to him only in times of extreme need.

The tone of Cooper's barks pressed Hawkeye's throttle wide open, and he was gunning toward nothing obvious.

20

———

HAWKEYE

Up ahead, Hawkeye spotted the smooth curve of a man in a deadman's float.

Hawkeye hoped like hell the guy was just conserving his energy and would turn his head to take a gasp of air.

How long had he been face down?

The boat rescue had been going on for a while now.

It could be that this guy had stayed upright and breathing most of that time.

Dead or on the cusp?

As he got closer, Hawkeye was debating best practices when, in fact, he had none.

Earlier, when he'd come upon Roy, Hawkeye had reviewed the few ways he'd seen rescuers get people onto a board. And he wasn't satisfied with any of them under these circumstances.

On his belly, this man would be a recovery. There was no way he'd make it to shore alive. Of course, that might be true no matter what Hawkeye did next.

If Hawkeye somehow got an unconscious man faced up and held in his legs the way he'd done with Roy, it wouldn't be the same outcome.

The guy would be dead long before they reached the shore.

What this man needed was CPR. And that was impossible on the water without a hard enough surface to use to compress his heart and pump his blood manually.

Still thinking the situation through, Hawkeye drew up beside the man. "Cooper, jump."

As the words left his mouth, Cooper was in the water, paddling up to the guy and nudging him.

Hawkeye appreciated the sharp barks because they would alert people on the shore that there was a find.

As Hawkeye got into the water, he flipped his surfboard upside down so the fins were facing skyward. Immediately grabbing the man's wrist, Hawkeye pulled it across the board and flipped the board back upright.

It was an easier maneuver than he'd imagined.

A child could have done that, he thought, as the board was once again turned down.

The man was on top, face down.

That was the problem with that particular technique.

If there was any chance of surviving, the man needed air.

Without mouth-to-mouth, there was zero chance for this guy. The distance to shore was too many minutes away. Minutes equal brain cells.

The guy's wedding ring glinted from hands bloated by sea water as Hawkeye dragged the man's arm above his head.

It wasn't pretty what came next.

Hawkeye grunted, pushed, and tugged.

An arm here, a foot there. A head lolling. A leg in the water.

Yelling, "Come on! Come on!" as he worked and maneuvered, knowing that time was tick-tick-ticking.

Finally, Hawkeye had the man on his back. He peeled back the guy's eyelid and touched his eyeball to check the corneal reflex, and by God, the man blinked.

Hope!

With his knees on either side of the man, contorting his body to align himself, Hawkeye did his best to give a first breath.

Then he untethered the board from his Ankle and held the cuff out to Cooper.

"Cooper, dude, get us to shore. Find Reaper. Cooper, pull. Find Reaper."

Trusting his dog, Hawkeye hunkered forward, performing the possibly life-saving breaths, hoping someone back on the beach would see this and get involved.

Cooper had been trained on how to drag something in the water. But that had been in the Cerberus pool, or a few times on a lake.

He'd pulled a lightweight raft and a swim ring, nothing as heavy and cumbersome as two men on a surfboard. And certainly not through an agitated sea.

But Cooper knew what was needed of him.

There seemed to be a point on the beach that Cooper had targeted, and he was swimming with all his might.

Hawkeye kept up the breaths—pinching the man's nose, sealing the lips, exhaling smoothly until he saw a rise of the chest. Turning his head and taking in more air, Hawkeye had never done this in real life. He'd practiced it on the vinyl dummies.

But never this long. Never in dire circumstances.

Like Cooper, Hawkeye just did the best he could with what he knew.

Reaper was calling something.

The sound carrying over the water was a staccato string of vowels and consonants that Hawkeye couldn't make sense of.

Hawkeye rose up momentarily. He needed to make sure there wasn't a warning in those words.

As Hawkeye rocked back on his heels, the man beneath him suddenly coughed and then was puking up lunch and seawater.

Hawkeye's fingers fumbled and slipped as he tried to get the guy over to his side so he wouldn't aspirate his vomit.

The volume coming out of this man's mouth was mind-boggling like he'd tried to drink the entire sea.

Hawkeye knelt on one knee, his foot planted on the board, holding the man in place as Cooper paddled along.

Suddenly, people were crashing in the water toward the surfboard, coming to lend a hand.

As soon as they reached him, Hawkeye fell backward into the water, letting the others take control.

By the time Hawkeye walked out of the surf, Cooper was on the beach, shaking off. Then, Cooper spun and jogged to Hawkeye, who rounded down to give him a whole-body hug and gratitude scritches.

That's when Hawkeye became aware that the phone in his waterproof carrier was ringing and ringing.

By reflex, he swiped and answered, "Hello?"

"Hello, is this Hawkeye? Man, where are you? Miss Armstrong is having an emergency. Did you get her message?"

"Petra? Emergency?" Hawkeye panted for breath. "Let me…One second."

Someone pressed a towel into his hands, and Hawkeye sent them a grateful "Thank you."

Hawkeye opened the messages app, swiping the screen, while movement pulled his gaze seaward.

The rest of Cerberus was heading to shore.

Halo had two people on his board. Levi had one.

Ash knelt on all fours, head down, as Hoover dragged him to shore.

There were citizens in the water ready to assist them, too.

That freed Hawkeye to read. **Man in a blowhole? Won't survive long.**

She was *at* an emergency. She wasn't *the* emergency. The relief that swept over Hawkeye was disorienting.

Petra needed him. She trusted him.

Per the message, he tapped the link to check the map showing where this guy was waiting, then Hawkeye lifted the phone to his ear. "Stay where you are, I'm on my way. Ten minutes tops."

21

____

PETRA

The tide receded.

"Terry! You aren't going to hear me for a minute. I've figured out how to get you out, but I need more equipment. My being gone is me getting you help faster. Do you understand?"

"Helping me. Hurry. Please." There was a sob. "*Please.*"

"You'll be back with Melissa very soon. Hang on."

Petra tipped her head and called up the chimney, "Okay, bring me up."

Even tethered the way she was, even braced with back pressed into the chimney opening and feet shoving her into place, the tide here was exhausting.

She was exhausted.

As inch by careful inch, the bystanders above pulled her up, Petra pressed against the stone wall realizing how smooth it was comparatively speaking. The sea buffed down the edges with the continual pounding of surf.

Hands reached under Petra's armpits to help her the last of the way up and out.

Sopping wet, Petra sat on her butt, hands under her thighs, breathing heavily.

"Terry?" Melissa was on her knees in front of Petra, her hands clasped as if in supplication.

"Talking. Able to do math." Petra loosened her helmet and held it in her hands, looking it over.

"Math?" Melissa whispered in confusion.

Petra didn't mean to be mean, but "Melissa, can you go away for a minute? I need to think about what I saw and what can be done, and I need my whole brain to do that right now."

Melissa blinked with her eyebrows held so high up on her forehead that the skin rippled. From a crouch, she backed away.

Could Petra have been nicer about it? More empathetic? Sure.

Did she have time for that right now?

Terry didn't.

Normally, Petra's head swirled with ideas that tried to catch her attention. It often made her feel claustrophobic and overwhelmed, even in the great outdoors.

But when the chaos of a crisis rose and those around her lost their minds in panic, she was calm, methodical, and able to function.

Petra always seemed to be experiencing the opposite of those around her. It was like she was in some kind of parallel existence where her rail held a reverse charge. Her brain was anxious and overwrought on the daily, and calm in crisis. Others were calm on the daily and panicked in crisis.

If Petra had to choose which rails to ride, she'd rather have everyday anxiety and clarity in a crisis than the other way around.

With people's lives on the line, that's when Petra wanted to be performing at her best.

In those instances, something in Petra's brain usually found the best possibilities for a successful outcome and lifted it into her awareness like a lantern being held aloft in a twilight wood, exposing the right path home.

But her brain *needed* both space and quiet to work through the data she'd collected in her descent.

The problem was that there was a tunnel that inclined from the sea to what she thought was a small cave. The water never fully emptied. Based on the cave entrance, it was a big enough space to shove a man inside. But Terry's silence followed by sputtering after a wave rolled in, meant that he was probably underwater with each wave. Then he'd use the time after to gulp at air and, to some extent, communicate.

There was something that was stopping Terry from coming out of the cave, at least to the area below the chimney.

Petra suspected a lack of a mental picture of what he was up against and a lack of air.

If she was chronically oxygen-deprived, it would be hard to prime her body to explore.

Right now, Terry knew he had access to air.

He didn't know how far under the rocks he was, how far it was to the shore, how the chimney worked where he could hear the voice instructing him.

When the water came in, possibly because of the slope, these waves seemed more forceful than she would have expected.

Terry might well have tried to escape his cave only to be further battered and pushed back.

Beans stood silently by her side.

"Do you know how long it is to low tide?" Petra asked.

"A half hour maybe more." He caught her eye. "Too long, right?"

"Too long." Petra looked down at her helmet. She was thinking of all the ways she could try to get a line down to Terry, but all of them presupposed that Terry didn't have broken arms, had the space to maneuver, and had strength left in his body.

But what if she affixed a rescue line to the top of the other helmet?

Petra tried to imagine what Terry's experience might be like. She imagined being in the cave, grabbing the helmet. Surviving a tide. Gasping for air as shaking, waterlogged fingers trying to get the clasp attached.

Then what would happen?

The tide comes in, and the tide goes out. Terry feels a slight pull to show him the exit.

He realizes that he is right next to the chimney.

Tide comes in…

If he held the rope—no. If Petra tied knots in the rope and he gripped above each knot, then she could help him stand up in the chimney and hold him in place as the tide came in.

Would it bash him?

At least somewhat. Yes, of course.

Was it better to come in from the front by the sea and try to send something in with a wave? Maybe something on a flotation so she could guide him out to the surf instead of up into the chimney?

Petra hadn't tested the way in. She didn't know if it traveled in a straight line.

If she had time, she could run experiments. But time was at a premium.

Up the chimney, then.

And the helmet seemed the most doable. But the timing had to be impeccable.

Petra called the rope team over, and she explained her thoughts.

Everyone had a clear idea of how this was going to work.

She readied herself to go down again and was surprised that convincing herself to make the descent the second time around was harder. Well, now she knew how claustrophobic and violent it was down there.

Petra let her gaze run along the cliff's top, wishing Hawkeye would suddenly appear. His rescue expertise and steady nature would be very welcome right about now.

She probably didn't make Melissa feel any better about the plan when she said, "Well, Terry, beggars can't be choosers."

Over she went.

Down. Down. Down.

"Terry, I'm here. We're going to get you out. We have a plan."

"Help." His voice was almost inaudible.

"Lower the helmet!" Petra called.

Here came the second helmet tied securely at the top with a rope.

Did she want Terry to dangle from his neck?

Heck no.

She'd at least get him into the chimney; they could add a harness under his arms from here. The helmet was to guide him out of the cave.

Please don't have broken arms, Terry.

Petra quickly called the plan to Terry so he knew what was expected of him.

He was ready.

She was ready.

Timing was everything.

Above, they'd weighted the plastic helmet by adding a rock so she could get it past the cave's lip.

Now, to test the theory.

With the next wave, Petra readied herself. As the wave receded, she dropped the helmet and released it to swing like a pendulum. The helmet skimmed the pool of water and under the lip.

It didn't come back out.

"You have it, Terry? You're putting it on?"

She didn't get a reply. He might have been too focused on the task at hand to hear her.

Or perhaps there was something about the structure that she didn't understand.

The wave came in.

The wave went out.

There was a hand on the line. An arm. A bright lime green helmet.

Holy shit. There was Terry.

In came the wave. Petra held the line tight. Terry's head was near her thigh, so his mouth was out of the water.

"Hang on," Petra encouraged. "We've got you."

He reached for her leg, and Petra swatted him hard. "Don't touch me. Terry, if you pull me down, no one is coming after us." She believed that was true. After all, no one else had offered to go back down with the helmet.

Petra lowered the second rope and worked it over his arms in the front.

He was shaking with cold and fear.

Petra kept talking to him about Melissa and how many people were helping, and they just needed to wait for the pull of the tide to go out.

With a quick release of the rope attached to the helmet,

Petra could get the lasso down around his chest and tighten the rope under his arms.

Was it the best way to get him out?

Absolutely not.

But it was the way they were going to do it.

"I'm going up. You'll be right below me. We have you tied in. Here comes another wave."

Petra had told the team about her fears about Terry grabbing onto her. There was only the breadth in the chimney for a single person to be rescued at a time. And she was on top.

These next few moments were the most dangerous.

"Apple," she yelled the code word her team had agreed on. She didn't want Terry to know what was happening next.

As soon as "apple' left her mouth, she was snatched up the chimney so fast that she thought she was Santa's elf riding a magical trail.

Not fast enough.

Even though Terry had his own line, a drowning man would pull a loved one under. It was the nature of the beast. This beast grabbed as her feet fell from the wall and extended outward. He clutched at her ankles.

And she kicked hard.

The borrowed tennis shoes came off in Terry's hands as Petra was dragged from his reach.

She came up hyperventilating. *Holy shit!*

When they got Terry to the top, Petra saw he was in worse shape than she'd imagined.

His clothes were shredded, his skin abraded. He was slick with blood.

Melissa was bent in two, screaming.

Terry didn't even look Melissa's way. He was going into shock. This rescue wasn't over.

Raw-skinned and broken, he needed to be at the hospital stat.

Petra looked at the cliff and at the people who were ready and willing to help, but how could they get Terry, in his battered state, from here to up there where they had vehicles?

It wasn't coming to her right away.

What did come was a sense of gratitude that in a crisis, all these people risked being near a turbulent sea in the service of a stranger.

Could she contrive a way for these good people to get Terry to the vehicles?

What she needed was a medevac helicopter.

No, she amended, that spray and the debris storm that came with a helicopter's downwash might be too much for Terry.

What she needed was the Cerberus team. After Levi had saved his fiancée, they had trained how to move people on steep inclines, and they'd know just what to do in a practiced formation.

Okay, Petra admitted to herself. While all that was true, she realized she just wanted to look into Hawkeye's eyes and know that he was there with her in the crisis because that had felt really good over the last couple of days.

"Hey!" Carlos called from the cliff. "Hey! Incoming!"

Petra whipped her head seaward.

The people here on the plateau couldn't survive another rogue wave.

22

———————

HAWKEYE

A teen on the cliff had his hand to his mouth yelling, "Incoming!" to let those below him know that their team had arrived.

Levi, Cooper, Mojo, and Hawkeye made out the essence of a path and took it at a speed that wasn't entirely safe.

Still, it took a long time.

As soon as Hawkeye got eyes on Petra, his stomach dropped.

She was covered in dried blood.

Her blood.

She was crouched over a rock performing first aid. Finishing up by tucking Mylar blankets and beach towels over the prone man.

A woman was wailing to the side, but she looked like a family member and not part of the rescue.

The second Hawkeye got down to her, he swept Petra into

his arms and buried his face at her neck. "I can see you're fine. But shit, woman, did you go in the blow hole to pull the guy out?"

She didn't answer. He didn't need her to.

She was the only one in wet, ripped clothes.

Even the victim, neatly tucked under a blanket with a jacket supporting his head, looked in better shape. But Hawkeye couldn't see what was going on for him beyond purple lips and full-body shivering.

Levi was commanding Mojo and Cooper into place on either side of the guy to offer body heat and keep him from going into shock.

Hawkeye turned back to Petra.

"I'm okay, just a little banged up. Terry's got broken bones." She pointed at the man. "Do you have an ETA on the ambulance?" Petra asked, looking past him to the cliff.

Leaving his hands on her shoulders, Hawkeye held her out from him. Her eye was less wonky but still not great. She had cuts and bruises all over her body—she hadn't sliced herself near her arteries. And the blood seemed to have coagulated. "We're on our own. Crises are unfolding all over the island."

The vein in her neck was throbbing, but that was the only sign that she might be stressed.

Safe enough for now.

Hawkeye leaned in to kiss her, then said, "Everyone is pressing the pedal to the floor. That's why it took me a while to get to you. I'm sorry it took so long."

"I have no idea how long it took—adrenaline tells me that we were working on saving Terry for five minutes, but also ten hours."

"That's about how it works," Levi said.

Levi moved over to the pile of equipment amassed on a flat

rock. It looked like the kinds of things someone might dig out of their hatch—ropes, first aid kits, blankets.

Levi pulled out two Tae Kwon Do long sticks from a black bag. "We're in business."

Levi efficiently constructed a stretcher by folding a sheet of plastic around either stick.

When he looked up, he caught Hawkeye's gaze, silently asking how Petra was doing.

"Good to go. Let's figure out the path before we load Terry up." His gaze scanned the bystanders. "Who calls this beach home? Who knows this exact area?"

A teen stepped forward. "Me. Beans." He put a hand on his chest, then pointed to the guy standing next to him. "Me and Lucky grew up just down the beach about a half mile."

"Getting Terry up that cliff is going to be a trick," Hawkeye said. "But that's where we have our vehicle parked. What's the safest way to get the litter from here to there?"

After Beans and Hawkeye conferred, the two Cerberus men moved the stretcher next to Terry. All four of his limbs were splinted. The one on the left leg was a traction splint made of walking sticks. That kind of splint was used to ease the pain of a femoral break and help keep bone fragments from cutting inside the leg. It could help prevent the femoral artery from being punctured. That was some advanced wilderness first aid.

He looked up to offer Petra kudos, but she looked too wiped out to care.

Levi and Hawkeye were feeling it, too.

With the boys leading the way and help from the bystanders on the stretcher, they got to the SUV. With the split seats down, Terry could lie fairly flat.

Melissa was in the far back with him. She'd been mum the whole time.

Petra and Mojo squeezed into one seat on the second row.

Levi was driving, and Cooper was between Hawkeye's feet as he sat shotgun.

"Twelve minutes," Levi said. "I'm taking it slow and steady to keep from jostling you too much, Terry."

Terry was going into shock, so Hawkeye cranked up the heat.

"Hospital knows we're bringing you in," Levi finished.

Hawkeye was watching Petra in the side mirror.

She caught his eye. "You were caught up in something, too?" Petra asked.

"The team pulled six from rip currents," Hawkeye said.

"We had the rip currents near the tide pool. But we could see them, and everyone stayed clear. Then there were these huge waves." She paused, her nose in the air. "You two smell like smoke and diesel."

"A boat caught fire. That was our second rescue mission today," Hawkeye said.

"I'm the third?" Petra asked. "Thank you both. Once I got the first aid wrapped up, there were lots of people who wanted to help, none of them had expertise, and I was getting afraid for—"

She seemed to realize who was in the vehicle and could be listening.

"Given the injuries, my thinking you were en route helped my psychology today. Thank you for coming."

Hawkeye turned his body so she could look directly into his eyes. "Petra, you sent us a distress signal. Of course, we're here."

Levi lifted his chin. "You know, we're pretty good at making do. But kudos to you. I've never heard of a bike helmet extraction before."

Petra's face drooped into a frown, and she lowered her voice. "It was riskier than I'd like to dwell on." She leaned forward and lowered her voice further. "It's hard to fathom. This poor guy was walking down the shore, having a romantic moment with his fiancée. A wave picked him up and took him out. He's talking to her one minute and gone the next. Near as I can tell, the ocean pulled him out, then pushed him under and into the blow hole. From romance to being pummeled underground." She dropped to a whisper. "His initial screams are sounds that will haunt my dreams."

"You heard him?" Levi asked. "I saw that hole. I heard the roar of the surf. You *heard* him down there?"

"I have heightened senses. My eyes seek out anomalies. I have the nose and ears of a dog."

Cooper drew his brows together until they wrinkled together.

"No, Cooper, not as good as yours. You are superior in every way. But you know I can hear things others can't."

"Like?" Levi asked.

"Electricity in the walls?

Levi chuckled. "Yup, part canine. I'd say."

"How is your team?" Petra asked. "Everyone healthy?"

"Reaper was taking Ash to the hospital for smoke inhalation. We'll meet up with the rest of the team when we get there."

"Two missions. You got everyone out of the water okay?" She put her hand on Hawkeye's shoulder.

He liked that she was reaching out for him. And he reached up to cover her hand with his.

"Unfortunately," Levi said, "we know of one guy who didn't make it. Ash tried to recover his body from a boat fire. But the smoke and fumes were too much."

"Swollen air passages from the chemical fumes. Back on

the beach, Ash was wheezing and having trouble breathing," Hawkeye said. "We don't mess around with that."

"Of course not. My goodness," Petra whispered.

"There were a few of our saves that might be touch and go," Hawkeye added. "Just all around, not a good situation."

In the far back seat, Melissa had laid her head on Terry's stomach, crying.

Terry was conked out asleep—not just the exhaustion of survival but the drop in adrenaline sucked the energy right out of his body, Hawkeye guessed.

"Okay, let's get a plan together," Hawkeye pointed toward the emergency sign. "Petra, the place is going to be packed. But coral can be dangerous. You'll need an antibiotic. You go in and get in line with the triage. If it looks like it'll take too long, we'll figure something else out."

"And you guys?" She reached past Hawkeye to scrub her nails behind Cooper's ear.

"Dogs and hospitals aren't a sanitary mix. We'll wait outside. The rest of our team is here. We need to find them and get an update. I can communicate with you via cell phone."

"Here we go," Levi flipped on the blinker, pulling up under the emergency awning next to an ambulance.

A nurse was waiting outside with a gurney.

As Levi and Hawkeye helped Terry transfer from the SUV, Hawkeye heard the nurse say, "Back again, huh? Your eye is looking better."

"Thank you for remembering me," Petra said.

"Were you involved in this too? You're going to need an antibiotic. We're slammed. Crazy day. The hospitals are full. How about you find a seat in the waiting room?" the nurse asked. "I'll corner a doctor as soon as I can and get you a script. Remind me of your name? Hermione?"

"Yes, Hermione Armstrong."

"You'll be in our system. I'll find you." She grabbed the end of Terry's gurney and was racing through the automatic doors. She caught Hawkeye's gaze and added, "The fewer people inside, the better. It's a zoo. Do you mind waiting out here?"

Hawkeye leaned down and gave Petra a kiss. "I'll meet you out here when you're patched up. Okay?"

PETRA

What was it that Tamika said to Petra the morning they were supposed to fly out of D.C.? "A body in motion tends to stay in motion."

Her time with Hawkeye had been one crisis after another. Was that the kind of chemistry they swirled when they were together?

Petra hated crises, though she thrived in them.

When something terrible was afoot, she was energized from beginning to end.

The problem was that they came to an end, and she always crashed hard.

She thought of past relationships when she'd try to explain it. She wasn't ghosting them; she was hibernating, trying to recover. But unless someone knew how burnout felt, yeah, it wasn't something easily imagined.

No, it wasn't a matter of eating more protein or hitting the gym harder.

It wasn't a matter of mind over matter or putting the pedal down on her inner drive.

She. Shut. Down.

And the last time she didn't listen to her body and pushed and pushed, she ended up in bed, unable to do even the rudiments of personal hygiene for months on end.

That was the end of her last long-term relationship.

And probably the end of all long-term relationships.

Petra had adapted herself to the idea of doing life solo.

She was fine with it.

Quasi-fine with it.

Alone had its good points and its bad.

She sure did like the idea today that all she needed to do was put up a bat signal and Hawkeye would be there by her side, helping her to navigate the challenge.

That and he could give a mighty fine kiss.

Petra held her index finger out in front of her face, forcing herself to focus there.

A lot had happened that day—over the last two days.

A lot.

And all her thoughts felt like they were crowding up on each other, pinging into one another.

It was as if she was hunkering in the middle of a swarm, one of which was a killer bee. She needed to find it and keep her eye on it.

Petra's survival brain had been on overdrive since she landed in St. Croix. It was too long.

Anxiety was a terrible sensation.

Coffee would be good—a generous hit usually helped her regulate her dopamine.

While coffee woke her colleagues up, it made Petra feel like taking a nap.

Coffee *would* help—but Petra couldn't motivate herself off her seat to see if she could find a pot somewhere.

Besides, she needed to be here so the nurse could find her and hand her the script. Petra wanted to get home and take a shower, wash the scrapes, and throw away this sundress.

Exhaustion was settling in as adrenaline left her system just like it had for Terry—like it would for any human after a day like today, she reminded herself.

Her thoughts flitted over the day from patch discovery, to doctor, to meeting Lucky and taking a ride over the rutted red earth being smacked in the face by tree limbs as they careened past.

She thought about Herb in the front seat and how her antennae had gone up. The look in his eyes. The tone of his speech. There was something shiny and plastic about him.

Something about him made Petra's teeth itch.

Petra patted the pocket of her sundress and was surprised to find that the girl's necklace was still there.

She didn't pull it out. She'd look at it later.

Petra wondered what happened when the girl's parents discovered the necklace was missing.

Jenny.

Jenny!

Shoot. Petra had used her connection with Holly Smokes to see if she could gather some information about the design of the pendant.

But now that Petra thought about it, maybe that was a bad idea.

Either way, Petra should definitely give Holly a heads-up.

Petra didn't have Holly's contact information with her, and it might be hours before she got back to the hotel and her computer.

Avery was Holly's editor.

Yeah, Petra's gut told her not to wait. Pulling her phone out, Petra quickly tapped a message.

Petra: **Hey, Avery, are you available for a phone call?**

The phone rang a minute later.

"Hey there," Avery's voice was bright and chatty, which didn't jive with the survival state Petra had been swimming through for the last two days. "What did you do today? Lay out with a pineapple drink and soak in some sun?"

"Sun happened. Drinks did not. Have I got stories to tell you when I get home." Petra worked hard to lighten her tone so she didn't worry her friend.

"Stories plural?" Avery's voice turned sing-songy. "Do any of them happen to include a certain handsome operator named Hawkeye?"

"In ways big and small, yes, he was along for the ride. Before I get too distracted, I'm calling you for an important reason. I brought up Holly Smokes' name in a conversation I had today."

"Mmmkay."

"There was this woman, Jenny Johnson, who reads Holly's books. And it turns out Jenny also goes all over the world doing adventure races. I thought it's such a small world at that level of racing that they might know each other."

"Were they in the same races? I'm having dinner with Holly this week. It would be fun to put them together."

"I can look in a minute and text you. "

"Holly is really Beth McNight."

"Yup. I remember. She said she doesn't want her kids to know she writes SEAL-populated reverse harems with whips and butt plugs. But I think she races under Holly, so she can use the images for social media, right? I'll look for both names."

Petra started to think that a combination of her job and the events she'd just lived through might have clouded her thoughts.

Before she disparaged this woman's name and warned Holly off, maybe she should do a little more investigating.

"Fun fact," Avery said, "while men can, on average, run faster than women in shorter runs. Women are faster when they run ultra-long distances."

"Which would be how far?" Petra asked.

"In my book? Anything over five miles seems excessive. I'm going to make this up. I think it's at the fifty-mile mark or around there."

"Just making facts up, tossing them out there for me to gobble up?"

"I know how you like to snack on a good factoid. But go back and check me. There's a website with women's adventure races and times. Just put it in a search engine."

"Okay, Avery, let me do a little searching around. I'll text you anything I find. Have a good evening."

"Petra?"

"Mmm?"

"That was why you called?" Avery asked.

"There's a lot going on. I think I called prematurely," Petra said with a sigh. "I need to clear my head."

"I get that. Call me when you figure it out."

Petra glanced around the part of the emergency department she could see, and her nurse was nowhere around. Petra's cuts were so minor compared to the injuries that were coming in. From the codes that were ringing out, near drownings, heart attacks, burns, and broken limbs were taking up everyone's attention. And Petra wanted that. She wanted to slide into the triage in such a way that she was merely the minor inconvenience of a scrawled signature.

She leaned back and looked out the window.

The Cerberus men stood in a circle, hands on hips, dogs sleeping or resting in the center.

Then she looked down at her phone, feeling like she was about to open a kettle of worms.

Here I go.

Herb and Jenny Johnson.

When culling through names, Petra had found that she could get to the right person the fastest by using both names of a couple.

When she pressed ENTER, Petra was not prepared for what she found.

Yes, there were lists of Jenny's races and pictures of her and her family.

But there were also news articles reporting on how the FBI had caught Herb and Jenny with so much evidence of their white-collar crimes that the couple had pled guilty in the hope of a lenient sentence. Even with a clean record and small children, a light sentence would be seventeen years for Herb and fourteen years for Jenny.

They were felons.

Sentencing was in two weeks.

Looking through this new lens, Petra thought about the couple and their behavior.

Did today make any sense at all?

Criminals.

That was so unexpected that Petra didn't know what to do with it other than to let Avery know to warn Holly away from any interaction.

Criminals.

Was that the explanation for the necklaces and the daughter's anger? Why did she yank it off and throw it? Was she mad at her parents for going to prison?

Those thoughts took up so much space in Petra's mind that when the nurse said, "Miss Armstrong?" Petra jumped and gripped her chest.

"Oh! Hahaha." Petra grinned. "You surprised me. I was in Lala land."

"The doctor says to take the medication until it's finished. If you have any red striations or unusual symptoms, seek further medical help." She held out a slip of paper with an old-fashioned prescription on it.

It had been a while since Petra had seen one of these, and she had to look at it for a moment.

"Are you okay?" the nurse asked.

"Fine. Tired. Going home to get cleaned up now. This can't happen very often, there would be more supports in place."

"Not necessarily. Supports in place is a funding issue," the nurse said. "But I can tell you what I've heard on the news playing in the different treatment rooms. They're saying that seismic activity just south of Puerto Rico caused rip currents and rogue waves throughout the Caribbean. Usually, when one island gets in trouble, the other islands rally. In this case, they're stretched thin everywhere. Teams are spooling up to come from the Florida and some other of the East Coast National Guards. But can they get here in time to be of any real help?" She shrugged as she pulled her gloves off and put them in a biohazard bag. "At least it wasn't a tsunami. Here on the island, there's really nowhere to run and nowhere to hide. I mean, what do you do? Go to the highest point and cling to a tree?"

"I hope the evening goes smoothly for you all. Thank you." Petra waved the paper in the air.

And the nurse headed back into the fray.

Petra turned to the window and saw a doctor talking to the Cerberus huddle.

Pulling the necklace from her pocket, Petra held it up.

It just felt dangerous.

It just felt like something needed to be said.

Beside her, the bathroom door slapped open, and a kid came running out.

Petra caught the door and slid into the single-toilet room. She locked the door, turned on the water, and without sending a warning text, Petra pressed the button to dial Rowan.

This was a matter for the FBI.

24

———

Petra

Petra had a quasi-secretive job, one that the FBI tried to keep on the down low.

Recruited to the Bureau by Rowan Kennedy when they were fellow doctoral candidates in the field of brain security—or whatever it was that people were trying to call it now—their diplomas said Doctor of Philosophy in Psychology.

But that was only because the field of study was so new that there wasn't yet a consensus on what else to call their research.

Rowan called himself a Doctor of Propaganda.

To Petra, that didn't quite get the gist of *her* work.

Things were changing so fast—every single day, innovations brought sweeping changes to how humans navigate the world.

Was that a burden on the human brain?

How well did the brain adapt to such constant shifts?

Did the modern world present unprecedented dangers to human wiring?

There was no data until someone asked the questions and looked for answers.

It was true that back in the first days of steam engine trains, there was fear that if a woman were to travel faster than fifty miles an hour, the speed would fling a woman's uterus from her body.

It was also true that fear of new technology was often just the fear of the unknown.

But this was absolutely a brave new world.

AI was changing a human's ability to tell what was real and what artificial intelligence had created on command.

Reality was becoming ever more malleable.

Was that image an actual image?

Is that video something that genuinely happened?

Is the voice on the phone that sounds exactly like my child really my child?

Who the heck knew?

What the government knew was that the human brain faced a shape-shifting reality and that con artists would swing in and manipulate people in unprecedented ways.

The FBI sought to understand how the new manipulations could happen and how to get out in front of it.

There were, in fact, few laws that protected a human's brain from a criminal attack.

Legislation took time.

Well-thought-out, effective legislation took even longer, requiring studies and a clear understanding of cause and effect.

Everything protective took time.

Everything calculated to con people changed at lightning speed.

Faster. Faster. Impossible to keep up.

The FBI hired Petra specifically to study doomsday cults

and the fact that people—in historically unprecedented numbers —were succumbing to the draw and falling to their sway.

Why was this happening, and what were the ramifications?

Petra hated the term "cult" because it came with ideas about Branch Davidians.

Where Rowan's expertise was in indoctrination and severing systems to gain power—much like what happened to Russia, then Türkiye and Hungary, and of course, earlier and most profoundly to women in Iran in 1979…

1979 wasn't all that long ago; Petra's mom was a freshman in high school. No, not that long ago at all.

Rowan studied how governments shifted people away from allegiances to family and friends, shifted morals and convictions, and shifted wealth from their citizens' pockets to someone else's.

And that all fell under the term psyops—psychological operations.

Psyops happened in spheres of influence as large as a nation or as small as a doomsday cult.

These were the thoughts that danced through her brain as Rowan's phone continued to ring.

Petra was exhausted, and she wanted to just drop the whole subject. But justice was a pressure that built in her until she came up with a way to find release.

And right or wrong, she wanted to hand this all over to Rowan.

Rowan, who had nothing to do with this kind of crime.

"Hey, sorry about that." Rowan was in her ear. "I walked away from my phone."

"I came across something. I'm sending you an article," Petra dove right in. She pressed send on the newspaper article about the Johnsons' crimes which summed things up more succinctly than the others. She waited, giving Rowan a chance to read it over.

"Jenny Johnson is the name you gave Avery a few minutes ago."

"It is."

"Guilty. Husband, guilty. Looks like you were hanging out with the riffraff."

"They're here on the island with their three small children."

"You have a narrative running through your head. You sound damned stressed."

"I've had a difficult couple of days. Listen, would it be okay if I rambled around a bit—sometimes processing out loud is the thing."

"Be my guest. I was just taking a scotch over to sit in front of the fire."

"Here are my thoughts in no particular order. Ask questions if you have them. The kids are young. I mean lovely young children, four, six, and eight are my guesses. If the parents go to prison—which is a given—even with a lighter sentence, they won't be getting out until the youngest is in his late teens. The oldest will be an adult. They will have missed their children's formative years. If I was a mother – and I am making this up from my imagination, obviously, but if I were their mother, I'd be freaking the hell out to be taken away from my babies. But she showed no signs of stress."

"You're also assessing that as a doctorate in psychology. There are norms in social patterns. But for this individual, you don't have a baseline," Rowan pointed out. "The woman could be a sociopath and not give a shit about her kids."

"Possible, I guess. But I'm telling you there was something completely wrong with the packaging. Putting the interaction I had, with this information about Jenny going to prison for a decade plus doesn't add up."

"You're a hundred percent sure it's her."

"And her husband. The articles I read reiterated many of the details I'd learned over the day. The number of kids, the state where they live. It's her picture, for goodness' sake. I cross-referenced with articles and pictures of her in her races. The husband and kids are there at the finish line."

"So, what was off?"

"The way she looked at her kids."

"More."

"If I were a mother on a last family vacation—not something in my experience, granted. But pattern recognition. This mom is two weeks away from not being able to tuck her kids in bed anymore, not give them a kiss when they wake up. I've seen other families have to deal with that kind of separation, so I do have a baseline. And this was *not* that. For example, let's say that they came down here for this last vacation with their young children, and the next time this was available to them, the kids would be grown. I'd try to give them the best possible memories of a happy, loving, caring mother."

"That seems reasonable. Is that not what happened?" Rowan asked.

"Mom and Dad were both laid back, kind of laissez-faire. It was just another day in the life rather than a time imbued with deep meaning. There should have been something buzzing under the surface, right? Like an undertone of bittersweetness. When the children were playing, and the mother was looking on, there should have been the sense that she was soaking it all in, imprinting her children and this event deep into her psyche to take out and remember on difficult days. There was none of that."

"These are mother observations, not father?" Rowan asked.

"Dads don't have 'fetal microchimerism.'" Petra said. "Fair or not, I expect more from a biological mom."

"And you're going to explain all that to me so I can follow."

"Fetal microchimerism is the phenomenon that happens when a baby is being born; part of their DNA passes through the placenta into the mother's body. It's stored in the mom's organs, usually the brain, liver, and skin, and persists there. That's the hard science supported by the scientific method and replications."

"Now, the soft science and speculation?" Rowan asked.

"There's the possibility that this connection is the source of mother's intuition."

"That research will never get funded," Rowan said.

"True. But in this case, I would think that if microchimerism did connect mother and child, it would be blasting this woman, lighting her system up like a Christmas tree."

"A chimerism tree?"

"You want me to laugh, but I'm too tired," Petra said.

"Okay, Petra, as a former FBI profiler turned researcher of state-sponsored mind security, offer me your theory."

"First, I have to talk to Avery when I get off from talking to you. I told Jenny about Holly Smokes. I need her to pass on a warning not to engage."

"Yeah, that's probably good. I'll—hey, Avery, Petra needs to talk to you when we're done."

"Okay, I'm just running next door for a second to check on Mrs. Glasser before the ice storm. Should I wait?" Avery called. "I wanted to ask Petra what she knew about all the rescues today in St. Croix and see if everyone's okay."

"I think you have time," Rowan called. He was back on the phone. "She has time?"

"I'm not in any kind of hurry," Petra said. "This is vacation."

Petra heard a door shut.

"What rescue today?" Rowan asked.

Petra briefly explained the situation on the island. "Avery saw that on the news? Must be a slow news day. And with a winter storm blowing in D.C.? Seems odd." And since Rowan had an association with Iniquus, she added, "I am worried about Ash. All I know is that he was having respiratory issues after the boat fire. I'll text you and let you know how he is."

"Grateful for the information," Rowan said. "The guy you pulled out of the blow hole is okay?"

"I'm not sure, to be honest. Broken limbs at a minimum."

"Shit, that's brutal. How old?" Rowan asked.

"Twenty-seven. The untouchable age."

"Not anymore." There was a clink of the ice cubes in Rowan's drink. "That fallacy's been blown. I'm going to help you focus. I'd like you to share the story you're telling yourself about the Johnsons."

"I imagine that the judge understood the stakes for this family. If they were to flee, they could try to get to a country without extradition."

"Could," Rowan conceded. "But surely they had their passports confiscated."

"Mmm. I was wondering if maybe someone should check on that."

"The judge?" Rowan asked.

"No. Could the Johnsons, knowing they might lose their passports, have reported them stolen at some point? Asked to have them reissued? That way, they'd have nothing to hand over to a judge."

"How would that be useful?"

"Depends on where they're going," Petra said. "They didn't need passports to get this far. If they were in a different country and needed to show them to someone, would it flag anything? I think that depends on the entity and the country."

"If I were on the lam, would I try to use my real passport? That seems risky." Rowan trailed the last word, then said, "Okay, take a step back. What would I do if I wanted to get gone? I'd sell everything to get as much cash together as I could. That would make sense if I were going to prison for the next ten years—house, cars, furnishings, cash out the 401(k). Liquify any stocks. I could say that this allowed me to give the money to the kids' caregiver – one would assume family. But you wouldn't hand over the money until you handed over the kids, right? But Avery, you can't pack that much money in a suitcase."

"Bitcoin."

"True," Rowan said. "Easily bought, then untraceable and accessible anywhere in the world."

"Exactly," Petra exclaimed. "Then I'd go to a place that's the farthest point from the contiguous US that I could without using my passport– maybe to a territory where federal laws have a lighter impact. Someplace like here."

"Uh-huh."

"And then I might go for a boat ride with the family one day."

"Fishing trip," Rowan said.

"With a cooler of food that's actually stuff I need, backpacks with our clothes. Then I'd head to South America, where I'd get off at any local dock and, therefore, not be watched by customs. Buy a car for cash. Travel over borders at non-border areas, move slowly but surely to Colombia or Ecuador."

"I'd probably head to the Solomon Islands," Rowan said.

"Laos would be nice." Petra looked out the window. Cooper knew where she was and was watching her. "Staying in Colombia or Ecuador would be a boat ride instead of a plane.

Anyway, that's what I'd do. I'd still be stressed about becoming a fugitive, but a lot less stressed than thinking I was headed to federal prison away from my kids."

"I see," Rowan sounded far away in thought. "It reminds me of an article I read about an Italian guy who committed fraud. Did you read about him?"

She shuffled her feet in the flip-flops that were thrust into her hands at the rescue with a "here, take these." She realized that they were two different colors and sizes. "It's not ringing any bells."

"According to the reporting, this Italian guy tried living in places without extradition, but it was always tenuous. He could be rounded up and repatriated at any moment."

"Where's this?" She traced a finger around the hole in her dress.

"Dubai was where he had been living."

"Okay, I can see where Italy might be able to craft some kind of diplomatic understanding if this was a big enough fish."

Rowan laughed. "More of a public fish, so they didn't want people to think they could get away with impactful financial crimes. Fish is an appropriate term here because the guy bought a barge and has been living on it in international waters."

"How does he eat besides fishing?" Petra asked.

"He has a garden and some chickens. People deliver food to him."

Petra stilled. "Isn't that aiding and…nope, it wouldn't be. When they hand over the supplies, they'd be on the high seas, too. Not that I understand the laws of the open waters. And I honestly don't want to. I just have a really funny feeling about this family, Rowan. They're so squeaky."

"Squeaky," he let his mouth play with the word as he repeated it. "I'm not sure how to imagine that."

"Think of a family that is social media perfect. You know

that she's the kind of mom who unpackages her groceries and puts them in containers to stock her fridge, and she has tens of thousands of people watching her do it."

"That's a thing?" Rowan asked.

"Very soothing, apparently. Does nothing for me. But you can imagine the family I'm talking about. Dad is handsome enough. Mom is an international adventure racer who also bakes bread and is unperturbed by reality."

"I'm pulling up social media and putting in a search for stocking a fridge." Rowan went silent. "There are all of these people on here doing something called fridgescaping. They're putting vases of flowers in their fridge."

"A nice little pick me up, and they last forever in the cold like that."

Rowan snort-laughed. "Tell me you do this."

"Me? No. Hey Rowan, I don't mean to take up your day off with things that aren't in your wheelhouse," Petra said. "Thanks for listening. Now that I've said it out loud to another FBI special agent, I feel like I'm no longer personally responsible."

"Yup, you went and involved me."

"There's no crime," Petra pointed out. "There's only a path I made up in my head."

"Still. I'm going to share this with Frost and see if she wants us to look into the passport situation."

"Sorry. Thank you."

"No problem." There was the slam of a door. "Avery's back and waving for the phone. Any other theories you wanted to share?"

"Nope. That's it. Could you just tell Avery about Jenny for me?" Petra asked.

"Will do. And Petra?"

"Yes."

"You're supposed to be on vacation, so maybe leave the badge in the room's safe and have fun."

Petra reached her hand into her pocket to finger the necklace. "That's the dream."

25

———

HAWKEYE

Hawkeye knew Petra was pushing through the hospital exit by the change in Cooper's posture.

It was still hard to see her in her ripped sundress, looking like she'd escaped through a briar patch with a killer at her heels.

A square of white paper was in her hand, and he hoped it was a prescription. He'd already found a pharmacy on the way back to the hotel.

"Good?" he called out as the team opened a space in their circle for her.

"I was about to ask you the same." Her face looked worried and exhausted. "Any word on Ash?"

"They've moved him to a room," Hawkeye said, digging the vehicle fob from his pocket. "He's going to see the respiratory therapist and should be released this evening."

"That's good news." She looked back toward the hospital. "Between Terry and the others, you all hauled out of the ocean, it would be nice to have an update. I mean, I understand privacy and HIPAA. But it would be reassuring to know the prognosis or to have an opportunity to give a hug."

"Maybe not the hug part," Levi said, "but we'll keep an eye on the newspaper to see if there are any reports."

"There were so many emergencies today, though." Halo shook his head. "They won't all be reported on. Probably just the deaths."

"Were there many deaths?" Petra asked, standing close enough to Hawkeye that he had to fight his instinct to put an arm around her.

"This affected the whole region. Sixteen confirmed deaths on St. Croix alone was the last count I heard," Reaper said. "There are a lot of people still missing out on the water."

Hawkeye caught Petra's gaze. "Iniquus Command ordered Team Charlie to rest and recover. In the morning, we'll check in with emergency services and see where we can lend a hand."

"Joining the search?" Petra sent her gaze to the dogs.

Cooper came over and nudged his head under her hand. When he did, her body relaxed a bit.

"There was a second seismic event," Reaper said. "The authorities are asking people to stay out of the water to give them an opportunity to assess. There are people on watercraft who haven't checked in. The Coast Guard is trying to follow up on mayday calls. My understanding is that a bunch of boats capsized before the calls could go out."

"Rescue has a few more hours of daylight," Halo said.

"But they're low in manpower," Levi said.

"Are they bringing in support from the mainland?" Petra asked.

"They are." Reaper rocked back on his heels. "Most likely, they'll be here by morning. That's where we're at. Tomorrow, we can figure out where to assist, maybe free up some hands or eyeballs."

"Rest and recuperation sounds like a good plan," Petra said. "If you're acting as volunteers tomorrow, I can join in. I'm FEMA-trained. Minimally, I could put pins in a map or monitor a radio."

Reaper focused on Petra. "You're pretty banged up. You might feel differently about being up and about tomorrow. If you're good to go, we welcome your assistance as a citizen volunteer, which is the capacity in which Cerberus will be working. But, if you're not a hundred percent—"

"I won't endanger or slow down your team. If I'm not up to the assignment, I'll back out."

"Very good," Reaper nodded. "We've concluded the hot wash, gentlemen. We'll meet in Conference Room B at zero seven hundred hours. You need to be fed, and your dogs need to be ready to go. That gives you twelve hours to get some effective calories and a good night's sleep." His gaze slid over the team. "I'll be here with Ash. Halo, I want you to manage Hoover."

"Sir."

"You all need to take care of your dogs and yourselves. Outstanding effort today. Outstanding." Reaper turned and sauntered toward the door.

The men peeled off, heading toward their various vehicles.

Hawkeye pointed his fob toward the rented SUV. "Good?"

"This is where we started the trip," Petra said as they approached the vehicle. "I've seen more of this hospital than the island."

"As far as adventure trips go, this one will be memorable. We'll tell these stories over wine at friends' dinner tables for years to come."

They were silent as they drove to the pharmacy and left the prescriptions at the drive-through.

It would be a fifteen-minute wait.

"Ten minutes," the pharmacist said as she looked into the SUV at Petra. "I can get it done for you in ten."

"Thank you," Petra said. Yeah, she looked like she'd been through a meat grinder.

Hawkeye drove to the other side of the lot to park under a tree. "When we get back to the hotel, it's straight to the shower."

"Are you joining me?" Petra asked with a tired smile. A little bit flirty, a lot of fatigue.

"If you're inviting, yes."

"I'm inviting. Maybe we could order a pizza and eat it in bed again?"

"Absolutely. Glad to get in bed with you any time. I think we have a plan. Somewhere in there, I need to take Cooper for his last walk of the evening."

"Cooper," Petra cooed, "you were such a brave helper dog today. Here you thought you were going to the beach to play with your buddies, and instead, you got a day of chaos."

"Speaking of chaos," Hawkeye started.

Petra looked up at him, and Hawkeye focused on her eyes. "Your pupils have evened out now."

"Oh?" Petra flipped down the visor to look in the mirror.

"Also, speaking of chaos, I've had a question I wanted to ask you since we were on the plane."

Petra slapped the mirror shut and pushed the visor toward the roof before turning back to him.

"On the plane, even when the animals were racing around, you—"

"Cooper and the other dogs were completely unfazed," Petra cut in. "Amazing."

Hawkeye saw the deflection. Was that habit, part of her neurodivergence, or that she really didn't want him to focus on her reactions to things that happened? "You were very calm and compartmentalized. You made me think of the phrase, 'Not my monkeys, not my circus.'"

"Chaos breeds chaos. And in a confined space like that, things can get really bad really quickly. The last time I took a flight, it was a demon racing around the cabin instead of a cat."

"Wait." Hawkeye was learning what he might expect from a conversation when speaking to Petra, and the bend that things took were not one and the same. "A demon?" He grinned. "What now?"

He was grinning a lot when he was around her.

His face wasn't used to it.

"True story. I had just got my new title. Before my current position, I had a job similar to Rowan Kennedy's. My field was mainly in the United States, where I tracked cults and their financial implications on finances. Track, not intervene. I was a fact-finder, not a taker-downer of dangerous felons."

"Criminal implications on finances?"

"Right," Petra said.

"But what did this have to do with the plane?"

"I was tracking a true believer who was going to see 'the guru.' I wanted the name and location of said guru. Up until that point, we couldn't find the charismatic. Imagine a beehive where all the worker bees are doing their job, and each of them serves the queen bee."

"Got it. You were looking for the queen. Did you find the leader?"

"I should add here that my focus was on monitoring doomsday cults. This particular cult believed that their guru could see the devil's minions amongst the humans. The guru would instruct the followers on how to act to avoid the various entities visiting the Earth's surface—sort of like taking little mini vacations from Hell. Only when the entities were here, they tried to find a body to steal."

"Soul to steal?" Hawkeye asked.

"Nope, whole body. The entity would just crawl into a body like it was putting on a new suit. And then the person lost their free will and had to walk around doing whatever heinous thing the demon wanted them to do."

"That's," Hawkeye paused, "something. I mean, people who weren't on drugs actually think that happens?"

"Absolutely. And as they follow what the guru tells them, they earn the right to be closer to the inner circle. With each step they took, the guru would perform rituals that would eventually open the third eye, allowing them to easily see and avoid these demons. It's in the newspaper. You can read all about the cult."

"That's all right, I'm good," Hawkeye said. "But tell me this, the belief is that once you can see them, you can avoid them."

"In theory."

"Is any of that against the law?" Hawkeye asked. "Fraud, maybe?"

"Could you prove it's fraud in court? I mean, I can't see the demons. But could I scientifically prove that they don't exist?" Petra shrugged. "Usually, with cults, it's a matter of free will. If a believer wants to surrender all their worldly possessions to become enlightened, so be it. It's when it crosses over into federal law that we get aggressively involved."

"And this group was?"

"Money laundering, drug running, human trafficking, and in that case on that day—"

"Your last trip in that position?" Hawkeye clarified.

"Yes, the funding finally came through for my research.

Anyway, yes, on my last trip in that position, I was trying to find the queen bee—and I'll stop to tell you that I love bees, and I don't love that analogy—"

"But it's the one that works." Hawkeye absolutely recognized that Petra's mind was firing fast and furious, and she was struggling to keep her thoughts linear in order to have this conversation with him.

He had a micro-amygdala, and apparently, too much neural pruning had gone on, leaving him with a neurotypical brain. As Cora liked to explain it, her software was faster and more robust, but since she was trying to run it on weaker hardware, she glitched.

Cora struggled to slow down to get words and thoughts in line.

Hawkeye had learned to be patient and insert leading questions.

He always thought that being in Cora's brain must be damned exhausting.

"Sadly true," Petra said.

And Hawkeye wasn't sure if she was responding to his comment about being the metaphor that worked or if she'd somehow read his mind and knew what he'd thought about her exhaustion.

"I'm on the plane following this woman," Petra continued. "I'm in the same row in the window seat. Me, then an older woman who looked just like my mark—mother probably—then this gal on the aisle. Imagine her. She's big for a woman. Not you big, but big, nonetheless. Not just height but all of her."

"Big," Hawkeye said.

"We take off, and we're doing just fine. I'm listening to the two of them talking, hoping to gather some tidbit of helpful information. They're bickering about the chores. Suddenly, the gal on the aisle—I'll call her Jane Doe—starts having a seizure-like episode. She's out of her seat, wedged into the aisle, convulsing. The mom looks over at her and says that, of course, the demons have shown up. She's obviously wrong about washing the dishes."

"She's seizing?" Hawkeye was in his head, trying to imagine this scene.

"No. She's not. Let me put that idea to rest right away. To everyone on that plane, it looked like a seizure. It was quaking. Her lizard brain was terrified because she saw demons all over the plane."

"A break with reality."

"I have no idea. I can't diagnose without an assessment and medical workup. But clearly, not a seizure because Jane Doe and Mom are yelling at each other in between Jane Doe's screaming at the demons to get away and leave her alone. Oh, and lest I forget, just as with me and my probable medical crisis, the flight attendants tried to help. They raced in with a first aid kit. There was an announcement about a medical event and that photography was not permitted. And asking if there were any medical personnel on the flight?"

"Did anyone step up?" Hawkeye asked, looking at the clock and starting the engine.

"To intervene with a break from reality? What could they do? No. Everyone hunkered down, trying to make themselves as small and unnoticed as possible. I mean, Jane kicked this one attendant down the aisle. The attendant hit his head and got whiplash on top of a TBI for his care and concern. He's still on medical leave."

"Shit. And this whole time, you're boxed in next to the window." Hawkeye put the SUV in reverse and backed out of their spot.

"The pilot comes on the speaker and says he's diverting to some small airport that's nearby. And I am pretty sure everyone on the plane would have been just as happy if the pilot found a stretch of empty highway. Anywhere down was good."

"The whole time?" Hawkeye asked. "The whole time Jane Doe is screaming and shaking? That takes a lot of energy."

"She had a strand of beads wrapped around her wrist, and at some point, she gnawed through the strand, and as she saw a devil demon approach, she'd swallow a bead and scream, 'Take that!' I was seeing it in my mind's eye like bulletproof cuffs that could ward off gunshot, but inside her body."

Hawkeye pulled his chin back, his brows pulled in tight. Then, he shifted to drive and started toward the drive-through window.

"The police were there with the paramedics. They put her in restraints and transported her to the psych ward. That same night, she was moved to a dedicated psychiatric hospital, and the bad part was I didn't get to follow Jane Doe to the queen bee. Now, it's up to the person who took my place to figure that out."

Hawkeye just shook his head in disbelief. "No wonder the cat and chihuahua show on the plane down here was a nothing-burger for you."

"Not a nothing-burger, but I couldn't allow my face to be identifiable in the social media circus that was sure to arise. Even with my new role, I can't be recognizable. I let my hair fall in my face. Kept my face averted. And hunkered down."

"I see. Well, let's get your meds and get you hunkered down at the hotel."

"With any luck," Petra said as he pulled up to the window, "the crazy is done for today."

"With any luck?" Hawkeye repeated. "What else could possibly go wrong?"

26

As Petra, Hawkeye, and Cooper entered the lobby, a large sign faced the automatic doors. Hotel guests were asked to check in with the main desk as Emergency Services tried to account for everyone's safety.

That made sense to Petra. After all, they were visitors and probably had no family or friends on the island to notice they were missing.

As they stood in line, waiting their turn, Petra wrapped her arms around Hawkeye's waist, and he held her to him protectively. It was a good feeling.

Stepping forward, Petra saw they had a printout with the guest names on double-lined sheets. "Hermione Armstrong."

"Yes," the desk staffer said, striking her name. "Thank you."

"Michael Kesse," Hawkeye said, and the woman flipped the page.

As she struck a line through Hawkeye's name, Petra read:

Herbert Johnson family (5). She leaned forward. "The Johnsons haven't checked in yet? It's late for them to be out with the children."

"You're friends?" the staffer asked.

"I know Herb and Jenny. They're here with their three children."

The staffer jotted, "Jenny + 3 children." She looked up. "Have you seen them today? Do you know where they might have gone? We're collecting the information for the authorities."

"I saw them this morning. I don't know about their plans. Sorry. Just while we're here," Petra pointed toward the supply cart behind the woman. "Could we get a couple bottles of water, please?"

When the woman turned, Petra took a picture of the roster, then slid her camera back away as she smiled and accepted the waters.

Did Hawkeye see all that? Yes.

Did he ask? No.

They moved to the elevators, where a large group was already waiting.

Hawkeye stepped back with Cooper. They'd wait for a clear car.

Petra moved over to the column, pulled up the roster photo, and sent it on to Rowan with a few choice shocked-face emojis. Then she held up her camera to record a selfie video, saying, "After a harrowing day on the island, the authorities are asking the people at the hotels to check in as they try to figure out who is missing. Guess who's missing. I have one more thing that I didn't mention before."

She tapped send.

A moment later, Rowan was on the phone, and without so much as a hello, he said, "What didn't you mention?"

"The whole family—mom, dad, and kids—all wore matching necklaces."

"A family gift?" he asked. "Any idea what that was about?"

"I asked. Jenny said that they wanted to renew their vows to each other and include the family. Then she amended it to say that she wanted the children to understand that they were telling them they were loved and part of a bigger happy family. I got stuck on the word 'bigger.'" Petra was quiet as she struggled with the best course of action. "Nope, I'm not going to say that out loud."

"Come on, Petra," Rowan reassured her, "you can say anything to me."

"Work colleague," Petra mumbled.

"Good friends," he countered.

"In this instance, work colleague."

Rowan sighed. "Give me a hint."

"Soldiers who I talked to at the base would tell me stories that freaked them out. Like, they'd be walking along and suddenly feel the need to tie their shoe, an overwhelming need. They'd bend over, and a bullet would fly over their back. That impulse would save their lives. Sometimes, it's a chill running up their spine that makes them freeze long enough for their buddy to say, "Hey, man, don't move. That next step is a trip wire."

"It's happened to me more than once," Rowan said.

"The daughter yanked her necklace off and jetted it toward the sea. When she wasn't looking, I went down and picked it up. I have it in my pocket."

"Text the picture to me. Let me see what you've got."

With Rowan on the line, Petra scanned the room to make absolutely sure she wasn't being observed. Hawkeye and Cooper stood patiently, giving her some privacy.

She surreptitiously snapped a picture of the pendant and

forwarded it to Rowan, then heard the ping as it landed in his messages.

There was silence on the other line.

"*Shit.*" Rowan hissed. "Are you *kidding me* right now?"

Petra's lungs lost their elasticity, making her next breath shallow and ineffectual. "This has meaning to you, then?"

"Yeah, Petra, it means stay away from these people. Don't be friendly with them, don't talk to them, don't let them eat or drink near you. Stay the *hell* away."

"Okay," Petra agreed. "I'll stay away. Anything else I should know?"

"I'm coming down there. I'll be on the first flight I can find, tonight if possible."

"Well, okay then." She blinked at the wall. What the hell? "Cheers to a sleepless night for both of us."

27

Hawkeye was in his head as they walked to the elevator.

It had been a long, trying day. There was no need for banter or smiles.

As a matter of fact, Petra decided that she wouldn't wear any masks at all with him.

She was simply going to say the words that sprang to her lips, express the emotions as they rose and shifted, not worrying if he could keep up or was uncomfortable with them. With her.

Because if any part of her could scare him off, she'd rather know now.

In past relationships, when she lowered her mask, it never went well.

It was a honed skill from childhood that she tried to present only the side of her that she thought was palatable.

Petra had figured it was an okay strategy for a casual date, or for a roll in the hay.

And she still thought that was true.

It had kept things calm so that she could have someone reasonably companionable accompany her to dinner parties, since she hated those miserable, smug questions about her being single.

She'd had fine talks and good meals, all very C+ when she naturally found straight 'A's to be easily in reach.

Well, academically and professionally, that was true.

Relationship-wise? Not so much.

She regularly pissed off folks when her neurodivergence made her ability to process quickly and extrapolate out the variety of endpoints, which inevitably proved true. And people found her odd in ways that they couldn't put a finger on. Mainly that had to do with how she communicated. A neurodivergent conversation was very different from a neurotypical one.

Better to mask.

Better to shapeshift.

When Petra had her wonky eyeball, she'd teased Hawkeye that she was an alien. But in some ways, she felt like that. It was just part of her variety of brain wiring.

Constantly second-guessing, always dealing with imposter syndrome.

She had a PhD. She'd moved through Quantico training. She was a badge-carrying supervisory special agent in the FBI's Behavioral Analysis Unit, where she used her knowledge of psychology and crime-solving skills to safeguard her country by spearheading the new world of propaganda and mind security.

And yet every time she badged herself into the J. Edgar Hoover building, Petra felt like she was wearing a costume— she was cosplaying—and at any moment, the guards would discover that she didn't belong there and toss her out.

Or she would be presenting research to her peers, and again, it felt like she was acting on a stage. It didn't matter that this, too, was a symptom of her brain wiring.

So little was known.

Medical research in neurodivergence was almost all centered around boys' outward inability to sit still. Girls' hyperactivity was often internal, with racing, catapulting minds.

Women of Petra's generation and older—like her mom and grandma—were just now getting their diagnoses. And at this late stage, they were pissed at the amount of time they had spent suffering through trying to be something they simply weren't and the amount of medical gaslighting they'd endured.

The light bulb goes off, and life makes a whole lot more sense.

Tamika got her diagnosis, too.

Yup, both friends sailed around in the same neurodivergent boat. Which probably explained why their relationship was so deep and such a relief to each of them.

Hawkeye, now he was interesting. He talked about his sister Cora like his relationship with her gave him a solid platform of understanding. And that he mentioned Cora's neurodivergence and not his own meant that he'd been through an assessment and deemed neurotypical.

Could a relationship work between them?

Petra *liked* Hawkeye more than she ever remembered liking someone. Liked who he was, how he acted, what he thought, and how he expressed himself. She liked the way he smiled, and how he interacted with his team and his dog. Liked how her body relaxed when he touched her. How he was a lightning rod, grounding all of the sizzle and spark that ran through her body when he held her hand.

She felt more aligned with and more "right" with him than she'd ever felt.

It seemed to Petra that they might be wrapping a warp of

understanding, shared experiences, and stories told, on which they could weave themselves a solid relationship.

"Here we are," Hawkeye said, coming to a stop.

He had been silent the entire way up. "Your mind is obviously whirring." Cooper came to a sit by his side while Hawkeye tapped the keycard on the locking mechanism. "Would you be willing to share that thought?" he asked.

"Darwin said it was survival of the fittest. And most people would look at someone like you and think that your kind of genes are the ones worth handing down. I was wondering if you have children."

"No." He pressed the door wide and gestured that she should go in first. "You?"

"No."

"Most people would look at someone like me..." he repeated, letting the last part drift off. It was an interrogation technique meant to elicit a broader understanding of a concept. Or maybe, it was confusion that she would say something like that. Which would be fair.

"I'm playing that sentence over and over in my head," she said. "It was quite rude, and then I coupled that with 'Did you procreate?' and it sounds terrible." Petra wanted to scamper away but made herself stand her ground. No masks. He wanted her thoughts. There they were. "My shower or yours?"

"Your preference. I didn't hear it that way. I heard that you had an alternative understanding of Darwin's phrase."

"I think maybe I do." Okay, that was a surprising response from him. "Who do you think is fittest?" Petra waited while Hawkeye gathered a towel and a pair of sleep pants.

"Cooper load," he pointed toward his bed and snapped his fingers. "I've never sat down and considered it. I guess I fall into the category of 'most people.' I'm going to pause and ask if you're nervous right now."

She blinked at him. Overwrought might be a better word. "It was an emotional day."

He reached for her hands and held them between both of his, bringing them up to rest on his chest. "But brainy stuff helps?"

"It does. It forces me away from my lizard brain and fight or flight."

"I'm going to take you back to Darwin in a second because I'm really curious. But first, I wanted to tell you how proud I am of you. On the beach today, you had everything in hand. You dealt with trying circumstances masterfully."

"Survival of the calmest. I like it when I can offer something. If I have nothing, I get anxious. A panic attack adds fuel to the fire. It's contagious, especially on a plane."

"Yes, we were just talking about the plane on the drive over here," Hawkeye let go of her hand as she turned and went to her room, and he followed behind her. "Why, especially on a plane?"

"Okay, you got me, I shouldn't have phrased it that way." She opened the bathroom door and leaned over the tub to turn on the water, letting it heat. "Anxiety contagion was studied in airports, and they found that a single person at a gate showing signs of anxiety increased the anxiety of everyone in the area, which stands to reason."

"My sister does that, too." He was grinning.

"What's that? Have anxiety attacks?" Petra threw a towel over the bar within arm's reach of the tub.

"Yes, to the anxiety attacks, and they can be difficult. Also, leap from thought to thought like rocks in a raging stream. But, just now, I was referring to the end phrase. You said, 'which stands to reason.' You made some connection, made some mental leap there, but if you don't take me along for the ride, I have no idea why it would stand to reason."

"I'm just going to undress and get in, and then you can follow," Petra said, and she couldn't imagine a less sexy introduction to their being naked together.

But honestly, she didn't have it in her to do anything more than peel off these clothes and maybe lift her foot over the side.

To be even more honest, nothing about this felt nervous. Petra could make it a thing, but that would be the stuff of novels and rated-R movies. Petra wanted the sting of hot water and the solace of Hawkeye's hands on her. The fewer steps getting there the better.

"Yeah, sure," Hawkeye said, shifting from foot to foot, then he turned his back to give her a moment of privacy.

Since they were about to be naked in the shower together, she wasn't sure she understood the move, but it had a charming, gentlemanly feel to it. And since she was wincing and gyrating to get out of her clothes, the gesture was much appreciated.

"Which stands to reason," she said, tugging at the string of her bikini top. "Think about a zebra on the periphery of a herd that perceives a possible threat. That zebra stills and focuses on assessing. The rest of the herd responds in kind. Danger for one could mean danger for all."

"Got it," Hawkeye said. "Sort of like yawning might have started as a signal that it was time for a tribe to go to bed."

"Yes. If someone yawns, it tells the tribe that things feel safe and sleepy. That they aren't on hyper-awareness. They can pass the feeling of safety around." Petra slid behind the curtain and was once again grateful for a moment of privacy as the pain of the first water on her abrasions made her face deform in agony.

She could hear Hawkeye getting undressed. Then he stepped behind the curtain to stand with her.

"Darwin?" he asked, bottles of shampoo and conditioner in his hands.

Darwin indeed. Ho-o-o-o-lyyyy shit.

She licked her lips and forced her gaze to meet his. "Survival of the fittest means that if you have the right traits, you have a better shot at living," she stammered. At least in the shower, he wouldn't see her drooling. Small favors.

He pressed her shoulder until she turned away from him. "You keep going with that thought. I'm going to start with your hair, and then I'm going to clean the blood out of your cuts. You're in worse shape than I thought. I'd hoped that once the dried blood was off, you'd have a few small cuts. I'm so sorry." He kissed her shoulder. "I'm so grateful you put yourself through that and saved Terry's life. God, woman, you are so damned brave. You are astonishing." He dropped another kiss —and held his lips there a little longer.

She liked how he lingered like that. "I…" Sensations and thoughts overwhelmed Petra. Panic clutched her lungs.

"Petra," he said, "you're okay. Everything's okay. You're safe. It's over. I've got you now."

She nodded her head.

"Put your hands on the wall in front of you. Go back to one subject. You're showing me something new about Darwin. Here are my fingers on your scalp."

Petra took a minute to breathe and center. She focused on her index finger, which lay on the white plastic wall, and the gentle swirls Hawkeye traced over her scalp. "Survival of the fittest sounds like pulling yourself up by the bootstraps, like rugged individualism. But, in human history, people have always depended on others for survival. People get good at one skill and market that skill from storyteller to shaman to stone cutter. It was—and is—a rare person who attempts to go it alone. And that's why ostracism was one of the worst possible punishments. Like being left alone on an island. Buck's Island here in St. Croix, for example."

"You're straying again. I'll ask about Buck's Island later. About Darwin, what I hear is that survival of the fittest means the one who can contribute in some way. Can follow societal rules. Probably the one that is seen as a good person."

"Exactly. That's… people who can form alliances and make easy friendships. That doesn't work out great for me."

"What are you talking about?" he asked. "You're friendly."

"Am I? Hmm. I don't think of myself as friendly. Since I'm neurodivergent, it's more likely that people think of me as odd. I'm fine with that," she threw in, lest he thought she was looking for compliments or even pity. "There are actually scientific studies which say that just from looking at the face of someone who is neurodivergent, neurotypical people think there's something off that they couldn't place, and so they assume a red flag and distance themselves."

Petra would love to know what Darwin thought about that.

Still, had she just told Hawkeye that people found her odd?

Petra was fighting hard not to make the mistake she always did—to mask, to shapeshift, to try to interpret what the other person was looking for and transform into that thing. It was a typical means of survival—since they were talking about survival—for people who were differently wired.

"We can debate how people perceive you," Hawkeye said, and his voice sounded like he was smiling. "My team thinks you're amazing. And if I saw any red flags waving, I wouldn't be naked with you right now. But let's focus on the word 'friendly.' Take Cooper. He's laid-back and accepting, but I wouldn't call him friendly. He likes who he likes and tolerates others. He does a good job. He's highly esteemed. He gets a lot of joy from his work, which helps people. But his behavior with you on the plane was atypical. He likes people at a distance. He's also my best friend."

"I think Cooper and I have a lot in common. I tend to keep my social circles small."

"And trustworthy?" Hawkeye asked.

"Yes, I'd say that's true."

"Always or as an adult?"

Petra was having trouble considering that question as Hawkeye knelt behind her, massaging his hands over her thighs, the bite of soap in her cuts, the gentleness of his hands. "It's more pronounced the older I get. I plan on being quite the curmudgeon in my old age."

"Thanks for the warning." He leaned forward and kissed her hip, then stood. He pulled Petra back into his arms, holding her against him, and she could feel his dick hard at her back.

"I'm going to say something, and I hope this isn't offensive in any way."

Petra braced for it. Nothing good could come next.

"We're both exhausted. Physically and emotionally drained from today."

This is the write-off.

"You're covered in bruises and abrasions. It looks like every part of you is in pain."

He doesn't want me despite my being naked and his dick standing ready.

"I want our first time together to be more than what I can give you tonight. I want it to be special and memorable. There's no need to rush us. We already have plans for a date at home." He paused, and she held her breath.

This must be the string-it-along kind of brush-off.

"You've told me how you ruminate for years and decades about events, and I wonder if it would be a bad thing to connect this particular day with a relationship milestone. I want to make love to you, obviously. But perhaps, this isn't the right time for significant firsts."

Significant firsts, she let that phrase somersault through her brain.

Significant firsts wasn't a phrase used for a stress-relieving roll. Or a "nice to know yah, that was fun."

It was something someone said when they believed there was a future.

His hands slicked down her sides, coming to rest on her hips, holding her tightly against him. "And I'm hoping it would be all right to wait."

Petra blinked at the wall in front of her.

She ran that conversation through her mind again without applying her "I'm not good enough" filter. Special and memorable, she cycled the phrase again and again.

That was so *damned* sexy.

Petra turned around, lifting to her toes to wrap her arms around his neck. She kissed him long and hard.

This experience with Hawkeye was absolutely a significant *first*.

28

HAWKEYE

Hawkeye hung up the hotel phone after ordering pizza.

Petra came into the room, walking tenderly. Dressed in a pair of panties and a T-shirt, she hugged a towel and comb to her chest with one hand, pressing the other into her lower back.

As hard as it was for him to ask her to wait, seeing her now was exactly why.

Did he want her? Hell yeah, he did. But not at her expense. Not when she was in such obvious pain.

He would always put her well-being first.

As she passed the open door that adjoined their rooms, Cooper whined for permission to come in to be with them.

When Hawkeye called him in, Cooper jumped down and came to sniff Petra, then rested his muzzle on the mattress.

"Load," Hawkeye said.

Cooper bounded onto the bed, circled, and then plopped down.

"He's exhausted, too," Hawkeye said as Petra pushed down the comforter and crawled onto a cool white sheet.

The feel of her skin, the curve of her ass, her sweet lick-able breasts had filled him with unexpected sensations. He felt *fiercely* protective of her. Not violent—though if violence were required to keep her safe, he'd bring it.

Talk about significant firsts; his reaction to her was a force that thrummed through his blood.

He reached for Petra's comb. "Come sit in front of me."

Hawkeye thought he knew why he was on high alert. He had questions. Lots of them. "In the lobby, you were talking to Rowan Kennedy?" Parts of their whispered conversation had floated over to him.

"I was," Petra crossed her legs in front of herself, then pulled the towel into a cape over her shoulders to catch the dripping water.

"It seemed intense. Did I hear right? He's coming to the island?" When he said that, Hawkeye's muscles banded, and he didn't know why. Had he stepped into her op somehow? "Are you here working?"

"I didn't lie to you," Petra said. "I came in service of a friend. I just happened to see something I wanted to bring to the Bureau's attention, which I did earlier today. Something else came to my attention tonight. I let Rowan know, and he leaped on it. Do I understand what it is? Not at all. The thing I brought to Rowan's attention was not what he reacted to."

The comb hit a snag, and Hawkeye held her hair as he worked the teeth through. "I'm not sure that I can follow that sentence."

Petra didn't answer, but he could feel the sleepy energy she walked in with shift to wariness.

"Can you tell me what you do for the FBI?" Hawkeye asked. "You were tracking queen bees, but you don't do that job anymore." When the comb slid easily through that section, he moved to the next.

"My title is 'supervisory special agent' in the FBI's Behavioral Analysis Unit."

"Supervisory, behavioral analysis. That's a mouthful," Hawkeye said. "What does it mean?"

"I'm a brain researcher in a lab. I'm working on the emerging concept of brain security."

"But you're not in the field now, tracking and observing."

"My observations will now be centered on content that Rowan and others gather, and when applicable, I'll study willing volunteers."

Hawkeye exhaled. "Safe, then."

She looked over her shoulder and smiled at him. "Has Rowan told you what he does for the FBI?" She faced forward again, and Hawkeye continued to leisurely comb her hair.

"He told me he has a doctorate in propaganda, but he was smiling when he said it, so I assume that wasn't quite it. I know he works over in the post-USSR countries studying how Russian psyops affects the world at large, but the United States in particular."

"That's right."

"I know that when he started dating Avery, she worked with him on some big case that included Panther Force, and after that, they got married and she became an Iniquus consultant. But you know that. That's why you asked her to identify Cerberus at the airport."

"That case you mentioned is an interesting one. Ongoing. Partly to watch it and see how that group adapts and what they do next. Partly because the laws haven't caught up, and a lot of what they do, while evil, is lawful."

"And somehow Avery was involved with that?" Hawkeye asked. "She's a romance editor."

"Mostly classified. I can't speak to that," Petra said. "What I can tell you is that the Russian psyops machine is extremely effective in some countries like ours."

"But not all countries, is what I'm hearing."

"Bordering countries like Estonia and Finland have worked to inoculate their people against the effects of psyops. They teach the subject in school from a very young age. Once you know how it's done, it's harder for the psyops to work. I spent a good deal of time over in that region learning from their experts about mind manipulation. And don't get me wrong, all mind manipulation isn't bad."

"How could it be good?" He pulled the comb from the crown to the tips, and she hummed a little under her breath as if she had enjoyed the sensation.

"Okay, here's an example—scientists have been studying how different sound frequencies affect the brain. Right now, you can pull up an app that will play sounds to help you get into the mind space you need for deep focus, creativity, or meditation," she said. "By manipulating the environment, you can budge yourself toward a desired state of mind. That helps in so many ways. I use it when I need deep focus at work or when my mind is on a gerbil wheel and I can't get to sleep. The music is specifically designed as a manipulation of brain waves."

"Do you do what Rowan does?" An existential threat painted over him. Could Petra become a target? "Are you going after Russian psyops?" he asked directly. Hawkeye was starting to see how Petra would sidestep a subject. It might not be that she was hiding something; it could be the direction in which her brain ricocheted.

"I'm a research scientist. As I try to understand how modern brains adapt to innovations, I focus my study on cult techniques."

"When you were a kid, you had to stand up and tell the

class what you wanted to be when you grew up. Is that what you said? Not doctor or ballerina, you said cult scientist?" Hawkeye chuckled.

"I said I wanted to be smart and have fun doing things I like."

Hawkeye held for a long moment while he processed how extraordinary that answer was. He blinked. "Wow, that went through me like a bolt of lightning. I never would have thought to answer that way." His hand held still in her hair. "I have to sit with that for a minute. It's a radical response. How old were you when you said that?"

Petra looked up to the ceiling, remembering. "Mmm, kindergarten graduation?" She lowered her chin again. "Yeah. I think it was graduation from kindergarten. The parents were there. I was standing on the blue rug in that itchy, yellow flower dress I hated."

"And what was the response?"

"Indifference from the kids. From the grownups, a bit like what you're doing now, unease. I thought I got the answer wrong."

"Which was painful for you."

"For a very long time, I was ashamed that I would want to be either smart or have fun. Then, freshman year in high school, I mentioned that story to my art teacher, and she reframed it for me as the best possible answer. That's what everyone should aspire to. A decade to carry that shame was more than enough. I'm forever grateful to her, to Mrs. Barnstrom."

"I'm sorry you carried it at all. I wouldn't call my reaction 'unease' as much as you damned well shifted my paradigms. It's so out of the box. So, while I'm going through this internal seismic event, I want to congratulate you. It seems to me you've met your goals. Amazing. You know you and my sister are going to get along really well. She does this to me, too, shifts my perspective. I like it. It keeps me nimble." He paused. "You're going to hear me mention Cora a lot around you. She's not just my sister. She's a very dear friend. I like to just laze about and listen to her thoughts. I can see you two becoming good friends. That is, unless you prefer to retreat into your curmudgeon shell, in which case, I can visit her and give you space."

He realized he was talking to Petra like they'd agreed they were in a relationship.

He needed to slow his damned roll. "Is talking about your work too much for you right now? Should we change the subject? Would you like to be silent?"

"Me? I love talking about my work. I'm sure it's the same with you."

"I love doing my work. I don't want to talk about it. I want to hear more about yours, to the extent that it's not classified. Rowan is into post-Soviet psyops, and he's jumping on a plane for St. Croix."

"Yeah, I don't know," Petra said.

"I see." He didn't see at all, but he knew enough about Rowan to recognize that he played among some very dangerous and despicable characters. And Hawkeye, selfishly, wanted Petra safe. "Federal employees aren't paid well. Your expertise is unique. You jumped into a brand-new world with brain security. I'd imagine there are any number of institutions and industries that would snatch you up and pay you royally to help them understand and exploit the human brain. Obviously, you don't have the personality or drive to do that. Are you frightened by what you're discovering?"

"As a scientist, I don't want to use the word frightened. Perhaps—mmm, I'm looking for a word that's more than cautious, less than hair on fire. I'm *braced*. The human brain is truly extraordinary. But living in a questionable reality is demonstrably bad. Underlying mental health issues will become more challenging. Depression, thoughts of suicide, anxiety, paranoia, anger control, and such. Our health systems aren't equipped. We don't have enough mental health professionals. Even if we did, the average person can't access them for financial reasons. The consequences are widespread. An increase in self-medication with drugs and alcohol, more violence borne of frustration, and a lack of control over our environment are expected. One of the responses we see in our research is the rise of small groups that tune into each other, eschewing wider society and societal norms. That too can be problematic."

Hawkeye drew his brows together. "Keep going with that."

"They fold in on themselves. They develop a reality apart from others, reinforcing those beliefs in each other. That's part of our history. The Pilgrims, for example, had unique world-views that they tied to their faith. They were first ostracized in England fled to Holland, then fled again to what would become the United States. History redefines who and what they were, but at the time, they were radicals."

"Sounds like you're talking about more cults. Your research is still cult related?"

"There's an argument for that. What are the elements of a cult?" Petra asked, pulling her knees to her chest and wrapping her arms around her legs.

"A charismatic leader. Brainwashing," Hawkeye ventured. He hadn't given it much thought.

"Can you imagine a world where we can't believe our own eyes, our own ears? Then what is reality? We need someone we trust to tell us what is true. A charismatic personality is, by definition, someone who can sway people. Imagine this—a human is floundering. They feel marginalized. They want to challenge the norms because the norms make them feel bad about themselves or their circumstances. Then someone says, you're right to be aggrieved and afraid. Come follow me, and I will show you the way to feeling content. The anxiety and anger will leave your body. The depression will lift."

"It sounds like self-medication, desperate people seeking relief."

She canted her head and fluttered her eyelashes at him. "Did you know that while facing a doomsday scenario like I did today, I might have fallen under the sway of a charismatic who makes me feel safe, and therefore, I put my faith in him? Does your cult have a name?"

"You're teasing me. But I hope that's true to the extent that I want good outcomes for you. In difficult circumstances, it's helpful—even hopeful—to lean on someone you trust. As I'm listening to you, I'm thinking about a German philosopher I read last year who lived through WWI and WWII. She postulated in an interview that if everything is a lie, no one believes anything anymore. And then she says that when you don't know what's the truth and what's a lie, you don't know what to do."

"You read philosophy?"

Deflection or a thought ricochet? He didn't answer.

"I'd say if you don't know what to do, you'd end up doing nothing, or worse, you do what you want." She turned back around.

Hawkeye continued to slowly comb her hair. He hoped she found it as calming as he did. "Why is that worse?"

"A whole different discussion. Is that the direction you want me to take?"

"I'll ask you about that another day. I guess I'd like to know how this applies to your work," Hawkeye said. "This is pseudo-spiritual?"

"Spiritual groups have been around for all of humanity. People connect that way. There's a lot of positivity. What I call pseudo-spirituality is about leadership gain at the detriment of the followers."

"That's an eye of the beholder kind of thing, right? The person may get everything good out of the association, but to the outside, people wonder why they might, for example, take a vow of celibacy or vow of poverty."

"I'm talking about Jim Jones and the like."

"That's who you study?"

"Right now, I'm particularly focused on a UFO cult that's been growing. They are dead set on the idea that the world is going to be overrun by aliens on a certain date in the future. Their origin story is this: After being abducted in his youth, their charismatic now has an alliance with the leadership of a distant planet. The planetary leadership contacts this guy with urgent messages, bringing him up to date on universal news."

Hawkeye could feel not just the smile on his lips but the smile reaching his eyes. How often did that happen? This wasn't a fun subject, but Hawkeye was jazzed by the kinds of things that Petra thought and talked about. "Nice to have connected friends."

"Isn't it? Right now, a battle is being mounted, and Earth's inhabitants can't survive it. That's the bad news. The good news is that the charismatic's alien friends have a ship en route to pick him up."

"Now?" Hawkeye asked.

"Right now," Petra said. "When the ship arrives to vacuum him into the sky, he can take only X number of people with him. People he cares about. People who are part of his extended family."

Hawkeye lifted a brow. "To go where?"

"Back to the friend-alien's planet."

"Where humans can exist on—air, water, food, gravity?"

Petra shook her head. "I suppose. I mean, how could you do that research?"

"Without becoming enslaved or a Guinea pig in some lab somewhere?"

"At a minimum, those would be my questions," Petra said.

"But no one's asking." Hawkeye's tone made it a statement, not a question.

"They depend on their leader, who has been there and is offering them Nirvana."

"In exchange for…"

"Well, just like in death, you can't take it with you. He's counseled everyone to divest themselves of their worldly goods. They'll accumulate it all in a central account, and the money will be meted out as needed."

"Why?"

"Why what?" she asked.

"Why divest?" Hawkeye put the comb down and pulled the towel from her shoulders. "Why put it in a single account? Who has control over that account, and under what circumstances will there be a withdrawal? What does 'as needed' mean?"

"You're so rational. And that shows you think there's a future on Earth when there isn't. They live on a farm in a barn turned into a dorm. They grow their own food. They're just waiting for the specific date and coordinates to show up for the great vacuuming—my term, not theirs. And as to your questions, they're good questions, but no one is asking them since it doesn't matter. They'll either be flying through space to their new home planet, or they'll be killed by lizard people—I'm making up the last part. I don't know what kind of alien they think is coming to destroy Earth."

"Isn't this against the law?" Hawkeye asked, pulling her back until he had her cradled in his arms, her head resting on his shoulder.

"People are acting from free will to the extent that the law defines it. We don't have brain security laws in place."

"But the leader is stealing all their money."

"Not stealing, Hawkeye, not even being gifted the money. It goes into a trust that the charismatic controls. He has declared it a religion or spiritual endeavor and jumped through all the hoops. In the eyes of the government, they have the right to assemble and the freedom of religion. They can believe whoever or whatever they like."

"And the other piece," Hawkeye pointed out, "is the leader gets all the money and doesn't even pay taxes on it."

"Bingo."

"So why is the FBI getting involved if it's not illegal?" Hawkeye asked. "Why are you studying it?"

"I'm studying it to understand how rational everyday people —educated people with no underlying pathological issues like paranoia or schizophrenia—fall under his sway. The FBI is interested because crimes are becoming ever more in the realm of mind manipulation and psyops. Breaking into houses with a gun and a money bag is so old school. With the right kind of manipulation, people just hand you everything they have with a smile on their face and a grateful, hopeful heart. Though, sometimes, with AI, it is much more of a cudgel. I'm talking about extortion."

"They already do that, don't they? They get teens to do something sexual on video for example."

"That's the old way to do that crime. With that method, many more variables could go wrong, which is much more dangerous to the criminal. Before, they had actual videos sent by the actual teens. Now, they don't need a child to manipulate. They can just pull a picture off someone's social media, put it through an AI photo or video generator, and boom. Not only that, but child porn is only child porn if a child is exploited.

What are the laws to stop people from creating child porn with AI? Who is harmed by it if the child pornography is merely an artificially generated image?"

"Shit."

"Exactly. We don't have the laws. We didn't know we'd need the laws. Here's another one that's shown up. Imagine a porn of you and your boss's wife. Someone sends it to you. They don't ask you for anything. You just see the images. What do you do? Are you in fear of losing your job? Your reputation? Your personal relationships? It's not illegal to make those images. It's not illegal to show them to you. It's only illegal if there's an ask or a threat. But, you may already know the ask, and you obviously understand the threat. That information exists in your brain. Is there a law that protects you from this kind of weapon?"

"That makes me feel oddly vulnerable. At Iniquus, for example, reputation and integrity are paramount. They hire people with those characteristics, so it's an intrinsic drive rather than an external fear. Yeah, this isn't a sensation I'm particularly used to."

"Confidence comes from a sense of safety. You present as confident," Petra said as she scrutinized his face. "I bet women like that because when they're with you, you represent safety."

"That's a sidestep, Petra. I'm going to have to go back and think about that later, think about my female friends, and if my presence makes them feel safe. My size and fighting skills are meaningless when up against an electronics crime. So, I'm going to put us back on AI manipulation. How does one protect oneself?"

"That's what I want to figure out. What makes people vulnerable, and how can it best be countered? I told you that I spent some time in Finland and Estonia. And that because they abut Russia, their populace needed to inoculation through education. They need to make sure their citizenry isn't going to fall prey to Russian psyops games meant to destabilize their countries. It was interesting to learn about and take some of their findings into my own study of cults."

"Alien Doomsday Cults."

"Exactly. I like to study alien doomsday cults because UFOs are particularly useful for gaining power and manipulation. Since UFOs are such an unknown quality, they represent an existential threat. When it comes to UFOs, folks are more likely to trust the leader with his special channel of information and do what they're told to do. Fear plus obligation plus guilt, and you have the tools you need to manipulate another human being."

"That's a narcissist's tool kit."

She canted her head, "That's right. How do you know that?"

"I've seen a friend date a narcissist. It's frustrating as hell to watch."

"You wanted to save the other person from something you saw plain as day. It's the same with families who see cults sucking their loved ones in." Petra laughed. "When all their loved one wants is to be sucked up by a spaceship."

The smile fell off Hawkeye's face. "But Rowan, he's coming down here."

"Yup."

"And you don't know why." Hawkeye didn't like this at all.

"I do know why. Rowan's coming down here because I saw something. I don't know why what I saw was so significant that he'd jump on a plane. I *thought* it would be a phone call to a random analyst in the basement somewhere." With a frown, she reached out to rub her hand over Cooper's soft fur. "I guess I'm about to find out."

29

———

Petra woke up to find that she had weaved her limbs with Hawkeye's.

He smiled at her. "Good morning." He dropped a kiss into her hair before he started to untangle himself. "Hey, I need to get up and take Cooper out. Would you like me to bring breakfast up like yesterday?"

She nodded not wanting to talk until she'd had a chance to brush her teeth.

She waited until Cooper and Hawkeye were out the door before going to pee.

It was nice to have some solitude to get dressed.

Once she was ready for the day, Petra had gone down to the desk with a sob story about the Johnson family she had met and befriended at the tidepool. When she'd checked in per the hotel's request last night, the Johnsons hadn't yet come in. "They have three small children," Petra continued. "When I came in from the hospital, it was late. I just want to make sure my friends are safe. Or if there's anything I could do to help."

"Johnson?" the staffer asked.

"Herb and Jenny Johnson? Room six-forty-two? I think I'm remembering that correctly."

"They didn't check in with the front desk. But that doesn't mean that they're in danger. Checking in was voluntary. And it was already late in the day when we started collecting the information."

"Okay. Yes, well, hopefully they're okay, thank you." Petra left the desk and found a bench away from the traffic flow.

When Petra dialed Rowan, he picked up on the first ring. "Where are you?" she asked.

"Miami. We'll be there in a few hours."

Petra scowled. "Wait. Who's we?"

"Finley and Prescott. We already had an iron on the stove. It just made sense for the three of us to come down to move our objectives along and get back faster."

"This is important enough that you left an unattended iron heating?" Petra scuffed her foot on the shiny granite.

"Timing was good. Let's leave it at that,' Rowan said. "What's this call about?"

"I talked with the front desk, and they said the Johnson family never checked in after yesterday's event. I saw the family on the cliff, away from the waves. I saw them go up toward the vehicles. My driver and Jenny's driver were helping me with Terry. I don't know how they got to their next place."

"What are your thoughts?" he asked.

"Three choices. Criminal. Innocent. Deadly."

"Okay," he said. "Take me through each."

Petra put one hand on top of her head. "Criminal—this was planned, and it went very well. Timing was excellent because everyone was caught up in myriad emergencies. The family had rented a boat and said they'd be out overnight to see sunset and sunrise. They're late, there's some worry. At some point, the Coast Guard would find the boat, but the family is missing. They fear the worst. There's a search. The family is possibly assumed to have drowned?"

"But in this scenario, what was playing out?"

"They met with a secondary boat and switched over."

"Left their belongings?"

"In this scenario, they left some belongings in the hotel. Pocket litter kinds of stuff. Stuff that they put out to convince anyone looking that they had planned to be back. But they took the basics they needed, passports, a change of clothes, and the kids' favorite toys—in a single bag. They climb from boat to boat, leaving the other adrift while their escape boat takes them to South America. Everyone believes there was an accident at sea. The family drowned and no one is looking for them after several days of failed Coast Guard efforts. And that narrative makes perfect sense after the coincidence of the seismic events yesterday."

"That's a lot to arrange even without the coincidence," Rowan suggested.

"Versus arranging to be gone from society for a decade plus and coming back to grown children and limited job possibilities."

"Here's some information I was able to gather. Ready?" Rowan asked.

"Maybe."

"One of the notarized letters in their file that went to the judge is from Herb's sister. She described her brother as someone whose whole personality changed in the last eighteen months. In her letter, she said it was like watching a bad actor on the screen who was trying to play the role of a saint in a movie. Herb talked about finding the light and living in the rays. The sister was worried enough that she went to the police before Herb's arrest to see if there was anything she could do because she thought that he might be having a mental breakdown."

"On the surface, that would make me think cult behaviors," Petra said.

"I checked their home address," Rowan said, "and it was recently sold. I checked with the Department of Motor Vehicles. Their cars were sold, as well. But all of that is what anyone would do knowing that they are going to prison. The only reason your antennae are up is that the mother didn't look at the child with bittersweetness. She could be on the autism spectrum." Rowan said. "She may be feeling the feelings and not expressing them in a neurotypical manner."

"Possible, sure," Petra agreed. "I could be very wrong. But you asked me how I'd play it out if this was their criminal actions."

"Okay move on to the next scenario, innocent."

"Yes, back to a boat scenario because I don't have one for them not signing in at the hotel if they're on land. So boat— they could have been having trouble with their boat. They needed help for some innocent reason, and they're dealing with the issue. That one doesn't make much sense to me at all, and I'm not even able to invent a good scenario to make it work, sorry."

Rowan sucked in a lungful of air. "That leaves deadly."

"It was a traumatic day in the islands from Puerto Rico down. The Christmas Winds, the rogue waves—granted, not tsunamis by any stretch of the imagination, but people got in trouble all over the island. The water was treacherous. Sixteen known dead as of the last count I heard."

"The deadly, then, is something like the kids got swept over the side, they weren't wearing their life vests, the parents jumped in and were able to grab the kids, but the current pulled them too far from the boat, and they never made it back."

"There were two seismic events and so two sets of giant waves. Why you'd go out on a day like yesterday, I have no idea. But, yes, that was exactly how I could see that working out."

"Great minds," Rowan said.

"You know, when people use that phrase, I can never tell if they're complimenting the person they're speaking with or themselves."

"Both." Rowan chuckled. "But okay, how about birds of a feather flock together."

"That's a stretch to make that act as a synonym for great minds, but I get the gist. What do we do?"

"*We* do nothing," Rowan's voice lost any levity. "I told you not to play. I'd like to discuss it with you when we're back in D.C. That file is classified for the moment. I'm working on getting permission from Frost to read you in back at the Bureau."

"Rowan, this has to do with the pendant, right?" Petra asked. "Do I *want* to be read in?"

"That I don't know."

***

Dressed in hiking clothes with her boots tied firmly in place, Petra sat down in the Cerberus conference room with a cup of coffee in front of her, a pad, and a pen.

Petra wasn't sure how she could be helpful. Honestly, she hoped she could do something sitting in front of a monitor. Adrenaline strength was a gift while she was helping Terry. But now, her muscles were tender, and her sinew felt too stretched. Being neurodivergent, she had to be careful of her hyper-mobility. And Petra wondered if the sensation was something to be worried about.

Sitting would be good.

Hawkeye was beside her, and Cooper was under the table with one of his paws draped over the toe of Petra's boot. It felt like they were holding hands. And it was very sweet.

As the men filed in with their dogs, Petra leaned to the side and asked under her breath, "Why do dogs smell each other's butts? There has to be a biological maybe chemical reason, right?"

"Well, yeah, dogs have apocrine glands back there. You could think of it like a social media profile. Their pheromones are like a post. The scents tell the other dog, for example, where a bitch is in her cycle, age, and how a dog is feeling that day."

"Feeling cute, may delete later." Petra reached under the table to scritch Cooper. "Is that why the dogs like to smell human crotches?"

"Checking our status. Humans have those glands in our armpits, too. But for most dogs, the crotch is more convenient."

"Helpful to dogs, but now I'm wondering if we used to smell each other for a status update. I mean, our tears change based on the why. Could we smell the difference at one time?" Petra asked. "Did we lick the tears off someone's face to taste them? Curious minds…"

"Wait. Tears aren't just tears?" Levi asked as he sat down. "Morning, Petra."

"Hey, Levi. We're talking about dogs sniffing butts. In human tears, laughing, lubrication, and self-cleaning from eye irritation are chemically different from emotional tears; those shed from sadness have high levels of stress hormones." She lifted a hand and waved. "Good to see you, Ash. All's well?"

"Good to go," He said as he settled Hoover. "Thanks for asking."

Reaper stood in the front of the room. "I have a list of potential assignments. When we're in the field, we'll let emergency services know which one we're tackling. The top two suggestions were a wellness check on a commercial boat owner and a search of Buck's Island. I'll go over the background of each case. First, Buck's Island. There is a tourist operation that takes visitors to Buck's Island where there is a national underwater park. Visitors snorkel along the marked trails to learn about the variety of coral and undersea animals and so forth. The boat went out as usual. The captain said that the current had been unusually strong even before the seismic activity. He encouraged everyone to stay near the pontoon. However, free will is what it is, and not everyone complied. After the first set of waves hit, the tourists were all over the place. It took him some time to gather everyone on his roster before he started back to the main island. The second seismic activity hit them hard. Luckily, he had everyone in a flotation vest. The pontoon was flipped with one wave and righted with the next. His roster was lost, the captain doesn't have the names of those with him anymore. He knows he couldn't find three."

"Were they within swimming distance of land?" Halo asked.

"They were a hundred yards from Buck's Island. They're either," Reaper held up a finger, "floating in the water on debris like our survivors from yesterday's boat accident." He held up a second finger. "They made it to the island." He held up a third finger. "They were picked up by another boat, or," his fourth finger went up. "They're deceased." He lowered his hand to the table. "A citizen boat is being lent to us so we can search the island to see if we can locate any survivors."

"You're doing that with your dogs?" Petra's voice rang with alarm.

The men turned to her.

"I—" Petra shook her head. Took a breath. Rolled her lips in.

The men waited.

"I don't mean to step out of line. But have you trained there before?" Petra asked.

"We just received the assignment and haven't done our due diligence," Reaper said. "Would you like to share your concerns?"

"My friend and I considered going there to hike. And as long as you're dressed properly, are aware, and stay on the path, it should be okay. They have scorpions, spiders, stinging nettles, and other things you guys probably deal with all the time on your searches."

Reaper nodded.

"But there's the manchineel tree, and that's what makes me worried about the dogs' safety. Every part of that plant—which grows prolifically on the island—is dangerous. Leaves, bark, sap, and fruit—all can cause chemical burns. If any of that were to get in the dogs' eyes, it could lead to blindness. If they were to eat one of the fruits, it could cause serious issues, especially because there is no quick way to get them to a vet. I know that sometimes working dogs wear muzzles and dog goggles, which, in this case, would be important. But if they were to roll or rub or otherwise get the poison on their skin it could be very bad. While humans should be fine, it's the dogs' behavior, especially as you search off-trail, that has me worried."

Reaper looked at her, his mind going.

"In the days of pirating," Petra added, "they would tie their enemies to the trees, so they died a terrible death from the chemicals. It's what I read. I felt compelled to share."

"Thank you, Petra. You're right. That environment needs a land team, not a K9 team. I'll reach out and talk to emergency services and get us assigned to a different mission." He lifted a sheet of paper. "I have a one-team assignment to do a well-check on a boater who didn't return last night. Witnesses on the wharf said they saw her go out, but the boat wasn't in the slip this morning. The sixty-year-old female is an experienced seawoman who always leaves her plans on her kitchen table. She lives in a cabin that is both off-grid and off-road. You'll be parking your vehicle and hiking in. Eyes on the subject or a picture of the itinerary."

"Cooper and I can take that one." Hawkeye turned to Petra. "Do you want to take that assignment, too?"

She nodded and looked at Reaper.

"All right. This is a reminder about the communication situation. We ran into some issues, such as dead spots with no cell phone service in the area and no landlines. Because of the tree canopy on much of the island, satellite phones are hit and miss." Reaper handed the paper over to Hawkeye. "Questions?"

"Is she paranoid? Armed? Animals? Any known medical issues?"

"She was described as a surfer who couldn't do the big waves anymore and enjoys the smaller waves they get here in St. Croix. They didn't have information about animals or medical situations." He rapped his knuckles on the table. "This will be our TOC." (He used the acronym for tactical operations center, pronounced "talk.") "When you two get back, check in here with me."

When Hawkeye stood, Cooper scrambled out from under the table.

Petra gritted her teeth as she lifted up from her chair. Surely, today would be easier than yesterday.

Right?

30

____

Walking side by side through the parking lot on their way out to the woman's off-grid house, Hawkeye was waiting for Petra to answer.

But Petra needed to watch her mouth. It was one of the hardest parts for her about being neurodivergent. If she was on a gerbil wheel with an idea turning over and over and over, it was a physical, mental, and emotional relief to share it. Petra liked to talk things through. By telling others, she could hear her ideas and echo-locate the holes. But in her line of work, her thoughts were classified and compartmented. Even Rowan, with the same level of security and the same job, had to be careful what he shared and under what circumstances.

Sometimes, she could speak hypothetically or talk about things in parallel.

And then there were topics that she needed to shut up about.

This was a shut-up-about-it topic.

Was this classified? *I mean, I ran into a woman on an*

island on my supposed vacation. It's not an open case. But Rowan was on his way here, so something had his pants on fire. I should shut up. Just shut up.

Petra's jaw locked as she finally said, "Yes, I spoke with Rowan this morning. He'll be here today. But I doubt I'll see him." Petra swallowed. "And as to whether or not I can explain the overlap between my studying alien bugout plans and Rowan doing Russian psyops, I can tell you what's already in the public sphere."

Hawkeye fobbed the doors open and jumped Cooper into the back seat before opening the passenger door for her.

"My team and I are looking at videos in social media feeds. We believe they are being generated by the Russian or the Chinese governments. But honestly, I don't know who is using this precise technique to go after America's mental health." Petra climbed in, and Hawkeye waited by the open door as she finished with, "The research question is: How do you use a social media post to get people to believe things that are obviously nonsensical?"

He held up a finger, shut her door, and jogged around to get in the driver's side. "So, how do you?" he asked as he climbed behind the wheel.

"You might have heard of the author Taylor Knapp and her books *The Unrest* and *The Uprising*?" Petra asked.

"I've read articles about her work and how she's able to frame her novels in such a way that they solidify the 'us against them' narratives. No matter your particular perspective, you're the 'us.' Everyone not of your perspective is the 'them.'"

"That's similar to the kinds of things we've seen in past videos. Recently, the video techniques have changed. We assume it's because people became aware and were less susceptible to the Taylor Knapp brand of psyops—books, music, and video games. Also, AI makes all this so damned simple."

"What are they doing now?" He tapped the GPS coordinate into his maps app. "ETA to the trailhead is ten minutes."

"Fast videos. By fast here, I mean the images and the words are presented quickly. I don't mean shorts. It seems the faster they are, the more effective they are at psyops. You have an influencer—in my world, that's a charismatic."

"Got it." He started the engine and backed out of their spot.

"The influencer says something that is factually true. In the next frame, they say a piece of propaganda. These are shuffled together like red and black cards. Truth then propaganda, truth then propaganda, layering fact and manipulation in quick succession. Now, to be effective, the truth has to be known."

"Got it, I think. But could you take me through an example?" Hawkeye asked.

"Apples grow on trees. The enemies use the apples to transport electronic data collection to your home. Apples have seeds —I'm making this up, by the way."

"Got it. Yes, apples grow on trees. Yes, apples have seeds."

"Those seeds aren't natural. They are put there by the government to be brought into your house and spy on you and your family. We all know an apple a day keeps the doctor away. But you must leave the apples on the store shelf to keep the government away. Apples are full of fiber and are good for your health. But not anymore because the government wants you weak, and so they are using the apples to get to you and your children. Apples are in the stores. Be afraid. You might have given an apple to your teacher as a child. But as an adult, you know the truth. Stay away from the apples! It flashes through the sequence very fast."

Hawkeye looked left and right, then pulled out onto the side road. "That's similar to a sales technique my dad used. He used a series of questions where he knows the answer is yes. You and your wife want to make a wise decision about your vehicle.

Yes. You told me that the most important thing about a vehicle is your family's safety. Yes. You both agree that you would prefer a car with good gas mileage. Yes. And you both want a black car. Yes. And so, it makes sense that you choose this car here because of its safety record, gas mileage, and black color. After saying yes so many times, the customers' brains feed them the next 'yes' as a natural progression, and then he makes the sale. Something like that?"

"He was manipulating the customer with that technique. But it wasn't nefarious or an enemy state trying to undermine the basic tenets of civilization. This is getting the brain to agree with a truth and then be presented with a non-truth. Your dad didn't do that. But to use that example, they try to get the person's brain to think, "I agree, yes, that's right." If the propaganda is inserted too fast for the brain to focus on it, it immediately focuses on another truth. The brain is acquiring that information in a factual string. With repetition, it will be perceived as a fact. It will formidably tie actual facts to the propaganda, so it's hard to untangle once the knot is made and pulled tight. More so when it's a trusted influencer or shared with you by trusted people—friends and family."

"Then what?" Hawkeye asked as he looked down at the GPS.

"Once these non-truths are accepted as truths, they add another layer of non-truth until all the true statements have been dropped one by one, and it's just a string of mind manipulation. Over time, the information is moved from the front part of the brain where executive function and processing live, and it moves to the back of the brain where facts are stored. There, it's no longer analyzed. It is a fact that lives deep in the brain."

Hawkeye flicked on his blinker.

"We go up this road until you hit The Social Club with the

beer-drinking jig and take a left," Petra said. "I came along this route yesterday on the way to the tidepool."

"Beer-drinking jig," Hawkeye sounded that out. "Don't leap around like that, please. Let's stick with the idea that social media videos are made as tools of foreign interference."

"Absolutely. And incredibly dangerous. Let me ask you this, Hawkeye, how hard would it be to change your mind from a known and accepted fact to a truth?" Petra asked.

"I don't know." He reached for his water bottle. "Give me a situation."

"Lincoln wrote the Gettysburg Address—a known fact you were taught. You weren't there. You didn't see it. It's learned from trusted resources, both from people and from writing. What if I came to you and said, 'Hey, look, Hawkeye. I hate to be the one to break it to you, but they were pulling the wool over your eyes. The truth is that we never had a president named Lincoln. In fact, the history books are lying to you because they don't want you to know that the sixteenth president was a woman. Her name was Abigail Melrose, and all mentions of her name, all images in any form, were destroyed by people who didn't want you to know the truth about that time.' Would you believe me?"

"No."

"Sit with that for a minute. What would it take for you to believe me?"

They sat in silence as Hawkeye's face clouded. "Nothing. Nothing you could tell me or show me would make me believe that we've had a female president in the nineteenth century."

"The Lincoln propaganda worked. A society believes in him." Petra held up jazz hands.

"Come on, Petra."

"Obviously, there really was a Lincoln, and obviously, I'm being illustrative with that scenario. But I wanted you to feel your stomach clench as you gripped at your belief and braced against me, telling you that your understanding of the facts is incorrect."

"You're right. It was a physical reaction. I braced." His *haha* sounded strained. "Interesting in a horrible way. And so, what do we do about that kind of foreign manipulation?"

"Throughout history, people who want power must find ways to make others conform. Psychology is easier and cheaper than weapons and bombs. What did America do in the Middle East when it went into Iraq? Shock and awe." Petra shrugged. "The psyops was to make the people think they had no chance against the might of the United States. That's not all. The motto in Vietnam, Iraq, and Afghanistan was 'win the hearts and minds.' The emotions and the thoughts."

Hawkeye exhaled.

"This is a form of that. However, foreign entities aren't trying at all to win the hearts and minds of Americans. They're trying to form fissures and make people doubt that truth exists."

"To what end?"

"A society that isn't cohesive is weak. Remember how we talked about survival of the fittest? Remember how we talked about those who were ostracized would probably die? Add this thought in—"

"Petra, how dystopian is this conversation going to get?"

"Off the charts dystopian. Brace yourself. In my lab, we're also researching how artificial intelligence and the ability to manipulate images and audio mean no one has a solid base to trust truth. Everything can be produced to support any line of thinking. It's going to get harder and harder to know up from down. I predict that this is going to lead to psychological trauma for the entire world. Our brains aren't built to look at everything and interpret whether it's real or an illusion. We'll exhaust ourselves and still never know. Yup, unless laws go into place on a global scale, we are really and truly going to have *serious* mental health issues."

Hawkeye stared out the front window. It looked like he was holding his breath.

"Yeah, this is the kind of fun stuff I think about all day."

"It must be terrifying in your head," he whispered with a quick glance in her direction.

"It can be. But someone has to think about this. Just like with the military, someone has to go outside the wire. Still."

"Yeah, still." He reached for her hand and held it tightly.

Petra had never felt so safe and protected.

If only it could be this easy.

31

———

The rest of their short ride was in silence. Hawkeye wanted to crush Petra's hand in his to hold her so tight that nothing could hurt her.

Was he glad there were brilliant minds quietly at work behind the scenes to figure this out?

Absolutely.

Did he wish Petra were a classical musician or a professor of medieval texts?

No.

Okay, a little.

During his time in the Green Berets, he had a sense of the pressures of protecting a nation. It must feel overwhelming for Petra to be a soldier on a new frontier.

He pulled the car off the side of the road under a tree, shifted into park, and shut off the engine. In silence, he folded the trail map, put it in the side pocket of his EDC—everyday carry—ruck, and opened the door, whistling for Cooper to follow him out.

Cooper bounded over the seat and out the door.

Hawkeye thought maybe he'd leave Petra alone. That conversation obviously got things percolating in her mind, and he didn't want to intrude.

When she walked around to join him, he pointed toward the faint trailhead.

The trees seemed to help. The farther they walked into the dense foliage, the lighter the proverbial cloud over Petra's head.

Finally, she said, "All right, I've been talking a lot about my work. Tell me about yours."

Cooper was off lead and walking to Hawkeye's side. "What do you want to know?"

"Uhm, we're on a search of sorts. Tell me a strange search and rescue story."

"Strange? Okay, I have one. Cooper and I were heading overseas to work with Strike Force, one of the Iniquus tactical teams."

"I know Lynx from that team, but I don't think she travels with them. She's a puzzler." Petra reached for his hand.

To Hawkeye, this gesture seemed natural and automatic.

But he had to remember that they had different brain wiring, and he didn't know how to interpret something even as small as this.

In his mind, people walk hand in hand when they're developing an intimate relationship. But he had a friend, Bruce, who held hands with anyone and all the time. For a hairdresser who was bubbly and a bit feminine, this worked. One day, Bruce asked to hold Hawkeye's hand while walking on a trail at dusk.

Hawkeye admitted it had taken him aback.

Bruce explained that a relatively typical neurodivergent trait was not being completely sure where his body was in space. It was why many neurodivergent people seemed clumsy and bumped into things all the time. It helped him to hold hands.

"I'm like your stability dog, then?" Hawkeye had asked, reaching for Bruce's hand.

Bruce found that hysterical. He said he held hands because he liked to, and he held hands to relieve the stress of walking.

How long had they been friends before Bruce explained that to him? And why had it taken him so long?

Hawkeye could see some challenges ahead as he got to know Petra better.

And he wanted to do both.

He wanted to get to know her better, and he wanted to be challenged.

While Lynx was a puzzler, Petra was a puzzle.

And Hawkeye liked that.

Their holding hands like this? He'd read it as companionable and trusting until she told him more.

And then he realized that, in the most positive light possible, this was a little bit like what Petra had been saying about AI. His neurotypical world and Petra's neurodivergent world overlapped, but what he perceived to be reality wasn't necessarily true.

Yeah, that was a mindfuck.

He'd have to spend time thinking about that and talking it through. But out loud, what he said was, "That's right. Lynx is our puzzler. I haven't quite worked out what that means."

"The search?" Petra asked.

"The search, okay. I'm at the airport. I see that this elderly woman is agitated. I began to wonder if she might be having an episode of disorientation, Alzheimer's, or what have you. Cooper is looking worried." Hawkeye rubbed his thumb between his eyes, "That thing he does with his brows where

Cooper squinches them in with concentration then looks at me to tell him how he should interpret the situation."

"Describe what she was doing," Petra asked.

"She was up and pacing back and forth in the waiting area, wringing her hands and moaning quietly. I'm not sure if there's about to be a medical crisis. I'm looking for anyone associated with her. I lock eyes with a different woman. She says that the woman is upset because her husband isn't there. 'Where is he?' I asked. Turns out they got separated when they were coming through security."

"It happens," Petra said.

"Then I hear a code over the loudspeaker. I recognize it as a missing person. In my view, I watch as workers pull out their radios and listen in. I always say the more eyes, the better. As a matter of fact, when we have a missing child, we don't try to protect the child by keeping things quiet. We get loud, and we get loud fast. We call out everything we know about that child."

"Give me a for instance. What does that mean to you?" she asked.

Hawkeye thought for a minute. "Okay, this isn't something that happened to me, but once Ash and Hoover got sent up to New York as a K9 team to help with a security contract after the protectee family had their non-verbal autistic child take off running. So, this is a hand-me-down story."

"Still," Petra said looking up at him, "what happened?"

Hawkeye noticed that she gripped his hand harder when her eyes weren't going in the same direction as her feet. That was probably why their hand-holding made him think of Bruce. "Knowing the child was at risk for running off, Strike Force practiced what they would say so that they could call the information off in a cadence as they fanned out. Imagine, say, four guys in security uniforms fanning out, calling that there's a— I'm making this up—boy, four years old, black hair, blue shorts, white tennis shoes, non-verbal. They said everyone had their head on a swivel, looking for the child."

"By the road."

"That was the danger, of course," Hawkeye said. "But this big, burly guy had scooped up the boy."

"What?" Petra gasped.

"Good guy. Had a neurodivergent child himself. He's singing all his words and keeping the stress as low as you can imagine. The kid is petting his beard, and when he starts to squirm, the guy tickles him with his beard. He was just an ace guy who would not give the kid over to our team."

"Wait," Petra squeezed his hand as her face flashed up to catch Hawkeye's eyes, "you said good guy."

"The best. He waited for a police officer to get over there to make a hundred percent sure that he wasn't handing the boy over to someone with bad intent. He stood there, singing his conversation and waiting for the officer to give the go-ahead."

"Marvelous. Okay, back at the airport," Petra said, "you wished they were blasting information about the missing husband?"

"Things might have gone quicker. The wife didn't have a photo but said her husband had a cane and a green jacket."

Petra stumbled, and Hawkeye tensed his arm so she could recover her footing.

"So, you went off on your search mission for him?" Petra asked. "Could Cooper get involved?"

"Cooper? Not really. Not unless there was a scent source. What I knew was that the guy was last seen going through security. And unless they arrested him for something, he should only be in one direction. Cooper and I went back to security, and we started there."

"Not knowing what the guy looked like, were you just

walking up to any guy with a cane and saying, 'Hey, do you know where your wife is?'"

"I wasn't looking for a guy or a cane. I was looking for a green jacket. That was the thing that would probably be the most different. So, out on a search, there are various techniques. For example, there are no straight lines in nature. If you see a straight line, it's manmade and might be a clue."

"A stick." She bent over to pick one up and examined it.

"Nope."

She pointed. "Those silk strands of spider webs."

"Have the semblance of being straight."

"Okay, I don't know," Petra gave in, "so I won't argue about it. You're looking for a green jacket, and you found it. Why did you land on that being the thing you'd be looking for?"

"Again, I've trained to conduct searches in all kinds of scenarios. We learned that the eye takes in everything all at once, millions of pieces of information, and your brain can't pay attention to all of it. It has to be selective."

"This is very true. My eyes see my nose all the time, but since it's not moving or doing anything of interest, I don't see my nose."

"Exactly, good, you're with me then. So, I label something that I want to look for."

"I want to look for straight lines."

'Which is true in nature. But in an airport, I can tell my brain to seek out the color green. It's surprising how little green is in the airport."

"Blue jeans, black shirts so no one sees when you spill stuff down your front. Neutrals. You said, 'Brain, find me something green,' and it worked? I'm going to put you back in your search story in just a second." Petra did a little quick step, "I wanted to tell you that I know this theory. When I woke up and got the call from Tamika that she wasn't coming to St. Croix with me, I knew my brain would be looking for all the crappy things that would happen that day—the day of the pseudo-stroke. My brain was primed for crappy. That's the reason why the Romans said they got up on the—"

"Wrong side of the bed." Hawkeye grinned. "Sinister. Exactly. That's exactly how it works on a search. So, looking for green, I came upon an elderly gentleman in a wheelchair."

"Wait." Petra stopped and squeezed his arm. "I thought you said *cane,* not wheelchair."

"*They* said cane. It's funny how people describe things to searchers. Stress is a part of the reason, but let's take your friend, the one who couldn't come along on this adventure."

"Tamika."

"Describe Tamika to me."

"She has long natural hair that forms a cloud of curls. She's about three inches taller than me. She runs, so she still has her track and field body type even though she's in her mid-thirties, like me. She's always put together—makeup, hair. Very vibrant with a big smile and friendly eyes."

"She's sick?" Hawkeye asked.

"Ah, I see what you're saying. If you went looking for the Tamika I described, you'd walk by. And that man's wife described how she knew him, up and using a cane. She would omit the wheelchair because it's temporary. Which is exactly what I did in the hospital when the doctor asked if I was taking medication. In general, I do not. The patch never occurred to me. Continue."

"It's a thing when we look for kids. Under the biggest stress imaginable, can a caregiver remember what their kid was wearing? When we're doing close protection, and the numbers are off, say one protection professional to a family, we take pictures front and back to show people and ask them if they saw that particular person."

"Front and back. I can see why that would be important. Yeah. Only certain kinds of brains have the ability to imagine what the opposite side might look like. And clothes would be easiest to remember, especially when something stands out—a color or design. Like the families you see wearing the same color shirt at the amusement park. If one gets separated, you know where they belong. Brains like that—categorization, recognizable systems."

"They explained to us that it would engage creativity to imagine what the other side of the clothing looked like. And we want the brain engaged in seeing what we're looking for, not draining energy."

"I agree with that. It would cut down on distractibility, false positives, and things like that. The guy who was missing, it sure would have helped find him quicker if someone had said 'wheelchair.'"

"I approached him because he had a green jacket folded on his lap. I introduced myself and asked if his name was Tom. He said yes. I told him his wife was worried because he wasn't at his gate, and he said they just parked him there in the corner."

"Corner?" Petra drew her face into a scowl.

"He was tucked away in a corner—away from the chairs—and in a shadow. It reminded me of someone leaning a broom on the wall out of the way."

"Wow," she whispered. "That's so sad. Thank you for finding Tom. You brought him back?"

"Not quite. I unlocked the brake and started wheeling him toward his wife. Then these two security guards show up. 'Tom, there you are. We found you!' They made it sound like Tom was a naughty child who had run away."

"That's nuts. Why would—ah, for liability. They didn't announce it over the loudspeaker so that it was only their people looking. Acting counter to that gentleman's best interest," Petra's scowl never left her face. "And if some rando in camo shows up with Tom and returns him to his wife, the family could make a stink. Rightly so, I think."

"Rando in camo.'" Hawkeye pronounced the words slowly with a bemused smile. "Is that how you think of me?"

"Until I got to know you better, yes. I don't usually let randos hang out on my bed with camo or without."

"Noted." Hawkeye stopped and grinned at her. They held the gaze for a long, comfortable moment.

When Petra started to look self-conscious, she started walking again. "You let them off the hook?"

"I made a bit of noise because I wanted people to know a civilian found him, not an airport worker. I didn't want to aid and abet their subterfuge. I thought the whole thing was poorly handled. Like you said, they handled it for corporate liability, not for that passenger's safety. Now, I make it a mission to make sure people know that if they have someone they care about in the airport and rely on airport transportation, a wheelchair or cart, they should have a tracker tucked onto a piece of clothing that they wouldn't take off."

"They could have gotten right over to him, and no one needed to suffer. His poor wife."

"My thoughts. Yeah, that kind of sits in my chest sometimes." Hawkeye took a couple of steps. "I have a question for you since we're out wandering through the woods."

"Following a well-worn path," Petra countered. "There's a stove pipe. I think we're—"

Her sentence was cut off when a Rottweiler charged forward.

His energy was coming for Cooper.

While he was doing a lot of barking, he headed toward them at an angle. Hawkeye read that as just wanting to warn Cooper and the strangers off.

"No one mentioned a dog up here," Petra said, moving closer to a tree.

"Problematic," Hawkeye said under his breath.

Even more problematic was that Cooper was out in front of them and lunged forward, his lips pulled back, growling deep in his chest in full grizzly posture.

The dynamic had suddenly changed.

Cooper was the aggressor, going after the other dog.

Hawkeye and Cooper trained for situations like this, but this had escalated too fast to get the right commands out—the Rotti jumped out of nowhere with no warning.

Hawkeye moved his attention momentarily toward Petra to make sure she wasn't going to run in for a rescue. He'd seen crazier things happen.

And now he got it.

While the Rotti had been doing a territorial charge at an angle as a warning, he had been angled toward Petra.

And *that* was not allowed.

As long as the Rotti wasn't backing away, Cooper would defend Petra.

Crouched and foaming at the mouth, scruff raised, focus unswerving, dog fights were dangerous as hell.

Especially with two alpha dogs, each protecting something important to them.

The shrill of a hurricane whistle split the air, and both dogs drew attention toward Petra.

Hawkeye crouched, ready to leap between her and either dog if they decided to charge the noise.

The sound was enough of a break for Cooper to see that Petra was safe and for Hawkeye to catch his attention and get him back to his side.

The Rotti had shied back into the bushes where he watched.

Now, they needed to figure out what to do about the Rotti.

"With all the commotion, if someone was here, you'd think they'd come out and check on this," Hawkeye said.

"If this is the woman's dog and the woman isn't here, I bet he's hungry. Do you have any food or treats in your pack?"

Hawkeye put some food in his hand and started tossing it out, kibble by kibble, praising the Rotti each time he approached the food. Hawkeye stopped praising when he skittered away.

"We may be here for a bit. Our assignment is to make contact with the woman or get into her house and find out if there's a float plan."

"This guy isn't going to allow that." Petra found a stump and sat there. "You don't carry some kind of dog tranquilizer?"

Hawkeye laughed. "I'm sure you're imagining something."

"It would be cool if you had a tranquilizer and a blow gun, and you could just shoot a dart into his thigh. We wait a few minutes until he goes night night."

"Book? Movie?" Hawkeye asked. He hadn't looked her way. He had his eye on that Rotti.

"I'm vaguely thinking of something fedora, whip, jungles."

Hawkeye kept tossing out the food one "good boy" at a time.

It didn't take long. Pangs from an empty stomach and a sense of calm from the intruders meant the Rotti was soon approaching.

When Hawkeye was finally allowed to give the Rotti belly rubs, he asked, "Shall we venture in?"

32

HAWKEYE

While Hawkeye put the Rotti in his crate, filled the food bowl inside, and ensured the bottle of water was full and fresh, Petra was looking at the map Reaper had given him with the assignment.

"When I get back, I'll make sure someone is coming up to take custody of this guy."

"Yes," she said absently.

Next, Hawkeye checked for signs that anyone had been there lately and took a picture of the notes left on the table, which were exactly as expected.

When he was done, Hawkeye checked in. "Okay?"

"This is a path." She pointed at the map.

"Yes."

She drew her finger along the path away from their vehicle. "At the bottom of the path, you choose to go to the tidepool, where I was yesterday, or over here to the boats."

"Your mind is on hypersonic," Hawkeye teased. "Little

curlicues of smoke are coming out of your ears." But she was sending up vibes that honestly sent a crackle of electricity across his scalp.

"The boats – plural – are here." She put her finger just to the south of the tidepool.

He stood silently.

"The tidepool to the boats." She stared at the wall. "Lots of bags. Too many bags for going to a tidal pool. Too many bags. I *saw* all the bags at the car. But I saw one at the tidepool with sunscreen and towels. And Herb was here on this ridge," she pointed to the land between the tidepool and the boat wharf, "away from the family. From this ridge, he could see the boats. Signal them with his bright orange hat? Could that…"

She looked at Hawkeye, who had no clue what she was talking about.

Petra focused back on the map. "And then, right there, the boats. Beans and Lucky were with me, helping Terry. They would have assumed the Johnsons got home some other way. This all could make sense." She turned to find Hawkeye's curious gaze on her. "Hawkeye, can we take a walk down to the boats, please?"

"Are you going to tell me why?" he asked quietly.

"No."

"Is this a case?" He kept his voice very soft. He didn't want to clang around and break her concentration. She was on to some discovery.

"I'm a brain researcher." But she blushed when she said it.

It was evident that with or without him, she'd be walking down that path.

"I guess we're walking to the beach," he said.

Off they went. Single file here where the path was so narrow. Silent.

Petra kept shaking her head. And squinting her eyes. "Colombia?" she murmured.

She reached up to squeeze her temples.

"You doing okay?" he asked.

"Headache."

"I have some pain meds." Hawkeye peeled his ruck off his shoulders. "What helps? Do you want to come back and take the path at a later time?"

"No. I think maybe a distraction." She held out her hand, and he tapped two pain pills onto her palm, still cut and scratched from yesterday. "Thinking other thoughts."

After sliding the meds back into his pack, Hawkeye pulled out a water bottle and handed it to her. "Okay, do you want to pick the topic, or should I?"

"I will," she said, handing the bottle back. "If we were lost in this jungle, could you keep us alive, Cooper, me?"

"Depends on your definition—heart beating, air going in and out? Very likely, yes. If we were in this kind of environment, we'd have to get less choosy about our food source. I'd bring in a snake on a good day."

"And a bad day?" She tried to offer a smile, but it felt weak to him.

"Worms, larvae, some tasty slugs."

"I can imagine getting to a level of hunger where all that would be gourmet."

"On the plane, you said that neurodivergence is highly esteemed in primitive hunter-gatherers," Hawkeye said. "And I've been thinking about why that might be the case. Hunting and gathering are different skills. Did the research explain why neurodivergent people excel at both?"

"I have my own untested theories and would be happy to speculate based on brain science and lived experience."

"I'd be interested." He pulled the ruck back into place, and they started off again.

"Researchers are only now starting to get the funding they need to better understand what's been true of our society since the beginning of time—people are wired differently. Now, we say neurotypical people and neurodivergent people. Primitive societies understand that some people are better at hoeing the ground, pounding the corn, tanning the leather, and making spearheads. And there are others whose efforts benefit their clan in a different way. Finding and honoring what your brain is tuned for and having those expectations of yourself are ways that help neurodivergent people and neurotypical people function as a cohesive and beneficial whole."

As the path opened up, Petra waited for Hawkeye and Cooper to take a step, so they were side by side and she was back holding Hawkeye's hand.

Hawkeye popped his brows and sent her a grin. "Those with micro-amygdala shouldn't look down on people who experience a healthy amount of fear."

"That goes without saying." Her eyes were a funny combination of laughter and pain.

They walked a while in silence, and then Hawkeye redirected her thoughts. "Hunter-gatherers?"

"People who are comfortable don't explore. Those who need a dopamine hit have a chemical push to get them up and searching for something new. That works for both hunters and gatherers—the chemical prod." Petra squeezed her hand around a leaf she was passing, then brought her palm up to her nose to sniff. "It would also be true for the healers who created cures—herbal or otherwise—observation, curiosity, drive to know and understand, test and assess, laser-focused on a specific niche expertise like energy meridians."

"What would happen if I stuck a needle in this guy's foot?"

Cooper stilled, ears on a swivel.

"I wonder how to use this root. I wonder if I can eat that berry. What happens when I prepare it like this and mix these things together?" Petra added.

"I mean, whoever figured out chocolate was a mad genius." Hawkeye pulled a bar from his side pocket and offered it to Petra. Cora had told him chocolate was a dopamine hit that helped her regulate her system like coffee was. That might be true of chocolate for Petra, too.

Petra smiled as she pulled back the wrapper and broke off a couple of squares before handing the rest of the bar back. "Thank you." She took a bite and pointed toward her mouth. "People with neurodivergence often have heightened taste perceptions, which has its good sides and its bad. That tasted so good, thank you."

"If that's true," Hawkeye said, "then exploration isn't just 'what's on the other side of this hill.' It could be 'I'll try that plant, but it subtly tastes of a chemical that made me sick before, better to spit it back out.'"

Petra said, "Which leads me to another unusual trait. Neurodivergent people typically forget to eat or drink throughout the day."

Hawkeye chuckled, "Cora says she isn't hungry until we put food in front of her. Then she's inhaling it like she's been starved for days."

"You ordered pizza that first day after I said I hadn't eaten. Once it arrived in front of me, I realized I was famished."

"Fascinating when you think about all of this big picture." He lifted his free hand in a sweeping gesture. "We were talking Darwin yesterday. When you think about it, yes, not having an appetite until the right time is game-changing. I'm thinking about being on missions where my stomach became a distraction during the boring points, on most long walks, for example.

If you can forget about your stomach, life is that much easier, right? And hunting, how does that play here?"

"A heightened awareness of how systems work, which helps the hunter capture their prey; and heightened attention to details, which helps them—"

"Stay alive while hunting prey," Hawkeye said. "I'm scanning through my brothers and on that piece alone, I'm starting to see patterns of who we relied on—and not to diagnose—but let's just say I have a bit more clarity on who rose in leadership because of elbow rubbing and who rose because their skills kept us safe."

"Right and thinking of the military, there are those who were at the base and those who sought out roles where they'd be far afield. Those who don't mind being away from society to accomplish their tasks. They probably prefer it to some extent."

Hawkeye thought back to all the books he'd read about anthropology, and he wanted to read them again through these new lenses. Petra was right; it took a village. Those who stayed, those who wandered; they had a variety of interests and talents, each doing what they could to keep their community safe—just like in the outposts when he deployed.

Survival of the fittest could very well have meant survival by doing the thing you were fittest to do in a community.

And now he had a good reason to answer that ice-breaker conversation, "Living or dead, if you could have a conversation with anyone, who would it be?" Hawkeye didn't have a go-to answer for that. His answer was usually tied to whatever caught his interest at that moment. Right now, Darwin would be top of the list.

"I'm still thinking about soldiers. Here's another trait," Petra said. "Neurodivergent people often have very high pain tolerance, and when called on in an emergency, they become laser-focused on resolving the crisis. Seemingly pre-trained strategic moves come fully formed into our heads, and sudden super strength."

"I really want you to meet Cora," Hawkeye said, his gaze casting out over the vista, where he could see a flash of blue ocean amongst the leaves as they approached the ridgeline. "I think she needs to hear your perspective on all this. I think my parents would benefit from hearing it, too. My parents did everything possible to ease Cora's life and help her fit in. But they were always told that she had to fight against her disability, which is—from what you're saying—an ability that isn't understood or properly utilized. We're back to the fish climbing a tree meme."

"Teaching someone to mask who they are to make others feel more comfortable and 'fit in'?" Petra used finger quotes. "That's exhausting and leads to burnout—like going to bed for five or six months, barely being able to crawl to the bathroom, being too tired to chew, kind of burn out."

He stopped and turned to her. "That happened to Cora. They said it was chronic fatigue, and they thought it was some virus that did it to her. She was fine. Highly successful at her work, a brilliant surgeon. And then she wasn't. And isn't. She's still brilliant. She's just not able to handle the surgeries anymore."

"Yeah. That's how it happens." Her voice sounded beaten down.

Hawkeye stopped to make sure Petra heard him say this and took it in. If Petra was anything like Cora, she'd be second-guessing every second of the day and finding all the ways that she didn't live up to the moment. "Petra, this whole weekend has been nuts, and you've been amazing."

She blinked at him.

"Not sarcasm—Cora always thinks my compliments are sarcasm. I say this with sincerity. You were remarkable in every way possible."

And instead of saying thank you and accepting his praise, Petra deflected by telling a story.

"Ever since I was a kid, it's like a switch goes off in me. I remember a friend was getting bullied out in the middle of the lake on the diving platform. I remember diving into the water, and the next thing I knew, I had this teenage boy in a hold with his arm locked up behind his back. I knew what word he was saying as I dove in. He hadn't finished the sentence when I had him constrained. Of course, I was in the middle of the lake with this guy's arm behind his back. I didn't have a next action in mind because I never knew I was going to do that first one. And the crisis was over, so the good idea fairy had flown away." She shrugged. "I don't remember how that resolved."

"One of my Cerberus brothers, Ridge, is married to an artist named Harper. She does that. She's moving along, and then her body is in motion, doing heroic things. She's put herself in peril to save lives that way. Often to her great detriment. Her actions have led to complications that have had dire ramifications for her."

Petra let her hand rest on Cooper's head and looked up at Hawkeye.

There it was, that sensation of—the words "hitch" and "coupling" were coming to mind. And Hawkeye could see in his mind's eye how two pieces were brought together and connected. He'd never considered those words and how the physical, tactile meaning was a good representation of their emotional meaning. Like the word "click," he'd thought before.

But the intensity he felt toward Petra wasn't the same energy he was getting back from her. He knew what he wanted —time to get to know her, a relationship that grew warmer and deeper. But he wasn't convinced that Petra was interested in him beyond this weekend and the calming of the hoopla.

Change the energy, change the outcome, a personal truism.

Hawkeye would have a direct conversation with her. Tell her his thoughts, and ask her about hers. Maybe they could do that over dinner.

Standing very still, Petra's gaze focused on the ground.

Petra mentioned that she didn't like surprises, so Hawkeye decided to ask her now if they might talk that through. He wanted her to have time to think, or maybe she didn't need to think. Maybe she'd quickly shut him down. He had to be prepared for that. "I—" he started.

"Shh," Petra yanked his arm. Her eyes flashed up. "Do you hear that?" she whispered.

Before he could answer, her eyes were on the ground again. She was holding her breath.

He didn't hear a damned thing. But after all the doors he'd breached in his career, his hearing was in pretty bad shape.

"There, that." She looked up at him, and seeing his blank expression, turned to Cooper.

Cooper stood rigidly, posture thrust forward, ears rotating then stilling. He obviously heard something, too.

"Could Cooper find it for me?" she whispered.

Turning to look over his shoulder at Hawkeye, Cooper waited for a command.

"Cooper, find it," Hawkeye said, wondering just what they were going to be chasing after.

When Cooper took off through the woods, Hawkeye and Petra raced to keep up.

33

———

PETRA

When Cooper got his order to "find it," things happened fast.

Hawkeye was crashing through the foliage, heading after his dog.

Petra didn't know how these things worked, but she got the general impression that this was not it. She tried to recall what she'd learned about K9 searches. It seemed to her that the dogs would go out sniffing around as a K9 handler walked in the general direction.

If the dog found something, they'd hustle back to their person and signal them. Then they'd track to the spot.

But that was a scent, wasn't it?

Was there a different technique if a dog was going after a sound?

To be fair, Hawkeye didn't hear it.

And Petra wasn't sure what it was she'd heard. Injured animal? Local bird?

She'd never heard that sound before. The cry was unmusical. It didn't repeat in the same way any of the three times she heard it.

And there was that essence to it—that quality of "call to the universe."

Melissa had done that yesterday when she'd stood on the rocks. She'd been holding hands with Terry one moment, a wave came and snatched him from her the next. She saw his head in the sea. Then he was gone. She was sure that gone meant *gone*.

And Melissa's calling to his soul was what brought Petra to the scene.

That event reminded Petra of the time she was in Hawaii on a perfectly beautiful day. She was looking over the cliff. The Pacific was like a lapis lazuli below her. Gorgeous.

When the group was called over to eat, Petra turned and as she stepped forward, she knew something unexpected was happening, but didn't have time for her brain to process. It felt like a water giant reached out its wave hand and tried to snatch her off the cliff. Her then-husband reached out and grabbed the camera strap that was around her neck, and that was enough of a counterbalance that Petra didn't plunge backward over the cliff to her death.

So even though he was a shithead, he did ostensibly save her life. Yes, she was glad to be alive, but still, she wished that wasn't part of their shared history.

She didn't really want to remember that day.

Or her ex.

But after yesterday, it was inevitable.

Not every relationship was like her marriage. Sometimes people could be mutually respectful and caring.

She certainly didn't have to think that if she tried for a relationship with Hawkeye, it would be destined for pain and grief.

What did he call her? Amazing. Remarkable.

That had been her experience with him. *I mean, here he is chasing through the dense rainforest with no clue what he's going after because I heard a noise.*

"Oh shit," Hawkeye said, coming to an abrupt stop. "Petra, maybe you need to—"

He stepped out of the way, reaching for Petra and guiding her forward.

There, on the ground, lay a little girl. Curled into a ball, she used an exposed root as a pillow of sorts. There on her neck was a bright red welt. The same welt Petra had seen at the tide-pool when the child had yanked her necklace off and tossed it seaward. This was the Johnsons's daughter.

This was not one of the scenarios Petra had envisioned and offered to Rowan, who was probably about to land in St. Croix with two fellow FBI special agents all because of the picture of that necklace.

Petra swallowed down her emotions. "Hello, sweetheart. Do you remember me? I met you the other day when you and your mommy were at the tidepool."

The child didn't turn toward Petra but scowled ferociously at Hawkeye. Anger and fear filled her eyes. Her body was fierce. She was a tiny warrior in a mud-covered bathing suit.

"My name is Petra. What's your name?" She took a step closer.

The child focused on Cooper who stretched out as a barricade between her and Petra.

Petra thought Cooper was using his body to give the child a sense of safety from the adults. But he was doing it strategically. He wasn't guarding her. If Petra reached for the child, it would be allowed.

Cooper's origin story came to mind, how he stopped Hawkeye's truck and kept the baby on the blanket. Cooper seemed to know what a youngling needed.

Petra would defer to Cooper and stay on this side of his body barricade.

"Where are your brothers?" Petra slowly lowered herself until her butt was on the ground.

"She has brothers? How many children are we talking about?" Hawkeye handed Petra his water bottle.

"It was a family of five," she said as she unscrewed the top. "And older brother maybe six or seven. And younger brother maybe three or four?" Petra showed the bottle to Cooper, then stretched it past him to set it down beside the child. "Parents in their mid-to-late-thirties."

Hawkeye shifted to the side and started inspecting the foliage and the dirt. Petra assumed he was looking for tracks.

Petra pulled her knees to her chest, wrapped her arms around her legs, and, in this position, remained perfectly still.

Just like earlier with the Rotti, Petra wanted to give this child a moment to acclimate. After all, two adults and a dog had burst through the foliage.

Something traumatic had obviously happened to this child between this moment and the last time Petra had seen her without her necklace on the cliff.

Did this have something to do with her necklace being missing?

Petra looked through her lashes as she scanned the child's body. There were no marks or bruises that looked like blows. Mostly, she was filthy, and her hair was wild with debris.

She had two white rivulets where her tears had cut through the dirt on her face, and her eyes were red and swollen from crying.

"What are we doing, Petra?" Hawkeye asked, his voice warm and low. He stood away from them, seeming to have taken the "who do you want in the woods, a man or a bear" responses from women quite seriously as he kept his distance.

"Did you find tracks?" she asked in return.

"They're single barefooted tracks that go on for a short distance. I don't want to go farther right now."

Petra pulled out her phone but before she looked, Hawkeye said, "No bars, no satellite."

She turned back to the child and showed her the photo from the day before. "That's you at the tidepool. There's your little brother. Did you hike out here with your brothers?"

The child glanced at the phone with disinterest. There was no spark of recognition. No *"Where is my daddy?"* Instead, she scooted closer to Cooper and threw a leg over him as she clung to his ear.

A thumb went into her mouth.

Call-back to self-soothing as a baby?

"You're out in the woods. Can you tell me how you got here?"

Nothing.

Petra was done pestering the child. These questions obviously weren't going to give her the answers she wanted. The child needed a hospital. The authorities needed to track down her parents.

Could the parents have left her behind purposefully if they were leaving the country?

Wow, that was a dark thought.

Sure, if Petra was making up a story about that, the family could have decided this was the throw-away child. They left her to be found, dead or alive, to further the story that the family had succumbed to some terrible event. No reason to look for their live happy bodies doing the rumba in South America.

That was how they'd treated her, like a black sheep. Kind of the outcast. And looking back, that could be why the child looked at her mom with abhorrence and why she'd dragged off the necklace.

Another crazy idea was that the child pulling off her necklace meant she was going outside of some teachings of "the bigger family' the mother had talked about. And so, she was dismissed from the fold.

But Petra would quickly admit these scenarios, while possible, were probably outlandish.

She, in fact, had no idea what was going on.

Petra slowly stood and moved toward Hawkeye. "I think she's in shock. Her brain should have had her drinking that water I set out without thought. Her skin is obviously dehydrated. She needs medical attention. I'd pick her up and take her to the SUV, but I'm worried about the brothers. If we take her, are we leaving them?"

Hawkeye crouched down, posting a knee and sitting on his heel. He pulled out the map. "We're right about here." He pointed to the map. "Another hundred yards, and I could come out by the sea here. If I don't have cell reception, I have my sat phone. Do we move her with us is the question."

"We'd be moving her farther from the shelter and supplies at the cabin as well as from your SUV if we need to transport." Petra turned her head from left to right. "The boys might be around here somewhere."

"Do you feel comfortable staying with her if Cooper is here to guard the situation? I can get orders."

"I think orders would be very helpful here. So would getting some medical personnel involved. I don't know what's going on right now, but her body responses are not normal."

Hawkeye slid the map into his ruck, "Let's be clear here, Petra. Nothing about this is normal."

34

Hawkeye

There was a lot going on behind the scenes, and Hawkeye sure would be glad to know what the hell it was and when it all started.

Petra's friend Tamika had to be Tamika Bradly. How many Tamikas were there in the world?

Tamika Bradly was FBI.

Petra Armstrong, FBI, was here making phone calls, flagging something she saw.

Rowan Kennedy was on the way here. FBI.

Rowan was a specialist. He wasn't jumping on a plane racing to St Croix for anything trivial.

Petra said she wasn't working.

Did Hawkeye believe her?

Absolutely. Yes.

The girl hugging the tree root. Now, that was a head-scratcher.

No matter the finger-pointing on the map, no matter the

mumbling under her breath about the number of bags, the look of shock on Petra's face when she saw that child was genuine. The girl's appearance was unexpected.

What had Petra seen on the map that made her want to get eyes on?

Did any of it matter?

Possibly.

Hawkeye wasn't at all sure that leaving Petra in the woods with a child—whom she'd protect—and Cooper—whom she didn't know how to command—was the best idea.

The choices weren't great. Sometimes, you had to do the thing that felt right.

The wind was picking up now. The foliage thinning out. A few more steps and there it was, a glimmer of blue. He'd made it to the top of the rise.

No phone bars. But a satellite overhead.

"Reaper, it's Hawkeye. We've got a situation." It took a moment to spell it out. All of it. Our subject, Molly McBeth, was *not* in the cabin. Her dog had been angry and famished but was now contained in a crate. He mentioned Petra's job, the phone calls, that Rowan was en route, that Petra seemed like she was trying to disengage, but something about the map made her want to check something out. But that was all background information. The issue was that there was a child alone in the woods in a muddy bathing suit who was conscious but non-responsive, and the possibility that there were two other children in harm's way.

"Given the situation on the island and emergency services slammed," Hawkeye concluded. "I'm looking for next steps."

"Is this an FBI op?" Reaper asked. "Are we stepping on toes? Obviously, we help the girl. But are we walking into a sting and messing something up if we continue with a lost-person search?"

Hawkeye stabbed a hand onto his hip. "Those are my questions."

"Let me work the phones and get a plan together," Reaper said. "Hang tight. Out."

Hawkeye sat on the boulder letting his booted feet dangle over the side. He had made it to their original destination, the wharf that Petra had pointed out on the map.

There was a single white boat tied to a cleat.

Molly McBeth docked her boat down there. But they said the name of her boat was *The Salty Margarita.*

That the slips were empty made sense; the island boaters were out on search and rescue.

Why the one boat?

There was no activity around the boat. No tell-tale anything other than it looked like it was in consistent use. Nothing was covered in canvas, protected against the weather.

Hawkeye lifted his field glasses to scan along the way, looking at the tidepool where Petra had clung. Seeing the rocks where Lucky had grabbed her hair to save her, seeing how she would have climbed over to find a screaming Melissa, it was tough terrain and desperate circumstances.

Her stories from yesterday were harrowing.

Had he left her in danger again today? Hawkeye thought they'd be taking a walk in the woods when he volunteered for this assignment.

Hawkeye continued to scan for anyone out and about, for anything to give him information.

But the tide was gently rolling onto the beach with a whoosh and a slosh that soothed the soul and was antithetical to his present purpose. *Come on, Reaper.*

As if on cue, the sat phone rang.

"Go for Hawkeye."

"Reaper here. Okay, we have a plan. Here's the dilemma,

they have no hands available. The concern is that the child suffered internal injuries, and that's why she's non-responsive. We want you and Petra to take the girl back to the cabin."

"I could get the girl to the SUV. Petra could take the girl to the hospital, and I can continue the search." Hawkeye pushed his field glasses into his ruck. "We're burning daylight, and the wind is pulling the scent cone for backtracking to possibly find her brothers or her whole family, for that matter."

"We considered that," Reaper said. "If it was a single lost person, we'd have Petra bring the child on in. But if you find one of the brothers and that brother is injured, you'd be stuck there without comms. Looking at the time statistics, you're right at the twenty-four-hour mark where there's a ninety-eight percent chance of survival. Each hour from here on, that drops the chance. By this time tomorrow, we're looking at a thirty-three percent chance the boys are alive."

"If they're even missing."

"Hawkeye, if it was only the girl who was missing," Reaper said, "we'd have a police report and frantic parents. No one's heard anything about a single missing child. As soon as Cerberus gets back from their mission, they'll join in the search. The authorities have posted that the Johnson family still has two missing adults and two missing children. Do you think Petra is willing to help?"

"I can almost guarantee it. Hey, there's a single boat here where Molly McBeth ties up her boat. This craft is seaworthy. The name is *Chill Out*. Do you want to document that in case it turns out to be interesting?"

"Documented," Reaper said. "Call in if this plan isn't a go. The nurse is en route with three volunteers to help with the extraction. She hikes that area and is familiar with it. You can consult with her if you have any questions about the terrain. She's bringing two of our wilderness medic bags. One for her to use as she stabilizes the child, one for you and Petra as you continue the search."

"The girl is covered in mud," Hawkeye stood and pulled the ruck strap over his shoulder. "Should we clean her up?"

"She might be part of a crime scene," Reaper said. "The hospital will need to do forensics on her, DNA under her finger-nails, for example. Touch her as little as possible."

35

PETRA

Sitting in the lost woman's cabin, the relief Petra felt when Cooper sat up and perked his ears was immense.

Whether this was Molly coming home safely or the nurse who volunteered to come package the child—yes, as long as it was one or the other—that was great.

But then her mind flashed with other possibilities, and Petra found herself scooping up the child, fast asleep, cocooned in one of Molly's blankets, and dashing to the bathroom.

"Petra?" Hawkeye had jumped to his feet.

"Someone's coming. I don't know friend or foe. I'll hide with the child until you figure it out."

"I figured it out. The woman is in scrubs, and they're carrying Iniquus wilderness medical cases."

When Petra came out of the bathroom, Hawkeye was standing angled at the window like a soldier. Could have been habit, might also be that she'd spooked him.

He caught her eye. "Good call to grab and go. Better safe than sorry."

The nurse came in, "Oh, she's tiny." She called over her shoulder. "If she doesn't have broken bones, I don't think we need the gurney, guys. Let's just take turns holding her if she's asleep. Can you sit down for a minute?" she asked Petra. "I want to do a quick physical and take a history."

"No history. We found her. Called it in. You showed up." Petra said. She was agitated because the boys were still missing. An enormous internal pressure swelled her veins, trying to force her into the woods with Cooper to start the search.

The nurse sent her a look of curiosity. But seemed to make an internal decision when Hawkeye didn't offer anything of any kind. After listening to the child's heart and checking her temperature, searching for bruises, bites, or other telltale signs, the nurse stood and signaled one of the men to pick up the child. "Thanks for making the find and calling it in," she said, and they all filed out.

"I was rude," Petra whispered.

Hawkeye hooked an arm around her and pulled her to his chest, kissing her hair. "Yeah, I'm worried about the boys, too. I'm all packed up. How about you use the bathroom, and we'll leave?"

That was two hours ago.

Now, the sun was starting to sink.

The sky was filling with bats.

Cooper was a machine. With his pink tongue hanging long, Hawkeye had to physically stop Cooper from searching to sit and rest and try a sip of water.

She didn't know what happened with the search once it got dark, but as the light dimmed, so did Petra's ability to tell where her body was in space. With the shadows and dark spots, Petra was tripping more frequently.

Soon, she'd be a liability.

Her plan was that if she fell, that would be her clue that her time of being a help was over. She'd just walk toward the sound of the sea, find a beach, and walk until there was a way to get back to the hotel. Nothing was but so far on this tiny island.

It was important that her disabilities did nothing to interrupt Hawkeye and Cooper's finding the boys.

But now, something was different.

Petra had to remind herself to breathe. They were close; she could feel it in her body.

Hawkeye said his ears got messed up during his time in the military. He probably couldn't hear the changes in the sounds of Cooper's travel patterns. From what Petra heard, she would surmise they were homing in on something.

When Cooper changed again, moving slower, feeling things out, Petra reached out and grabbed Hawkeye's arm.

When Hawkeye stopped, she stood on her toes to whisper in his ear. "Cooper found something he doesn't like. Do you want to recall him silently and let him take you in quietly until we know what we're dealing with?"

"Are you psychic?" he whispered with a bewildered look.

"Not in the least," Petra said. "I'm listening to him."

Within minutes, Petra, Hawkeye, and Cooper were crouched outside a hillside house.

Hawkeye was surveilling the situation with his field glasses. He lifted to speak into her ear. "I see three adults. A fighting-age male is brandishing a gun. An adult couple is tied to a column. Two young boys are playing with a ball in the yard."

"Well, shit," Petra whispered, then stuck a finger in the air as Cooper perked his ears. "There's a car coming," she said.

An off-road vehicle with the fabric top folded down popped over the ruts and roots and found its way to a stop.

Petra and Hawkeye moved closer. They inserted the earbuds for Hawkeye's parabolic ear, so they could hear what was said.

The guy with the gun came out and leaned onto the hood. "What's happening down there?" the house guy asked,

"It couldn't be better. Lots of boats are missing, people. It's a mess. Also, there've been people over at Molly's house."

"Her boat didn't come in yesterday," house guy said. "Was it supposed to?"

The car guy reached for a bag and dragged it to him. "The letter on the table said she was out for a day cruise. I bagged up everything that was edible. She likes the vegan crap, so it wasn't much."

"Do we go?" house guy asked. "Do we not go?"

"I called the Prokhorovs for instructions. The issues all over the Caribbean make this so much easier. But since Molly's missing, this area is going to get attention. I told them our boat was the only one in the slip, and people might wonder why it's not out helping. They said to wait until ten or eleven o'clock and head out as planned. The Coast Guard and searches will be happening north of us."

Prokhorovs? Wow. Well, now Petra knew why Rowan and two other members of his joint task force were headed to the island.

"Are we going to do *it*?" house guy asked.

"Get this guy's money? Hell to the yeah, I am. You do what you want. But if you help, we get half in your Bitcoin account, half in mine. Get down to Panama, sell the boat. Go off in the world."

"But if we have the money, why are we putting up with the family?" house guy asked. "We get the money and move on."

Car guy was twirling his keychain on his finger. "Because you're an idiot. What's happening down there?" He lifted his chin toward the boys kicking the ball.

"Parents are still tied. I let the kids run around in the yard for a bit. They're kids."

"So first, what happens if we go and we don't take them?" car guy asked. "They're here, and they tell the cops about us. We're fugitives instead of them being the fugitives. Right now, they're not breaking any new laws. Second, the Prokhorov family paid us to do a job."

"So?" house guy asked.

"So, the Prokhorovs can't let someone off the hook, even a small fish like us. If they let us off the hook, everyone thinks they can come and go as they like. We deposit the family as we said we'd do. We never said we'd deposit them as anything other than healthy. I never said a word about depositing them as wealthy. That's a separate transaction, as far as I'm concerned." Car guy stopped talking for a moment. "Hey, I'm only counting two kids."

"What?" house guy asked.

"There are three kids. I'm only counting two." Car guy motioned toward the yard.

"The house guy looked into the vehicle and held very still. "I thought you had the girl."

"What do you mean you thought I had the girl?" car guy yelled. "I told you to watch the family."

"But you were gone. The girl was gone," house guy whined. "I don't know what gets your freak on, man. You want the girl? Take the girl. Not my thing, but you do you."

There was a smack. "Are you telling me you don't know where the girl is?"

"Ow shit, don't do that." House guy was rubbing his arm. "I don't know where the girl is."

The car guy ran to the house.

Hawkeye leaned to her ear and whispered, "Do you know who the Prokhorovs are?"

"Yes," Petra said. "They're not my monkeys and certainly not my circus."

He caught her eye. "It's Rowan's circus, though?"

Petra shook her head. "I can't speak to that."

"Got it. And you saw something that tied this family to the Prokhorovs and sent up a bat signal?" Hawkeye asked.

"I did no such thing. This is all very much different than what I had imagined." She held up a hand to signal that she was listening. It was harder to hear with the men inside, but the parabolic ear—that Hawkeye carried on searches to help him locate people who were calling out—was, in fact, very helpful.

"Where's the girl? Where's the girl?"

They heard fist to flesh and Jenny crying out.

"She's a child. I have no idea. Children get things in their minds."

The next bit was garbled. The men talked over each other, sometimes screaming at the parents, sometimes hissing softly. "We're so deep into the trees that a child has no chance of finding her way out. If you helped her to escape, you only sent her to a painful death from dehydration, hunger, and animals. If you think it's a good idea to try to get another child out, they'll die just as badly."

Then the car guy was yelling at the dad about finding a WiFi signal at dark. They would be transferring his Bitcoin monies to the men's Bitcoin wallets.

"But how will my family live? That's all we have." Herb sobbed.

"Yes, well, at least you will live, right?" the car guy said. "Then we'll take the boat and get you to Panama. Your mule will take you to Columbia from there."

"With no money, we won't survive. Leave a little in pity for the children." Jenny was begging.

Hawkeye signaled to Cooper to keep quiet, and the three backed deeper into the foliage.

"What's the play Petra?"

"We use the sat phone to call Rowan and dump this onto his plate."

It was a quick relay of information and GPS pins, then the three—Petra, Hawkeye, and Cooper—were right back in their spot, watching and listening, waiting for the FBI team to show up.

It felt like a very long time.

The house was eerily quiet. Nothing was coming over the parabolic ear.

In the last of the daylight, the kidnappers were back by their vehicle.

"Stop it and listen. When you take guy to a Wi-Fi signal and get the money, take the gun." From her angle, Petra couldn't see who was speaking to whom.

"Man, if I end up shooting him, it's murder. Right now, I'm doing some Robin Hood shit, stealing from a robber baron to feed the poor—me."

"Shoot him in the leg."

"You think I'm a good enough shot to shoot a running person in the leg? Dude, I've never shot a gun before."

"Then let him run. We have his wife and kids. We tell the Prokhorovs that the guy ran off with the girl. We're supposed to transport them, not jail them. Yeah, I know we've got them tied up, but you know what I'm saying."

Cooper signaled, and moments later, Rowan came squat-walking through the foliage.

After a quick update from Hawkeye, Rowan said. "Okay, you two, you're done here. My team and I will handle it." He touched the gun at his hip.

Petra blinked at him.

"You and Hawkeye need to eat, hydrate, and decompress. Petra, you've done amazing work. You're done here. This isn't for you."

Yeah, hostage rescue wasn't part of Petra's skillset. She moved to go.

"Hey," Rowan whispered. "Not a word to anyone. This is an active mission." Rowan caught Hawkeye's gaze. Hawkeye gave an affirmative nod.

"Off we go," Petra mumbled when they were well out of earshot, "to have a relaxing evening." She turned back to the house with a deep frown. "As if that could really happen."

Hawkeye took her hand, and they walked away from the kidnapped children to get themselves something to eat.

It felt *so* wrong.

36

___

PETRA

They didn't feel like going far.

Exhaustion wasn't enough of a word to explain how her body felt. Neurodivergent burnout didn't quite cover it either. And she was too tired to find a more appropriate descriptor.

She didn't want to eat at all, chewing felt like it would take too much energy, but Hawkeye insisted. He also wanted her to sit outside and see the stars so she could calm her mind before she tried to sleep.

So here they were.

With pre-made picnic boxes from the fridge by the front desk, they'd wandered outside and down the wharf where they sat, dangling their feet above the water.

"I've always heard of fight, flight, or freeze. But you have fight, flight, or chill. I don't know that I've ever seen anyone respond like you in a crisis before." Hawkeye pulled his sandwich from the box and unwrapped it.

"Fight, flight, freeze, but for women, there's a fourth and a fifth, fawning and fine. Women have a human bomb in front of them, tick, tick, ticking. There's no way to run away or freeze." She spread her hands wide. "How would that serve?"

"Fawning." He seemed to be trying on the word for the first time.

"Smiles, laughs, placating language."

He shook his head.

"When women are near dangerous men, they aren't smiling because they're happy. They're not laughing because they find the situation funny. They're placating, emotionally petting the man interacting with them—someone known or a stranger. A hurt ego is dangerous. Violence is always possible."

"So, when I turn to a woman, she's smiling at me—" Hawkeye said.

"You're huge and solidly muscled. What chance would a woman have against you even if she were a trained fighter? I'm a trained fighter. I'd never go up against you. I'd fawn."

"With me? Have you done that?" he asked with a look of shock and disquiet.

"No." Petra unwrapped her sandwich and lifted the bread to see what textures were underneath. "But I have friends who vouched for you. And our mutual friends would hold you accountable if anything happened to me at your hands."

His brows came in tight.

"If you'd just stepped into my sphere and started chatting me up, and I knew nothing about you? Yes, I'd fawn out of self-protection. Few women wouldn't. You're an unknown quantity."

He took a bite of his sandwich and thought about that while he chewed. "I've heard that before from my female friends that the most dangerous thing in a woman's life is a man."

"What do you think is the biggest danger to a man?"

"Stupidity?" He shrugged.

"By that, I think you mean taking irrational chances and pushing things too far?"

"Yes." He opened his bag of chips and angled them toward her, so she knew she was welcome to share.

"I guess you're living with that on the daily in your career. But you're trained to do it. And that's the difference between danger and stupidity."

"Fawning," Hawkeye said again, but this time, it was like he was tumbling the idea around. "So, I can't trust a woman's smiles to mean they think they're having a pleasant exchange. They may be frightened. Wow. That's difficult to swallow. I mean, if I'm turning to speak to a human being near me, and they happen to be female, how would I know if they thought they were in danger?"

"I doubt you're saying things to a stranger like, 'You're beautiful.' Or 'Can I buy you a drink?' Or other smarmy things?"

"I don't know that I never did that. But usually, I talk to people more conversationally."

"And if they were saying I'm not interested, I came here to have a quiet meal and read?"

"Obviously, that's clear communication they don't want to engage in a conversation with me. 'Have a nice night.' Move on."

"Dog handler," Petra said, taking a bite from her cheese and veggie sandwich.

"What?"

'You're a dog handler." She held her hand over her mouth so he wouldn't see her half-chewed food. "No means no when you train your dog." She swallowed. "You thoroughly under-stand the concept. Good on you that you can extrapolate that out, and you know that when women say that to you, it's the same thing."

"That's kind of you to say. But at the same time, I don't think you can apply that as a blanket truism to all dog handlers. Let's just say when they're not with their dogs, they might not act as upstanding, and now that I'm pulling up pictures, I'm remembering episodes where I've witnessed fawning. I don't know what to say. It feels like a 'sorry' should slide in here, but it doesn't make any difference to the grand scheme."

Petra sighed.

"Fight, flight, freeze, fawn, go to the fifth one you said, fine. What's that one?"

"It's that it doesn't occur to you at the moment that there's a danger where it's possible that if you acted like there was a danger, it wouldn't be dangerous." Petra heard that tumble of words and even she wasn't sure they made sense.

"Nope," Hawkeye said. "I'm not going to try and untangle that sentence."

"I'll give you an example. I went to Alaska. I had a bucket list item I thought I might try to check off. I wanted to see a mama bear catch a salmon and feed it to her cub."

"Wow." He laughed. "That's oddly specific."

"I know, right?" Petra smiled. "It got into my imagination that I really wanted to see this happen. When I found an Alaskan cruise on sale for next to nothing and only four days long, I twisted my friend Tamika's arm, and she came with me for the cruise. She stayed on the boat. I went out on a bear walk. Two hundred dollars, no guarantee that you'd see a bear."

"Worth it."

"Absolutely." Petra took a bite of pickle. "We're walking down the path, and we see a black bear, fat and happy, getting ready to go into hibernation. He's off in the distance. We walk a little further, and there's another black bear waddling her fat bottom in and out of the bushes."

"You're down on a path in sight of black bears?"

"There's a wooden walkway fairly high above the ground," Petra explained. "There are two bear guides with us, though their depth of bear behavior knowledge was pretty low. Imagine the kind of young man who would bag your groceries. The only reassuring thing about either guy was that they each had a car flare taped to their chest, ready to deploy. Apparently, it's the smell and not the flame that's the deterrent."

"Interesting," Hawkeye said, then creased his brow.

"What was that thought?" Petra asked.

"We practice in the forests around Northern Virginia, black bear country, as you know."

Petra nodded. "Easier to get to, but no salmon."

"True. But we have different ways of dealing with bears if we see them. It mostly means being aware and minding our own business while we sing a song or talk out loud, so the bear is aware of us and knows we're not looking for a fight."

"It's *fine*, move along," Petra said.

"Ah. I'm getting it now. So, bears in Alaska…"

"We were walking on the path and spotted a cub lying in the sun, balanced belly-down on the railing. So cute. He was there for a while, and nobody saw his mom. Finally, he gets down, and we see him wander away. I turned around the bend and went to the railing to see down. There I am, face to face—I mean, feel her exhale on my skin kind of face to face—with this mama bear. Her cub is by her side."

Hawkeye pulled the potato chip away from his mouth. "Shit!"

"Nah. I saw that mama bear and said, 'Hey, mama, you're doing a mighty fine job with your cub. I'm so proud of you.' The mom looks at me like – I agree, thanks for noticing, and she and the cub lumber off."

He ate the chip. Then another. And a third. "That could have gone so badly."

"She could have eaten my face. Easily. But I didn't send off any scared vibes. She didn't feel any danger from me. We were good. And guess what?"

"No clue."

"I saw her by the river about fifteen minutes later, and she pulled a salmon from the water and fed it to her cub."

Hawkeye gave Petra a high five. "Congratulations." He ate another chip. "I have a question for you. I'm leaping a cavern to a whole new topic."

"Leap away," Petra said.

"Actually, it's not such a leap," Hawkeye corrected. "I was thinking about this because of the fawning topic when I was asking if I could buy a lady a drink."

"Okay."

"Is there a scientific way to know if a person is your person?" Hawkeye asked.

"Wouldn't it be nice if there were a blood test for love? 'I see, Miss Armstrong, that your blood is saturated in X and Z. Congratulations. May you live happily ever after.'" Petra looked out to sea as she said that.

Her brain was busy.

Hawkeye waited.

"That was flip," she turned back to him. "You want a real answer."

"I would, if you don't mind."

She nodded. "I think this goes back to the word crush. You used it the other day. Some people have an experience where, because of an emotional connection, life seems bright and shiny. They think, oh, this is what the poets were writing about. This is how it happens in the movies. This is real. And then the light switches off, and you almost hate the other person because the joy you felt feels like it was stolen from you?"

"That second part I've never experienced. I'm referring to the first part."

"Yes," Petra said, "that's just chemistry."

"Literal chemistry—not like the phrase 'we just had good chemistry.'"

"Is there a difference?" Petra asked.

"I don't know." Hawkeye rubbed his thumb along his jaw. "I feel like we might be in an odd loop here."

"Okay, let me take a stab at answering you, and then you tell me if I'm off the mark. I'm approaching this first part from the perspective that one person in the relationship is either a psychopath, a sociopath, or someone who survived a high-trauma childhood. When you're with this person, and you feel seen and appreciated and cared for, you feel safe. The conversation flows. You are glowing."

"Okay."

"Now, walk away. The new love went home. You're left standing in your living room alone. How do you feel in the following minutes, hours, and days? What do you feel after you've had some space from this person? Are you depleted? Do things seem grayer? Do you relive your time together and have bad feelings about how things went? Places where you felt unease? You see, a manipulator will have figured you out. They are experts at it—cult leaders reign supreme in this way. What they're giving you chemically is dopamine."

"Dopamine, okay."

"It's one of the reasons why, in a cult," Petra said, "you need to be kept away from others, kept close, and continually fed the dopamine so you constantly glow."

"They know they're doing this?"

"Some do. Cult leaders do," Petra said. "Survivors of childhood trauma aren't as aware. Their goal is to keep things calm and stay on the good side. It's a safety measure, not malevolence. Think of it this way: there are people who kill for a living —you did, I have to assume. People who kill without moral impetus are psychopaths. People who kill for the greater good —the security and protection of their clan—are warriors. The reason for the kill is defined by whether we, as a society, think of them as good or bad."

"Got it." He took a swig from his water bottle and then set it down on the rough wood. "Psychopaths are bad. Survivors get our sympathy. Security gets our gratitude."

"What happens if you walk away from the dopamine rush?" Petra asked with her hand over her mouth to hide the bite she'd taken from her sandwich. "You crash. You feel bad. If you want the dopamine back, you seek out that person again."

"Like an addiction." He leaned forward. "Cooper, leave it," Hawkeye said as a fish jumped from the water and Cooper pushed up to a crouch.

Petra grinned at Cooper, then reached for a potato chip in Hawkeye's bag. "It can very much be like an addiction. Again, the cults want you to need that hit, so you do what's necessary to feel good. Now, on the other hand, you walk away, and when you think back on your time together, you still feel warm and fuzzy."

"You think back, not only was it good then, but you feel positive and happy in the now," Hawkeye said. "Life feels good."

"That's oxytocin and serotonin—those are the connection chemicals."

"The tell is that you shouldn't feel desperate to get back to them." He chucked the last bite of his sandwich toward a gull, pecking along the rocks.

"Be a little careful with that last sentence. You can miss someone and look forward to seeing them soon. It's more that you're not—"

"Depleted and looking for a refill. Not an addict looking for a high. There's no crash between."

"It's a good indicator," Petra agreed. "It's not a litmus test. But to answer your original question, 'Is there a scientific way to know if a person is your person?' That's the best answer I have."

"Check the chemical reaction. I like it." He smiled and brushed the hair from her face, gently tucking it behind her ear before he bent in to kiss her. Holding there, he whispered. "And I like you—the serotonin oxytocin kind of like." He sat up to see her reaction.

Her reaction was joy.

"That's one of the most romantic things I've ever heard." She scooted closer, tucking into his arm. "Thank you. I serotonin oxytocin like you, too." Petra cuddled into him, his warmth radiating into her. Then she reached over to play with his fingers, resting on his opposite thigh. "Do you want a significant relationship in your life, or are you good?" She ventured.

"I've always considered myself a man who should be a husband."

"That's an interesting way to phrase it. You seem to be a man who sets a goal and reaches it—Green Beret, Cerberus Tactical. Of course, personal and professional aren't the same. So how is it you're not married?"

"Here's how I saw it," He rubbed a finger under his nose, looking up as he formed his thoughts. "The person I could devote myself to was out there, just not 'out there.'" He chuckled. "Not out there as in woo-woo. I think the kind of person I wanted to be with isn't in the places where people meet for the dating scene."

"Apps," Petra said, slipping Cooper a bit of cheese.

"Apps. Bars. Dance halls. I'm not into the party scene. I always thought that my person was probably at home playing with her animals, doing her hobbies, having friends over, going out hiking on the weekends." He turned and captured her chin in his fingers as he smiled at her.

Petra liked the warmth in his eyes and the genuineness of the crinkles at the corners.

"See I was right. And, of course, I needed Cooper with me so he could give his stamp of approval. The universe needed to put me in the right place at the right time."

"So that was the universe at play, the whole thing on the plane?" Petra asked.

"I imagine as an FBI special agent, you're not putting all your deets out for the public to see. The universe took some time to figure out how to put us in the same place, under the right circumstances that we got a chance to know each other a bit."

"Good of the universe to finally get the job done. I used to think of myself as a woman who should be a wife. I was even married for a while back in my twenties."

Petra always struggled with the idea of timing. Her brain was able to figure out early on if a person was someone she liked and enjoyed. Unfortunately, she acted that way. It seemed off-putting, even overwhelming to neurotypical people who seemed to know the dance steps that she did not.

But Petra wasn't going to mask. She'd promised herself to be genuine with Hawkeye. If she was going to scare him off, earlier was better.

"Yesterday," she said, "you talked to me about the importance of preserving significant firsts for a time when they could be savored. This weekend has been desperate, scary, painful, miserable, and sad. But through that, I'm stuck on significant firsts. Through all that, what's going on between us feels like a significant first to me. I haven't felt this settled and comfortable amidst all the discomforts before. I feel like this time together has been important."

"Absolutely. Yes. I'm looking forward to getting home and —" Hawkeye stopped when his phone buzzed. He pulled it out from his thigh pocket. "Go for Hawkeye." He paused. "I have Petra here with me. I'm putting you on speaker. No one else is in our area to overhear."

"Petra? Reaper here."

"Hi?" She leaned forward to speak over the phone as Hawkeye held it out.

"I'm looking for information you might have about the girl from today's search. She's in the hospital and had a seizure. She remains uncommunicative. The hospital is seeking information that might help them to understand her medical situation. When you saw the family at the tidepool, was anything mentioned about her health? Did you see any medications?"

"No. Nothing. I can tell you that I never saw anyone say anything to her, and she didn't talk to anyone. She seemed in a bad mood, and they let her have her storm cloud at a distance. That's her brothers, too. They didn't try to get her to join in as they played. Also, they were staying here in the hotel. Is it possible for the manager to go into their room? I know they were leaving the island, but it's possible that a bottle was missed, or a pill fell onto the floor with identifiable markings."

"We already looked," Reaper said.

"The girl," Petra said, feeling the warmth and joy of the conversation she was having with Hawkeye recede into the distance, replaced with fear. "Is she in imminent danger?"

"I can't say. That they were calling and asking for any possible information is a big red flag. They have to be worried. They couldn't go into her case much more than to ask for information specifically around what might have caused the seizure."

"Okay. I'm going to think about all this and see what I can come up with. Off the top of my head, I have nothing."

"Thanks, Petra. Out."

Hawkeye's body had changed. He sat up straighter as he expanded his muscles. The word that came to Petra was that he was "primed." His focus was hard on her. "I don't know you very well yet, but I know you," he said.

Petra blinked at him.

"You have a plan to get that information, and it's not a safe one. When you said you were going to see what you could come up with, what you meant was that you were about to go find out why that child is in a medical crisis."

Petra paused. "Yes. You're right."

"All right. Cooper and I are in." Hawkeye stood, gathering the last of his food and balling it up to shove into the trash. "What's the plan?"

37

———————

Hawkeye

Petra said that from her experience with communication while saving Terry from the blowhole, the place that made the most sense for the kidnapper to take the dad was The Social Club with their famous drinking jig. From the off-grid house, the dirt road would come out onto the pavement only a quarter mile away, heading south. To the north, it was a much longer drive to get to the next piece of civilization.

So, they headed toward The Social Club.

"Petra, why would he want or need civilization? All he needs is connectivity."

"Not true. He needs connectivity and control. If you had a gun, a phone, a recalcitrant human being, you'd also want a light source, right?" Petra asked.

"I would, but not when it risked being seen."

"I've been in the passenger seat of cars that have driven by there a few times this weekend, so I've had the advantage of looking around. The sign says that it closes at nine. But the lights that are near their parking lot are public streetlights. And I'd bet the light over the club itself stays on. There's a copse of trees just to the south of the entry. I'd bet this guy is taking Herb there because while he'll be able to see, he won't be seen. They could probably make a bunch of noise, but they're too far away to be heard. Few people on the road. And most of all—"

"Connectivity. I'm not doubting you. That all sounds right to me. But he has a gun, and we do not."

"I have a badge." Petra tapped her belt. From his place in the driver's seat, Hawkeye couldn't see it, but was sure it was there.

"You were in Afghanistan. You up close and personally know the power of the gun. He won't lay it down and cower under the power of the badge."

"Of course not. But the kidnapper said out loud to his buddy that he wasn't interested in killing anyone. In his mind, he will hesitate."

"Uh-uh," Hawkeye said. "That's not a good enough strategy."

"I sort of have one," Petra said, watching the trees—a dark violet against the deepening sky—blur by. She turned back to him. "I'm wondering what Cooper's capacity is. My understanding is that all Cerberus K9 are—what do they call it?—a nose and a bite."

"Not true. Truffles is a caving rescue dog. Valor is a search and comfort dog."

"But Cooper is."

"Yes," Hawkeye acknowledged. "A nose and a bite."

"I don't want to put you in any kind of trouble, Cooper," She crooned as she reached over the seat to rub Cooper. "And I don't think I would be putting you in harm's way. I want to apply a little shock and awe. Imagine this, you and Cooper get out of the SUV and position yourself in the area as my backup."

"Whoa. No. If you're going in. I'm going in."

"You? All six-feet-three of you?" she asked.

"Six-feet-four. But that's right. All of me will be standing next to, if not in front of, all of you."

Petra nodded slowly. "I made a mental note of what you just said. I'm folding it up and sliding it into a memory pocket to go back and read again later. It was probably very romantic and gallant. I'm too focused on a child in danger to appreciate it fully at this moment. What I want you to hear me say is that your standing next to me, Hawkeye, would be much more dangerous," Petra told him. "Look, Rowan et al. are waiting for the two kidnappers to split forces so they can free the Johnsons. I don't want this guy to go sprinting home and endangering people. I think he's the only one with a gun. So, having said that, my plan is that you and Cooper hide as backup. I wait until they drive in and settle."

"*If* they drive here and settle."

"If they don't, I was wrong." Petra said, "My lips are buzzing with adrenaline—the helpful kind. The kind that turns up the volume on my senses and makes me feel bigger and stronger." She licked her lips.

Hawkeye felt the adrenaline coursing through his body, too.

"While I'm waiting for them to show or not show, I'll try to figure out where else they might have gone. My thoughts as of now: I think they want this over with. I think they'll take Herb out as soon as the guy is reasonably sure that the club is closed and everyone drives home. Remember, they want their cake and to eat it, too. They plan to get on their boat and head out tonight so they can deliver the Johnson Family to wherever it is they're supposed to deposit the family. Send the pictures to the Prokhorov Family. The Prokhorov Family pays them and checks the task off, so these two guys don't go on a Prokhorov Family hit list." She held up a finger. "Okay, I'll tell you that one in a second. Back to this scenario. I think the kidnapper will go to the club because he's doing a scary new thing, and the club is a known and comfortable site." She took a breath. "Okay, in my plan, you're in place. I drive into the parking lot and roll down the window."

"From inside the SUV?" Hawkeye asked.

"Yes."

"Could you park so the engine is between you and them?" Hawkeye asked.

"Sure. I can do that. I pull in, park so my engine is between us, roll down my window, and turn on my interior lights so they see I'm alone. I yell, 'Hey, Herb I need to talk to you about your daughter for like half a second. She's in the hospital.'"

"Just like that. 'Hey, Herb.'"

"I know his name. I know where he is. I'm not being an aggressor. I mentioned his daughter—who is missing, and they think she's dead—"

"And this so shocks them that—"

Cooper started whining when Petra pulled her hand back.

"No begging, Cooper," Hawkeye said. "We're on a mission. Working."

The whines immediately stopped, and Cooper scrambled to sit up in his seat, gaze scanning. Hawkeye would laugh if this wasn't such a crazy-as-shit plan and if he wasn't about to agree to it.

"This is the place?" Hawkeye asked, as a car pulled out from the side and turned south.

"That's it."

"So, you yell, then what?" Hawkeye asked, driving a hundred yards farther, then sliding off the side of the road to park in the shadow.

"From there, we wing it," Petra said, undoing her belt. "My presence there is going to be a bit of shock and awe. Head scratching for sure, possibly a flight response. If the kidnapper flees, he may take Herb, or he may abandon Herb in order to get back to Jenny and the kids and warn his cohort. But I'm going to start talking right away. My voice is going to be so laissez-faire, so 'everything's fine' that—like that mama bear story I was telling you about—it won't occur to either of them to do anything other than tell me what's wrong with the girl. I say thank you. Maybe a little finger wave. I roll up the window and drive off. Once I've driven off, I'll wait for you and Cooper right here with my lights off. It's far enough but not too far."

"And Herb?" Hawkeye asked.

"Herb isn't my mission. The girl is my mission."

"You held up your finger," Hawkeye said.

"What?" Petra canted her head.

"You held up a finger and said, 'Okay, I'll tell you that one in a second.'"

"Oh, another place we might be able to get the information. But that one, I think, would be more dangerous. It's if they evade Rowan's team and are running for their boat. I might be able to scream toward the boat that I need to know about any medicines the girl takes, and Jenny might try to scream the information back to me. Fetal microchimerism being a thing. I think she'd try."

Hawkeye shut his eyes and shook his head. "No idea what you're talking about." He opened his eyes and held up a hand. "I don't want to know."

"Fair enough." She climbed out of her side of the car and scooted around the front to take his place in the driver's seat.

"I hate this," Hawkeye exhaled. "I care about you. You'll use every cell in your brain to stay safe, right?"

"Absolutely. And you will, too." She stretched up and

kissed him. But this wasn't a warm lingering kiss. This was tight and cold. And somehow, that reassured Hawkeye. It wasn't a possible-last kiss; it was a 'let's kick ass and take names' kind of kiss. It must mean that in all the scenarios she ran through her brilliant head, she believed in good outcomes.

Did he?

38

———

PETRA

Petra was fine with this.

She really was.

Pulling out from the shadows, she did a three-point turn, drove past where potentially the car with Herb in it would exit onto the road, did another three-point turn, and positioned herself so she could see without being seen.

Had Quantico been a while back?

Yes.

Did she practice this kind of fieldwork on the daily?

No, not even annually.

Stakeouts weren't Petra's thing. Riding on planes next to demon-dispelling, prayer-bead-munching acolytes was her thing. Attending meetings to know what was going to be allowed on one's person during the great vacuuming flight into the cosmos before the lizard people arrived—no plants, soil, or polyester—was her thing.

But honestly, how hard could this be?

Pull in and block their car.

Don't put your vehicle in park but reverse. Get the steering wheel lined up properly for peeling out. Be ready to drive crouched low in the seat.

That last one was a little bit fingers-crossed thinking. Hawkeye was right that the only thing that might stop a flying bullet was the engine block.

Out and away.

Their vehicle had been a cloth top, and that top had been folded down. They didn't need to get out of their car to use the light source.

That could be problematic—Oh! Oh! Here they came.

All right.

In Petra's head, the plan was so much easier than the doing.

Focus. There's a child in the hospital. She's having seizures, and the doctors don't know what to do.

For Petra, when she presented a couple days ago as a medical mystery, as a conversant adult with a "fiancé's" support, they let her walk out the door unsolved. The hospital couldn't release the child until someone fixed her, right?

The child—that's why Petra was here.

This was what she was doing.

By the light of a full moon, Petra put the SUV in neutral. Slowly but surely, the gravel began to crunch as gravity tugged and her tires rolled. After picking up momentum, she moved the shifter to L to engine brake without needing to tap her foot brake with their red look-at-me lights.

She felt a shiver go through her body as the kidnapper's vehicle eased into the parking lot and over to the space she'd predicted.

Petra loved it when her predictions were right. And

honestly, it wigged her out a bit. If she didn't know enough about brain science, she would call this psychic.

Once her SUV edged up on the parking lot, she turned on her engine, flipped on her lights, and followed all the steps.

Car in reverse, the wheel turned, the engine as a bullet blocker, and the window goes down.

"Hey, Herb, it's me from the tidepool. Hey, got a sec?" Cool as a cucumber. "I won't interrupt what you've got going on. But your daughter is in the hospital, and the doctors need to know what's happening with her health because she's not doing well. Is she on seizure meds?"

"I don't know what to do here," Herb said in a voice that sounded like perspiration.

"Who is she?"

"An author," Herb said. "She was in the car with me when we went to the tidepool."

"How did she know you'd be here?"

"She took a wild guess," Petra called in a singsong. "Just the medical info, and I'll be on my way."

"Amanda, my daughter Amanda, she had measles when she was an infant."

"What's happening right now?" the kidnapper asked.

Shock and awe is happening.

As a breeze picked up and the branches swayed, Petra saw a gun pointing at Herb.

"Measles," Petra repeated. "What did that do to her? They said she had a seizure?"

"Uhm. Yeah. She's—" Herb had to stop and pant. And when he did, the gun inched closer and waggled to get him talking. "She's Deaf," he stammered, "and has a learning disability that makes her about the mental age of a three-year-old, and she has epilepsy. But that wasn't a problem when she took her medicine."

"Move on now. You need to go and tell the doctor. Go on," the kidnapper called.

"Sorry. I'm sorry, two seconds more. I need the doctors to know because if she were to die, the authorities would want to know who to blame. Better to keep her alive, right, Herb?" Petra came very close to threatening a guy with a gun. *Shit.*

"My wife said that she thought Amanda would be fine with a natural syrup that she was making. It takes her all day to make it. It's got lots of steps and lots of ingredients. I don't know what to tell you other than we needed some medicine that would work if a pharmacy was too far away."

"Shut up," the man hollered. "Actually, you, in the car. You come and talk to me."

"No need. I'm leaving now." Petra shifted her foot from the brake to the gas pedal, draped her arm over the seat, and looked over her shoulder as she pressed the pedal down to back out of the lot.

"I said, come talk to me." The bang was as unexpected as the pop that followed.

Petra jumped as high as her seatbelt would allow, her shoulders came up protectively around her ears and stuck there, her elbows tight against her body.

The SUV's steering wheel pulled hard to the right. The guy had taken out her front tire.

Petra worked to organize her body into following her plan, peel out, screech off into the distance, and circle back to collect Hawkeye and Cooper.

But Cooper was having none of that.

A streak of black against black pulled her attention around. Cooper bunched his haunches underneath him and leaped.

The shrill of Petra's scream filled the air.

She supposed her limbic produced the sound in service of Cooper by pulling attention her way.

Petra hated when she was both living the emergency and also, somehow, an onlooker sitting on a stool in the corner, calling out her observations.

That's what was happening to her now.

Cooper flew over the top of Herb and locked onto the kidnapper's gun arm.

Petra had her belt unlatched, her door open, and was rolling away from the SUV.

Herb was racing across the parking lot.

And somehow Petra was on his heels. Then she was diving, arms scooping around his knees, and they both went crashing to the ground.

In her mind, she was back in the lake, protecting her neighbor from the bully.

And just like at that lake, once she had the guy in a hold, the good idea fairy flew away.

Hawkeye was calling Cooper off the terrified kidnapper, in the glow of the overhead lamp, Petra could see blood dripping down the bad guy's injured arm.

Good. He should be in pain.

Petra pulled her badge around—the one she swiped through the machine to identify herself as she entered the J Edgar Hoover building—and commanded, "FBI, don't move!"

Nope. This didn't at all go to plan.

***

While they waited for Rowan and his buds to finish up at the house, Petra had called the hospital with the information about Amanda Peterson.

It was a long wait for the gun-toting, actual badge-wearing special agents to show up.

Prescott was back with the family and the other kidnapper.

Finley and Rowan climbed from the car.

Rowan was shaking his head at her. "Spot on," he called as he walked over.

Herb and the kidnapper lay side by side on the ground, knees bent, shoelaces tied together, hands laced behind their heads. Cooper—who was thoroughly pleased with the way the evening had gone—sat guard.

Gun or dog? Petra would probably choose the dog every time.

After all, you can't snuggle with a gun at night.

And the dog came attached to a wonderful man.

"Checking on you," Rowan said, stopping in front of her. "This was genius. But I told you to step away."

"I—"

"You were saving a child. I know." He gave her a hug. "How are you?" Rowan turned to stand by her side and observe.

"A little wigged out, thanks for asking." Her eyes were on Hawkeye and his on her. "Cooper's happy."

"Cooper's always happy when he gets to eat the bad guy." Rowan chuckled.

"You're not arresting Herb, are you?" Petra asked on an exhale.

"This is a big case. We think it's best if we turn the Johnsons. Having informants on the role might help us figure out what the Prokhorovs are building next in terms of their psyops."

"Herb's been over there processing his life and his choices out loud. Seems like the Prokhorovs have figured out how to leverage doomsday cults. Not just big money to pay for the family's psyops endeavors. There's an army of adherents who no longer think. It's like those gamers using Taylor Knapp's video games only on steroids. The fast videos you gave me to process work really well. Too well. It's insanity. We can't let this happen." Petra said. "Tax-free church money and a variety of First Amendment rights protections. I think the Prokhorov Family has landed on the legal means to leverage America against itself."

Rowan kicked at the ground. "A goal that they have been pursuing for generations."

They stood silently side by side while the kidnapper and Herb were moved to the back of Finley's car.

"The brain is a magnificent thing. It looks like all of this magically fell into place, but it can be traced from one step to the next," Petra said.

"Walk me down that path." Rowan crossed his arms over his chest.

"From Hawkeye's point of view, this will probably look too neat. Too coincidental. The world doesn't work that way."

"Let's go through this logically."

"I'd prefer that," Petra said. "Because I wasn't sent down here on fairy dust to take down another Prokhorov cell."

"You weren't at all." Rowan insisted. "You were going with Tamika to spread her parents' ashes. It had nothing to do with work."

"No?"

"Petra, this wasn't an op. Tamika's parents got married down here, and she didn't know what to do with the ashes. She figured she'd do it here."

"Why did Tamika land on the idea of spreading the ashes in St. Croix? I would postulate that it was because, about six months ago, your team suspected some activity was going on in the United States Virgin Islands."

"We couldn't find it," Rowan said. "Now we know from Jenny Johnson it was the jump-off spot. They asked their adherents to commit crimes. If caught, they pled guilty, and then The

Family moved them to safety and gave their followers a new name. Exactly as you suggested, no passport, no worries. Go to the islands and get a boat. From that boat, jump to a new boat, and everyone vanishes. Pockets get lined. Kudos. That was some masterful speculation. You were dead on."

"That's fine. I don't need kudos. Just back to my list. We can both agree this area was on Tamika's mind and probably influenced her to come. Once we were here . . . *me*. Once *I* was here, I found that St. Croix is a small island. Visitors are grouped in hotels and guest houses along the shore. There are only so many restaurants. There are only so many places to go and only so many tourist things to do."

"To make the Petersons look like they were here on family vacation they'd have to do those things, right? Go to the beach. Take the family to the tidepool," Rowan agreed.

"In this case, that was part of the Johnsons' escape. But before that, sure, they probably did things to blend in. Because the Christmas Winds were unusually strong, a lot of the tourist things—hunting lionfish, snorkeling, swimming with horses— were unavailable, tightening an already limited number of things to do. That's how I ended up in the vicinity of the Johnsons. And then there's you."

"Me," Rowan said.

"Why are you here? Because of Avery." Petra answered her own question. "Avery was talking to me on the phone when I was at the airport. And when I think of Avery, I think of you."

"Thank you," Rowan said with a smile.

"When I saw Herb there, that necklace bothered the shit out of me. It made me feel vulnerable, and I didn't know why. But I felt compelled to tell you about it. And up until the moment you and Finley pulled up in this parking lot, I didn't know why."

"Okay, I'll bite," Rowan said.

"I was in your office last July. I was running in and didn't knock."

Rowan pointed at her. "I remember that. You ran in. The image was on my monitor. I flipped it off immediately. You must have seen it."

"Not seen it," she corrected. "Clocked it."

"How's that?"

"If you left the image there and acted like it was a nothing burger, it wouldn't have stood out to me. That your reflex was to hide the image meant my mind tagged it as significant."

"You're a thousand percent right. I'll have to figure out how never to do that again."

"Lock your door?" She shrugged.

"I see the whole thing unfolding just the way it would for a brain wired like yours. From the beginning, the necklace bothered you. You knew it was associated with something bad—which it is. Your conscious brain kept looking for the answer, so you went and pressed the mom. You followed the child. You got the necklace. You tucked it into your pocket and kept thinking about Avery, who is tied in your brain to me. All of this makes perfect sense. You had all the steps, but you just didn't have enough information to put them together. And as you and I know so well, the brain is an incredible thing."

"It is that. But here are the things that were starlight and pixie dust," Petra held up a finger, "the unexpected seismic activity." Another finger went up. "A young girl who was not putting up with that mess. A third finger, "Hawkeye and Cooper." She smiled over at them so they knew she was still okay, and Hawkeye started over to her.

"Looks like you two are getting on," Rowan said as he stepped aside. "I need a word with Finley before they take off."

"Everything okay?" Hawkeye asked as Cooper thrust his head under Petra's hand.

"Rowan and I were just going over how this all happened, how we got to this place."

He leaned down and gave her a kiss. "Destiny?" he asked.

Petra snuggled into his arms, laying her head on his chest where she could hear his heart beating strong and steady. "Yes, that's exactly what I told him. Destiny."

EPILOGUE

A man stood at the podium. "And so, a year ago, we were all hard at work pulling people from the water. It took a lot of brave men and women, citizens, all working together to save lives. We honor each and every one of you."

A woman took his place. "As we call your name, please come forward and accept your plaque."

The local government had arranged for the citizens who survived to hand the thank you plaque to the person who made it possible.

Seeing Melissa balancing Terry on his arm crutches, wedding rings on their fingers, was an enormous sob that sat in Petra's chest.

Petra knew Hawkeye was feeling his emotions too when Roy—whom he pulled out of the rip current—and a guy named Tony—whom he'd pulled from a deadman's float and given artificial breath—stood up. Tony held a beribboned dog bone for Cooper, who, apparently, dove into the water and pulled them to safety.

The only one that was missing who Petra really wanted to

see was Amanda Johnson. She was returned to her parents after Jenny and Herb became FBI informants.

Petra wasn't sure how she felt about that.

Not good.

But she wasn't going to let that mar this day. It was a day of celebrations.

They all went outside to a lovely cocktail party on the beach.

Hawkeye came over. "I hope you'll forgive me for what I'm about to do."

Petra froze.

"I try never to surprise you," he said, taking her empty glass and handing it off to a server.

"I appreciate it."

"But you mentioned that while you were down here last time, you wanted to swim the horses." He reached for her hands.

"That's true," Petra said. "I'd met a guy named Mitch."

Hawkeye nodded toward the beach where Mitch held the reins of two horses. "We can't swim them because of the—"

"Christmas Winds." Petra smiled. "This surprise I don't mind because I already imagined having this experience, and I've met Mitch. So, thank you."

"Good. Will you go for a ride with me?" He held a hand out to usher her to the horses.

As they were leaving, Hawkeye waved at Halo to let him know they were going.

Cooper ran beside Petra's horse as they rode along the beach. The sky was painted with a tangerine sunset. The warm air was magical.

Petra thought she might even look the part of a romance heroine since she'd worn a flowing sundress to the ceremony.

Hawkeye pulled up on the reins and dismounted. He walked over and lifted her down.

Kissing her gently, he said, "This is the part you need to brace for a little bit. We're going to round the corner. And some people are there. People you know. No strangers."

"But why?" Petra asked.

"Because I wanted them to share this day with us. This celebration is meaningful not just because of the lives saved but also because of the life we started together. I invited them down to mark this time. But if it's too much, we turn around."

"I think I'm okay."

Hawkeye had the reins in one hand, leading their horses; he held her hand in the other, and Cooper danced at her feet as they turned the corner.

There, Petra found a heart made of flickering votive candles in the sand. At a distance, sitting quietly, were Avery and Rowan, Tamika and Diamond, Hawkeye's parents, his brother, and Cora, both Hawkeye's sister and now Petra's dear friend. The Team Charlie brothers were there with their K9s.

And Petra started to cry.

"Happy tears or stress tears?" Hawkeye asked.

"Very happy, thank you."

Hawkeye led her into the center of the heart.

When he knelt in front of her, Cooper came to a dignified sit beside him.

"Petra." Hawkeye pulled a ring box from his pocket.

"Yes," Petra said. "The answer is yes. I'm full now. You can say more later. Okay?"

"More than okay. Perfect." He quietly slid the ring onto her finger.

Hawkeye stood and was enveloping Petra protectively in his arms when Tamika called out, "Okay, y'all. I know we were told to sit still, and all. But we got to clap. That's some beautiful romance right there."

The laughter of their loved ones rode the breeze and wrapped around them.

Hawkeye was right, this was more than okay. This was perfect.

The End

Readers, I hope you enjoyed getting to know Hawkeye, Petra, and K9 Cooper. If you had fun reading Shielding Instinct, I'd appreciate it if you'd help others enjoy it too.

Recommend it: Just a few words to your friends, your book groups, and your social networks would be wonderful.

Review it: Please tell your fellow readers what you liked about my book by reviewing Shielding Instinct at your favorite retail store. If you do write a review, please send me a note at hello@fionaquinnbooks.com. I'd like to thank you with a personal e-mail. Or stop by my website, FionaQuinnBooks.com, to keep up with my news and chat through my contact form.

If you would like to know the reading order of the World of Iniquus books, flip the page to find a chronological reading list.

WORLD OF INIQUUS NOVELS
IN CHRONOLOGICAL ORDER

Year One

Weakest Lynx (Lynx Series)

Missing Lynx (Lynx Series)

Year Two

Chain Lynx (Lynx Series)

Cuff Lynx (Lynx Series)

WASP (Uncommon Enemies)

Year Three

In Too DEEP (Strike Force)

Jack Be Quick (Strike Force)

Relic (Uncommon Enemies)

Mine (Kate Hamilton Mystery)

Deadlock (Uncommon Enemies)

Instigator (Strike Force)

Yours (Kate Hamilton Mystery)

Open Secret (FBI Joint Task Force)

Thorn (Uncommon Enemies)

Gulf Lynx (Lynx Series)

Year Four

Ours (Kate Hamilton Mysteries)

Cold Red (FBI Joint Task Force)

Even Odds (FBI Joint Task Force)

Survival Instinct (Cerberus Tactical K9 Team Alpha)

Protective Instinct (Cerberus Tactical K9 Team Alpha)

Defender's Instinct (Cerberus Tactical K9 Team Alpha)

Danger Signs (Delta Force Echo)

Hyper Lynx (Lynx Series)

Danger Zone (Delta Force Echo)

Danger Close (Delta Force Echo)

Year Five

Fear the Reaper (Strike Force)

Warrior's Instinct (Cerberus Tactical K9 Team Bravo)

Rescue Instinct (Cerberus Tactical K9 Team Bravo)

Hero's Instinct (Cerberus Tactical K9 Team Bravo)

Striker (Strike Force)

Marriage Lynx (Lynx Series)

Guardian's Instinct (Cerberus Tactical K9 Team Charlie)

Beowolf (Iniquus Certified Cerberus Tactical K9)

Red Line (CIA Color Code)

Sheltering Instinct (Cerberus Tactical K9 Team Charlie)

Shielding Instinct (Cerberus Tactical K9 Team Charlie)

Year Six

Radar (Iniquus Certified Cerberus Tactical K9)

Trusted Instinct (Cerberus Tactical K9 Team Charlie)

Acting on Instinct (Cerberus Tactical K9 Team Delta)

Whiskey (Iniquus Certified Cerberus Tactical K9)

With more Iniquus novels to follow!

For the most up-to-date list, go to FionaQuinnBooks.com

ACKNOWLEDGMENTS

MY GREAT APPRECIATION

To my publicist **Margaret Daly**
To my cover artist, **Melody Simmons**
To my editor **Rossana Tarantini**

To my Street Force, who support me and my writing with such enthusiasm and kindness.

To all the professionals who shared their knowledge of working K9s, especially the various Virginia search and rescue teams.

To all the wonderful professionals I called on to get the details right as I conducted my research, especially **M. Carlon** for her medical expertise.

Please note: This is a work of fiction, and while I always try my best to get all the details correct, there are times when it serves the story to go slightly to the left or right of perfection. Please understand that any mistakes or discrepancies are my authorial decision-making alone and sit squarely on my shoulders.

Thank you to my family for your love and support.

I send my love to my husband, thank you for sharing my exploration of St. Croix and all of the adventures.

And, of course, thank *YOU* for reading my stories. I always smile joyfully as I type this sentence. I so appreciate you!

ABOUT THE AUTHOR

Fiona Quinn is a USA Today bestselling author, a Kindle Scout winner, Amazon Top 40, and an Amazon All-Star.

Quinn writes suspense in her Iniquus World of books, including Lynx, Strike Force, Uncommon Enemies, Kate Hamilton Mysteries, FBI Joint Task Force, Cerberus Tactical K9 Series: Alpha, Bravo, Charlie, Delta, and Certified Cerberus Tactical K9, the Delta Force Echo series, CIA Color Code Action Adventure, and now, an Iniquus cookbook!

She writes urban fantasy as Fiona Angelica Quinn for her Elemental Witches Series.

And, just for fun, she writes the Badge Bunny Booze Mystery Collection with her dear friend, Tina Glasneck, as Quinn Glasneck.

Quinn is a Canadian author rooted on the shores of the Atlantic, where she lives with her husband and children. There, she pops chocolates, devours books, and taps continuously on her laptop.

Visit: www.fionaquinnbooks.com

COPYRIGHT

Shielding Instinct © 2025

Published 2025, Fiona Quinn Ltd.
Halifax, NS, Canada

All Rights Reserved.

No part of this book may be scanned, reproduced, or distributed in any printed, or in any electronic form, nor can it be used to educate AI or used in conjunction with AI in any form or for any reason, without the express written permission from the publisher or author. Doing any of these actions via the Internet or in any other way without express written permission from the author is illegal and punishable by law. *It is considered piracy.* Please purchase only authorized editions. hello@ fionaquinnbooks.com

This book is a work of fiction. Names, characters, businesses, organizations, places, events, and incidents either are the product of the author's imagination or are used fictitiously. While some recognizable historical events or real-world locations may be mentioned to provide a sense of setting, they are used solely in a fictitious manner. All other characters and events are entirely fictional, and any resemblance to actual persons, living or dead, or actual events is purely coincidental.

Kindle eBook ISBN-13: 978-1-966221-13-5
Print Paperback ISBN-13: 978-1-966221-14-2
Print Hardback ISBN-13: 978-1-966221-15-9

Cover Design by Melody Simmons from eBookindlecovers

Publisher's Note: Neither the publisher nor the author has any control over and does not assume any responsibility for third-party websites and their content.